I Wish
I Could
Remember
YOU

L.J. EPPS

This novel is dedicated to my father, Henry, who always believed I could do anything I set my mind to, and to Aja, who always tried to help me break out of my shell and have some fun.

TABLE OF CONTENTS

CHAPTER ONE. 1

CHAPTER TWO 14

CHAPTER THREE 24

CHAPTER FOUR 32

CHAPTER FIVE. 44

CHAPTER SIX. 54

CHAPTER SEVEN. 74

CHAPTER EIGHT. 81

CHAPTER NINE. 98

CHAPTER TEN 112

CHAPTER ELEVEN 118

CHAPTER TWELVE 134

CHAPTER THIRTEEN 149

CHAPTER FOURTEEN 169

CHAPTER FIFTEEN. 185

CHAPTER SIXTEEN. 193

CHAPTER SEVENTEEN 210

CHAPTER EIGHTEEN. 221

CHAPTER NINETEEN. 233

CHAPTER TWENTY. 238

CHAPTER TWENTY-ONE. 245

ACKNOWLEDGMENTS 263

CHAPTER ONE

Emily Montgomery tossed and turned in her bed, as the sheets tangled around her bare legs, thrashing awake from the nightmare about her upcoming divorce from Steven, her estranged husband. She cowered away, unable to run, rooted to the spot, trembling, even in her sleep. She woke with a gasp and jerked her body up in bed. Her skin was on fire, as her heart tried to run right out through her throat.

It was the same as every other night—the fitful sleep and terrible nightmares where she felt so helpless and exposed. Emily grabbed the remote off the nightstand and flicked on the TV. Maybe an old movie would take her mind off her troubles. She wasn't going back to sleep. She knew, too well, what awaited her.

The alarm clock flashed four a.m. She groaned. Normally, she didn't get up to get ready for work until six a.m. It was going to be a long day. How would she face her English class of teenage angst and be any good to them today?

Emily shivered as the morning chill got to her. She saw her bathrobe was within reach, so she grabbed it to cover her thin, pink nightgown. Why was she trembling so much? Why was her heart pounding through her chest?

Sadness overcame her. She had looked the papers over a hundred times, but she needed to look at them again. Her heated divorce was the reason she couldn't sleep at night.

Her husband, Steven—an attorney—didn't want the divorce to go through. Her court date, next week, was always at the forefront of her mind. How could her marriage of six years be over? How could a marriage that started out so happy go so wrong? Life was supposed to get better once you hit thirty, not worse. Having an abusive husband was not what she wanted, or needed.

Emily couldn't keep thinking about that. She had to stay positive and focus on the happy things in her life. And there was plenty of good, like her boyfriend, Robert. Robert was kind, thoughtful and generous. To think, she hadn't wanted to go out with him, at first. Now, she couldn't imagine her life without him. Besides her newfound relationship, there was also her teaching career which she loved so dearly.

She shoved the papers away. She didn't want to dwell on them anymore. It was time to get her day started. Hopefully, it would be a good one.

❧

"Hey, Emily, how's everything going?" Christina was a good friend as well as another teacher at the high school.

"Okay, I guess." She frowned. "But I need to finish my lesson plan for tomorrow."

"Your facial expression doesn't imply okay. I thought you were going out to dinner with Robert. You should be happy." Christina tucked a strand of blonde hair behind her ear.

"Yes, and don't forget my sister, Monica, and her husband will be there as well."

"And, there's that look again. What's wrong?"

"Monica put this little dinner together as a celebration—it was one year ago, today, that she introduced me to Robert." Emily stood and walked toward the window. "Don't get me wrong. I'm grateful to her for giving me the extra push I needed to start the divorce proceedings and to move on…" Her voice drifted off and so did her thoughts.

"Go on—what's the problem? You don't seem happy."

"I do love Robert, but…" Emily hesitated.

"But what?" Christina's blue eyes blinked. She sounded impatient.

"I feel bad because I found myself staring at the divorce papers, again, this morning. I still have some unresolved feelings for Steven that shouldn't be there."

"This kind of reaction is normal; you were married for a long time." Christina put her hand on Emily's shoulder. "As long as you know in your heart, after everything he's done, you can't take him back."

"I know that. I just wish the emotions would go away." Emily was mad at herself for having affection for a man who had hurt her over and over.

"They will in time, Em. Don't beat yourself up over it. After all, Robert loves you. He knows you're going through a tough divorce, and he supports you." Christina turned to walk away. "Try not to get so down. I have an appointment I need to get to. But I can stay, if you need to talk more."

"No, thanks. I still need to finish my lesson plan." Emily waved bye to Christina. "But thanks for the listening ear."

Emily knew Christina was trying to help. But what Christina didn't know was Emily hadn't told Robert she still had unresolved feelings for Steven that she couldn't explain.

The divorce papers meant the death of her marriage. A marriage that she'd hoped would last. No matter what they were, she hoped, in time, they would go away; and then, there would be no need to tell Robert.

A few minutes had passed, but she still was unable to concentrate. Emily opened her desk drawer and took out a small mirror that she kept for makeup emergencies. Holding the mirror up to her face made her sigh because she saw worry lines under her hazel eyes.

Her long hair was a mess. Could her messy hair be a metaphor for how messily her marriage had ended?

Her mother would say she hadn't raised her that way, that she'd raised her to be a stronger person.

You don't need a man to survive. How could you stay with Steven for so long while he had multiple affairs? How could you let him put a hand on you without you leaving him? How could you be with someone who badgered you because he didn't want you to have your own life or career?

If only her mother were still around to chastise her.

All Emily wanted was a marriage that lasted forever, like the one her parents had. Was that too much to ask for? She tapped her nails on her desk. Now that she had finally found the strength to get out of her marriage, why couldn't Emily shake the thought that it would never be over.

The smell of chalk never bothered her before; but today, a slow ache developed in the pit of her stomach from its odor wafting in the air. It was like being sprayed by a skunk on a warm day. The clock ticked on the wall, and car tires screeched outside the window. Every noise disturbed Emily, and she knew no good could come from staring off into space. Like someone who was lost and couldn't find their way, Emily closed her notebook. She would finish her lesson plan later, when she could concentrate.

Emily swung her leather purse over her shoulder, and clutched her briefcase in one hand while opening the squeaky classroom door with the other.

She heard a soft voice call her name. "Mrs. Montgomery." It was Maggie, one of her tenth grade students.

"I'm glad I caught you," Maggie said, brushing a strand of red hair from her green eyes. "I got halfway down the street and noticed I forgot to turn in my book report."

"Maggie, it's not due until tomorrow."

"I know but I won't be here for the rest of the week, and I didn't want to be marked late turning it in."

"Is everything alright?" Emily's eyebrow rose.

"My father is having heart surgery in the morning over at Ceder Hospital."

"I'm sorry to hear that, but I'm sure everything will be okay." Emily placed her hand on Maggie's shoulder. "You know my brother-in-law is head of cardiology at Ceder Hospital."

"No, I didn't know that."

"Well, he is," Emily said, with a smile. "And, he's a stickler for making sure everything is in order. So I'm sure his staff will take excellent care of your father."

"I hope so." Maggie's voice quivered. "I'm on my way to visit with him, now."

"Do you need a ride?" Emily asked. "I go right pass there on my way home. I could drop you off."

"I don't want you to go out of your way." Maggie shook her head. "I was going to catch the bus."

"It's not out of my way." Emily's briefcase rattled as she unsnapped it to put the book report in. "My car's outside in the parking lot."

"Okay." Maggie nodded.

Emily didn't make a habit of driving her students around; but, she felt this was appropriate, under the circumstances. Maggie was a good student. And she hated to admit it, but Maggie was one of her favorites. She was bright and smart and kind; and, if one of Maggie's family members was in a bad way, it was her duty to be there. Yes, the hospital was in the opposite direction from her apartment; but, that was okay, it would give her an excuse to drop in on Monica.

The walk down the long, dank hallway took longer than usual, and the air was stale and dry. Nearing the back door, Emily squinted, trying to block the piercing sun, coming through the windows, from her view.

There was a cool breeze blowing, and her hair swirled around her neck like a rope.

"My car's just over here," Emily said, brushing the strands from her eyes.

The employee parking lot and the student parking lot were one and the same. And there was commotion everywhere. A few teenagers were talking, with high-pitched voices, on their cell phones. Others were wrestling on the cement, like they were in a gym. Some stood near the fence, watching the school bus screech to a halt in front of them. While others sat in their cars eating, like it was feeding time at the zoo.

"Let me get my keys," Emily said, rummaging through her purse. Her old, green Ford was a few feet away.

"There would be no need to search for keys, if you would take back the expensive car I bought you. Just one click with the remote, and you'd be in your vehicle—all safe and sound," a deep voice said. "I don't understand how you can ride around in that old rust bucket. If you would come to your senses, and come back to me, the car would be all yours."

The voice was Steven's. Emily hadn't seen or spoken to him in months. Her body trembled, and her feet became unmovable, like she was stuck in quicksand. The purring of his car stopped, and she heard his door slam; but, she still couldn't turn around to face him.

"Mrs. Montgomery, are you alright?" Maggie asked.

"Yes," Emily said, with wide eyes. "Why don't you take my keys, and get in my car." The keys clanked together. "It's the green one, over there. I'll be right over, in a minute. This won't take long."

"Don't worry, she's in good hands with me," Steven said, with a sneer. "You can run along."

"That was uncalled for," Emily said, turning to him. The rope she had felt around her neck, earlier, tightened.

"I'm sorry, but this is grown-up business." He stalked closer to her.

Seeing him again was like a kick to Emily's stomach. She was frightened, angry and curious, all at the same time. Steven had on a striking, dark blue suit with pinstripes, a black tie, and matching shoes. He was dressed to the tee. Every light brown hair on his head was in place. And his light brown eyes stared right through her. Steven always looked as if he was walking into a courtroom, even when he wasn't.

She mustered up the courage to look in his eyes, and asked, "W-what are you doing here?"

"I thought we should talk."

"I don't know why. E-everything we needed to say to each other has already been said." Her voice was shaky.

"I don't want a divorce. I will not add my signature to those papers." He shook his head. "Not now, or at any time in the near future."

"And, we both already know, I don't need your signature. So once again, why are you here?"

"Because I wish you'd give me another chance to right all the wrong I've done." His eyes softened.

"And, you know, as well as I do, it's too late for that." She shook her head. "We've discussed this before."

"We can go to counseling, like you wanted." His tone was gentle. "I never meant to make light of your feelings. I think counseling will show you that."

"Oh, so now you want to go to counseling." Emily couldn't believe what she heard.

"Yes, like you wanted," he repeated, for emphasis.

"Yes, I wanted to go. But that was after we first separated; and, you refused. Now, you waltz up here, after all this time, stating you want to go. What am I supposed to do with that?"

"You're supposed to say yes."

"I can't," Emily said, standing her ground. "I've moved on, and so should you."

"Speaking of moving on." His eyes slanted. "Do you know how much it hurt me to find out you are dating? We haven't been separated that long. You walked out on me, and you didn't even give me a chance to make it right before you moved on." His voice cracked.

"Just because I didn't want to go to counseling didn't mean I didn't want to work things out." A look of hurt was on his face. "My point being—I'm trying my hardest to change. I know my conduct during our marriage was out of order. But now, I'm taking into consideration your viewpoint on things. And even though I never wanted you to work, if this job makes you happy, I have no problem with you keeping it."

"I hurt you? Do you realize how much it hurt me when you had one affair after another? And all of the times you shoved me into walls, and tables, for no reason." Her voice grew louder. "I still don't think you do." She shook her head. "That's how I know it's too late, Steven. It's too late for apologies. I no longer need your permission to have a career."

Since they'd separated, Emily had been avoiding him. She thought that was best for everybody. How could he be here, now, with love in his eyes? How could he, all of a sudden, want to go to counseling? Emily's heart pounded, and she couldn't breathe. She felt like a train was coming, and she was tied to the tracks, unable to save herself. Her head was spinning, and she glanced over at her car to make sure Maggie couldn't hear their conversation.

"This isn't the time, nor the place, for this." She glared at him.

"I don't care if you're worried about someone overhearing us." He shook his head. "In this moment, all I care about is you and me. And I need to get my point across. I tried calling you to apologize, but you wouldn't answer." He continued on his rant. "I even came to your apartment, several times, but you wouldn't come to the door. I still had hope, even after I found out you were dating someone else. I figured it was just a rebound phase. I thought you'd come to your senses and realize how much we love each other. I left you alone for a while, so you could get this new guy out of your system and come back to me. But that never happened." He ran a hand through his neat hair. "Then, when you served me with divorce papers, I knew you were serious; so, I mustered up the nerve to come and talk to you."

"You've never been at a loss for words before. I'm surprised you would have to muster up anything." There was pain in his eyes that she hadn't seen before. But it didn't matter.

"Well, I did." He leaned over and whispered in her ear. "I'm sorry. I never meant to invade your workplace. But I needed to tell you this, in person. I needed you to listen and hear me, this time. And this couldn't be left on voice mail or screamed through a door."

"I can't do this, right now. You should go." Emily turned to walk away, but Steven grabbed her elbow.

She glanced back at him and their gazes met. She hadn't been this close to him in a long time. The leftover feelings Emily had for him bounced around in her stomach. But those emotions needed to be put to the wayside. She couldn't forgive him—not after everything that had happened, not after a year and a half had passed. It was too late for counseling. She was moving on, and he needed to do the same.

"You're trembling." His gaze bore into hers. "You don't have to be afraid of me. I won't hurt you." He let her arm go. "I came here to get some things off my chest."

"I've heard all of this before. I think you should go." Emily felt her face stiffen.

"I need to say one more thing. After that, I will leave you be."

"Go ahead," Emily said, shaking her head. "Just say it."

"I refuse to give up on our marriage." His eyes were sincere. "You're the first woman I ever loved." He grabbed her hand. "If you find it in your heart to give me one more chance, I predict a very different outcome for us—a happier one."

"If that's true, then why did you go and ruin everything we had together? Why did you do things to hurt me?" Unwanted tears flowed down her cheeks. "You ruined everything." Emily pulled her hand away and glanced down at the ground. Her shoulders shook.

"I didn't mean to ruin it." His tone was sincere. "It's just...I had a tremendous workload. And it was unfortunate that you got the brunt of that stress. By no means am I making excuses for myself, but you knew all of the issues I struggled with." He brushed a hand through his hair, again. "But you abandoned me by going back to school to become a teacher."

"Abandoned you? So now our unhappy marriage is my fault."

"That's not what I'm saying, at all." He raised her chin so their eyes could meet. "But we can be happy again; it's not too late. I love you."

"No." She shook her head, stepping back from him. Emily's heart raced and her hands trembled. "I don't return your feelings," she continued. "So, if you still love me, you won't put either of us through this." Her voice cracked. "All I ask is that you give me what's mine. Then, this can all be over, in a matter of minutes."

"You understand, I can't do that." His eyes hardened. "I can't take our relationship and sum it up in a neat, little package and forget about it, like it never happened. It's unfortunate that you don't share my feelings. I guess I shouldn't have come." He turned toward his car. "Just so you know," he said, glancing back at her. "If you really wanted to get rid of me, you wouldn't take this to court. Instead of dragging this out and fighting over possessions, you would leave with nothing. In my head that means it's not over. Your little boyfriend, Robert, will never be able to give you what you need. You remember that." The glass from his car window shook as he slammed the door behind him.

"He's never going to change," Emily mumbled, watching him glare at her from his black Bentley Continental GTC.

She wiped the tearstains from her face and turned toward her car. In the distance, she could still hear the buzzing of teenagers all about; but, she ignored them.

"Are you sure you don't want me to catch the bus?" Maggie asked, handing the keys over.

"No, I'm fine." The motor roared as she started the car. "And, like I said before, it's on my way."

She turned up the radio to drown out the awkward silence. There was some thumping, hip-hop music playing that Maggie would probably enjoy. Hopefully, it would help Maggie forget her troubles for a moment; but, it wouldn't help Emily forget her own. Her hands shook, gripping the steering wheel. Was Steven right? She turned toward the traffic ahead. Was she dragging this out because she didn't know how to let him go for good? No, she shook her head. And how did Steven know Robert's name? Emily's mouth went dry and, like a deer caught in headlights, she continued to drive.

⋘

Steven's heart dropped to his knees as he started his descent down the street. Being a criminal defense attorney, he spoke to courtrooms full of people and never got nervous. But he had been nervous to see Emily—so nervous that his palms had been sweaty. He had blown his last, desperate attempt at winning his wife back—at least face-to-face. Now, all his dreams of her running into his arms and taking him back were dead and buried.

She hadn't changed much. Her hair was a darker shade of brown, now; but, it was still long and flowing. Her skin was flawless, and her high cheekbones made her even more attractive. Thinking about Emily made his chest tighten and his skin felt like fire.

The path Steven took while driving led him down many side streets. Faint sounds of a ball bouncing made him look off into the distance, where he saw children playing in their front yards. He didn't have kids and that was his fault. But maybe it was for the best because he already saw far too much of his father when he looked in the mirror. How had he fallen into the trap of becoming the one person he never wanted to emulate? He wouldn't be able to live with himself, if he treated a child the way his father had treated him. Yes, the lack of offspring was probably for the best.

After riding around for a while, Steven turned onto his street. He lived off the corner of Nine Mile and Blooming Hill, in a spacious house in the suburbs of Precone, Illinois, near Chicago. Pulling up into the driveway used to make his chest puff up with pride, but now it saddened him. At thirty-six years old, he had everything a man could want, except for a wife to share his home with.

He tried to associate all of his memories in the house with good times, but he knew Emily didn't feel the same way. Knowing she linked the house with bad things made his heart ache. After all, he'd had the house built for her. There were four bedrooms and seven baths. The kitchen used to be Emily's favorite room. Funny, since she didn't cook much; but, she loved the décor. When he had first shown it to Emily, her eyes had lit up with joy. The kitchen cabinets were made of Sapele mahogany. The countertops were Tourmaline granite and there was a beautiful island in the middle of the room. The living room had a stone fireplace and a large bay window.

Brooding wasn't doing him any good. Maybe different scenery would help, so he headed for the Victorian, spiral staircase that led up to the master bedroom. Once upstairs, the situation hadn't corrected itself because the exact same thoughts came to mind upstairs. The bedroom had Emily's favorite colors—dark gray, silver and white. A glass chandelier hung from the ceiling, and sliding doors led out onto the terrace. From the terrace, you could look out along the backyard and see the swimming pool and tennis court.

The dresser, which held pictures of Emily, wasn't helping either since it showcased his life with her. Picking up the crystal frame holding their wedding photo brought back so many memories. Remembering her laughter echoing around the house was like a blow to the head because he was the one who'd taken her laughter away. The only sounds left in the house, now, were the faint sounds of his maid, Anita, vacuuming in the hallway.

His pity party continued as he plopped down in the cushioned chair in his bedroom. Yes, friends and acquaintances told him he needed to move on. Yes, he was fortunate to have had six years of marriage under his belt. Most couples didn't make it that long. But his feelings for Emily had never diminished. So he paid the others no mind, and kept on his quest to win her back.

Emily now lived across town. How could she go from a mansion to a one bedroom apartment? Steven knew in his heart that was all she could afford on a teacher's salary. And it was his fault that she'd ended up that way. When she'd left him, he told her all their property belonged to him. Steven had said Emily would get nothing from him, unless she came back to him. Why had he been such a jerk to her?

Seven years ago, Steven had met Emily while she worked as a waitress at Chiers, a small restaurant. Her smile had been infectious, and her beauty had overtaken him. Never had he met someone so kind and sweet. But now, that sweetness he so fondly remembered was gone, and she refused to give him another chance. She refused to let him make things right. But if Emily thought she could dismiss him, and he'd go away quietly, she had another think coming. Steven took out his cell phone and made a call.

CHAPTER TWO

Monica was hard at work at Ceder Hospital. She loved her job as a pharmacist. She counted out meds for a customer, when she heard footsteps approaching. Looking up, Monica found Robert standing in front of her. He often came into the hospital to provide drug information and to offer product samples to physicians. Now that they were friends, his visits became more frequent.

He looked great in his dark gray suit. His height, mixed with his broad shoulders, made him look good in anything. And his sandy brown hair and pale green eyes set the suit off, nicely. Not only was he handsome, he was a good guy. That's why Monica had introduced him to Emily. Monica thought they would make a nice couple.

"I didn't think you were stopping by today." Monica beamed. She was always happy to see him. "Are you distributing samples in the hospital?"

"No, I had a sales meeting down the street and thought I'd stop in to visit."

"Shouldn't you be getting ready for dinner? Our reservations are for eight p.m." Monica glanced down at her watch. "It's almost six-thirty now."

"I still have plenty of time to change." He smiled. "Unlike you, I know how to change quickly." He chuckled.

"Is that a crack against women?" One eyebrow rose.

"No, just against you."

"If you must know, I'm finishing up for the day. This is the last order I have to fill, and then I'm on my way upstairs to retrieve my husband."

"How is David?"

"You can ask him yourself when you see him, later."

"Why—don't you know how he is?"

"Our schedules are so busy that I haven't seen much of him these days." Monica glanced down at some pills on the counter.

"I guess that's to be expected. You two have been married forever," he said.

Monica gave Robert a stern but playful look. "So, are you saying me and my husband are all washed up and too old for romance and fun?"

"Yes, that's what I'm saying," he said. "Seriously, though, there is a reason for my surprise visit. I want to show you something."

Monica's eyes widened when she saw Robert taking a ring box from his pocket.

"What's that?" Her mouth dropped open.

"It's an engagement ring, for Emmie." He opened the box and showed Monica a small, but elegant, round-shaped diamond ring. "I want to surprise her with it, tonight. Do you think she'll like it?"

"I think any woman in her right mind would love it." Monica smiled. "It's gorgeous. It's just…"

"It's just what?" Robert looked doleful.

Monica knew he saw her enthusiasm fade. She didn't want to hurt his feelings, but she had to be honest with him.

"I think, maybe, you're moving a little too fast." She put the bottle of pills she had counted on the shelf behind her and turned back to him. "Don't get me wrong. I'm the one who wanted you two together. But Ems is not divorced from Steven yet."

"I realize that." He shrugged. "It's just…I've only been in love once before in my life. And you know that relationship ended badly because I was scared to commit. I'm not going to let that happen, again. I want Emmie to know how serious I am about her."

"I think she already knows that. You don't have to give her a ring to prove it. You've been standing by her side during all the drama she's been going through." Monica placed her hand over his on the counter. "Take my advice. Put the ring on hold, for a while. Just until her divorce is finalized."

Monica looked down at the ring, again. She gently squeezed Robert's hand. She knew he was serious, but she hoped he would take her advice.

"Here." Monica closed the box and handed it to him. "Just put it up, for now."

"I'll think about what you said, but I can't promise anything. I'll see you later." He put the box in his pocket and bleakly turned toward the door.

Monica felt bad for bursting Robert's bubble, but her heart was in the right place. She knew he was the right man for her sister because he was nothing like Steven. But Monica also knew this wasn't the right time for an engagement. Monica told her assistant she was leaving for the day, then grabbed her small purse and headed for the door. She wanted to make her way upstairs to find David and get his opinion on the surprise engagement ring.

"Monica," Emily shouted, spying her sister standing at the elevator.

She made her way past the front desk of the large lobby where the walls were light and the carpet was beige. The front desk was cherry mahogany and reminded her of a check-in desk at a hotel. A female staff member dressed in a burgundy jacket cackled on the phone, while another male staff member typed on a computer—the keys clicked loudly. The grand chandelier in the middle of the room seemed out of place.

"Ems, what are you doing here?"

"I dropped off one of my students whose father is in the

hospital, and I thought I'd stop in to visit. She's in the gift shop, now, picking up flowers."

"That's nice of you. I know how you hate coming here—to the hospital, I mean."

"It's not that I hate it—it's just that it brings back so many bad memories of Mom and Dad. I know it was years ago, but I don't handle it as well as you do."

"I have my good and bad days," Monica said, shrugging. "But it's not always easy."

The elevator dinged and a few nurses in blue scrubs got off, complaining about how bad their day had been. Another elevator arrived and a young man in burgundy scrubs pushed a man on a stretcher with tubing coming from his nose. At the same time, a code blue was announced over the intercom.

Emily shuddered since those were all the reasons why she didn't like coming to the hospital. Hearing things like that made her wonder who the person was they were calling the code on. What kind of life did they have? Would they make it?

She inhaled and there it was—the odor of the hospital. All the smells and all the sick people who were praying they would get well. It brought back too many memories of her parents and what they had gone through. Her parents had been in a car accident on a snowy night. The roads were slick and they hit a pole. They had never made it out of the ER, and Emily didn't know if that was a good or bad thing. That had been a terrible time in her life. But out of it came some good because that's how her sister had met David.

"Robert was just here." Monica hit the up button for the elevator, again.

"Was he showing you a new product?"

"Yes, something like that." Monica smiled. Her brown eyes brightened and they matched the color of her hair.

"What's that strange grin for?" Emily asked. "You look like one of my students when they've done something wrong." The elevator dinged again.

"Oh, nothing." Monica shook her head. "There's the elevator, I have to go. See you at dinner." She stepped inside.

Monica left so abruptly Emily never got to talk about Steven's surprise appearance at the school. Maybe it was for the best, she thought, as she walked to the gift shop. Monica had never cared for Steven's arrogance. This bit of news would probably put Monica on edge the same way it had put Emily on edge.

Once she was out of the hospital and back in her vehicle, a fog of remembrance washed over her. Ceder Hospital was about ten minutes from the home she used to share with Steven. If Emily turned left out of the parking lot and went farther north, she would end up there. The tires on her old Ford screeched as Emily turned right, out of the driveway. She wanted to go to her new home—well, new as of a year and a half ago. Her apartment was on the south side of town, and it was about an hour's drive from Hill High School.

The stretch of blocks Emily took to go back past the high school, and toward her apartment, housed many memories of her life with Steven. There was the expensive, fancy Italian restaurant with the green trim around the roof where Steven always liked to eat. Down the street from that was a tailor where he had his suits custom-made. There was a row of small, brown bricked businesses where Emily often got her hair done and went for massages. Next to the massage parlor was an old-fashioned ice cream shop where they served the best vanilla ice cream she had ever tasted. Emily hadn't been to those places in so long that it seemed like a lifetime ago. But she couldn't help dwelling on the past, every time she drove by. Her new apartment was not in as upscale of an area as she was used to when living with Steven. Instead of fancy restaurants around the corner, Emily now had convenience stores and gas stations on every corner.

"Are you sure you want to go through with this?" Mitch asked.

"Yes, I'm sure." Steven plopped down in his chair in his office. The walls were black which matched his somber mood. He shoved his Montblanc ballpoint pen to the other side of his desk. It screeched while rolling away and stopped just at the edge of his harvest cherry, Saratoga executive desk.

"Look man, we've been friends for a long time. And I've been handling odd jobs for you, for a while now." Mitch sat down in the chair across from Steven's desk. "I mean, following your wife here and there—when you two were together—was fine. I understood, during the rough years of your marriage, you wanted to know of her comings and goings, you wanted to know who Emily confided in."

"So, what's the problem?" Steven leaned forward in his chair.

"You need to think about this." Mitch scratched the bald spot atop his head. "Because once it's done, there's no going back."

"Don't you think I know that already?" Steven's voice was bleak. "I don't know what else to do."

"Try talking to her, again."

Steven shook his head. "I spoke to her, a little while ago. And it didn't do any good. Emily still wants the divorce. Or, at least, that's what her lips say."

"What do you mean?"

"I believe, somewhere deep down inside, she still loves me." Steven stood. "I believe, if that Robert person wasn't around, Emily would give me another chance. All I need is a little more time to convince her that I'll never cheat on her again or harm her in any way. I love her."

"If it's any consolation," Mitch stood, as well, "I've seen the changes in you. You don't flirt with every woman you see, now. And I think, if Emily spent some time around you, she would see that as well."

"So now you understand why I'm doing this?" He felt Mitch's piercing black eyes staring right through him, as if he knew what he meant.

"Yes, I understand. But if Emily ever found out, I don't think she'd understand. And then, all of your professing to her that you've changed will be moot."

"Yes, I know." He held up his hands. "Like I said earlier, I don't know what else to do." He reached in his drawer and took out a yellow envelope. "The money's in here. It should be enough for you to get the job done. Let me know if you need more."

"I'll get right on that." Mitch took the envelope and put it in his pocket. He headed for the door.

Steven knew in his heart he had only given Mitch instructions as a last resort. And maybe Mitch was right, and he will regret his actions later. Mitch had a brother named Jerome who could never hold down a steady job. Jerome would take the unsavory jobs that Mitch gave him. Jerome needed the money and never asked questions.

Should he listen to Mitch? His thoughts all jumbled, now. He had met Mitch in law school and they had become good friends. Mitch often gave him sound advice, but today he couldn't take it. This was something he had to do. He wasn't a horrible person, and he needed Emily to finally see that.

"Thanks for staying the night." Emily smiled. She sat on the brown, circular sofa in her apartment.

"There's nowhere else I'd rather be." Robert leaned over and kissed her forehead. He sighed as he plopped down on the sofa beside her.

"Is everything okay? I was surprised when you called off dinner with Monica and David. I'm sure they were surprised as well."

"I wanted to spend some alone time with you. We've both been so busy, lately, that I feel like we don't do this enough." Robert grabbed her hand and squeezed. "I should be asking you if you're okay."

He tried to change the subject. The ring burned a hole in his pocket. But he had decided that it wasn't the time to bring up an engagement.

"Emmie, did you hear what I said?" He saw a faraway look in her eyes.

"I'm sorry. I guess my mind is elsewhere."

"Would you like to talk about it?" He was concerned, but he didn't want to push her.

"Not really. But I know I should. Steven came to visit me today. It was so unexpected. I haven't seen him in months—it unnerved me a little."

"Just a little?" Robert lifted her chin so their eyes could meet.

"Maybe a lot. I didn't expect to see him until the hearing."

"What happened? What did he want?" His fingers clenched.

"He wanted the same thing he always wants—another chance. He wants us to be a family, again. I thought he'd moved on, since I hadn't heard a peep out of him for a while."

"I guess the reality that the divorce hearing is in a matter of days is hitting him."

"Yes, that's what I think, too." Emily stood and headed for the kitchen.

"So, how did you leave things?" Robert followed her. He watched her open the refrigerator and take out a bottle of water. From where he stood he could feel the cool breeze from the refrigerator.

"Emmie." Robert grabbed her hand before she could walk back to the living room. Eager to hear what went on, he stopped her before she could get away from him.

"Yes." Emily's eyes widened as she looked back at him.

"I asked you how you left things." He became impatient with her silence.

He knew Steven could be overpowering, sometimes. He needed to know what happened. Her silence was deafening—even a baby crying would be better than this.

"I told him that I couldn't return his feelings. And then, he left."

"And, that was it?"

"Yes, that was it."

Robert knew Emily wasn't telling him everything. But he

decided to let it go, for now, because he didn't like confrontation. His parents had argued, constantly; divorcing, finally, when he was a teenager. After the divorce, they still found ways to put him in the middle of their arguments. Loving them both, equally, he didn't like to pick sides. Once Robert was grown, he moved to Precone, leaving the petty arguments behind in New York.

It did no good to dwell on actions that caused him to develop a fear of commitment, along with a fear of being hurt—but he thought about them anyway. Never wanting to end up like his parents was at the root of all his problems. It's what caused the one and only other serious relationship Robert ever had to end; she had wanted to get married and he had not. He had vowed to never let his fear get in the way of a relationship again. And then, Emily came into his world. She was so kind and sweet that he fell for her. The way she cared about others, especially her students, made him proud to be with her. At thirty years old, it was now time to make a real commitment and to settle down.

Robert leaned over and kissed her temple. The scent of her strawberry shampoo engulfed him. No, he couldn't give her the riches that Steven could, but Emily said she didn't care about those things. Never once did he feel like the rebound guy or the replacement guy. The only problem was Emily was still a married woman, and Steven didn't want to let her go. But their divorce would be finalized soon, and then he and Emily could concentrate on each other.

"There might be a sales manager position opening up soon at work." He tried to change the subject.

"Really? That's wonderful." Her eyes brightened a little. "Are you thinking about applying for it?"

"Maybe. It would mean less travel and more office time."

"But I thought you like to travel. You said going around to different hospitals and doctor's offices made for a less boring day."

"There are a few different openings. I don't have to apply for that one, but it's the one that pays the most. I would be supervising a whole team of people."

"What's really going on?" Emily tapped his nose in that playful way he liked. "When did you start caring about making more money?"

Robert stood and grabbed Emily's hand. "I think we should both get some rest."

"I know what you're doing—you're changing the subject." Emily smiled. "But I am tired, so I'll let it go, for now."

He followed behind her to the bedroom. He sometimes spent the night. They got undressed and ready for bed. He was happy she'd let it go. He needed more money if they were going to be married. But she didn't need to know that. Robert slid under the covers next to Emily, holding her until she fell off to sleep.

CHAPTER THREE

Steven's hands shook as he squatted down near the cold, hard ground. He laid a bundle of multicolored flowers down in front of the headstone. He made this journey at least once a month. It was his duty, since it was his fault. Noticing a slight chill in the air, he zipped up his jacket.

His teeth chattered, as he whispered. "Hey, little one—Daddy's here. I promised I would visit you once a month. So far, I've done a good job at keeping that promise."

He rubbed his trembling fingers across the engraved name. A tear nestled on his cheek. Before he could wipe it away, it trickled down and fell upon the flowers.

"I guess I better move the flowers. We wouldn't want them to get wet, now, would we?"

His hands quivered as he moved the flowers out of the area where his tears could dampen them.

"I know your mom doesn't come to visit you. It's only because it hurts her too much to be here. But she loves you so much. She loves you just as much as I do." Feeling like he was lost on a deserted island, he took in a deep breath.

His attention was distracted by a noise, close by. Some other visitors were down the way, and there was a faint sound of someone crying. A blue eyed, pigtailed, little girl was with a woman—probably her mother—knelt at a grave. They were saying something about how much they missed Daddy. Steven's heart knotted. He should have a little girl like that, right now. She wouldn't be old enough to speak, but she would be just as beautiful. The lump in his throat grew bigger. For a minute, he felt as if he couldn't breathe. Somberly, he turned his attention back to the grave. His hand was still unsteady as he went back to stroking the name on the headstone.

"Lindsey Montgomery—that's the name your mom wanted for you." Steven managed to muster up a smile. "I wanted Anna Marie, after my mother, but your mom won out. She smiled so much when we talked about you that I couldn't deny her."

His knees ached, so he sat down on the cold ground. Feeling like he was drowning, Steven continued, "If only you were here, things would be so different now. We would be a family. I've tried to get your mom to forgive me. But she refuses to reopen her heart and let me back in. I don't know what else to do. I know it's my fault we lost you, and I don't know how many more ways I can say I'm sorry. I was so unreasonable during that time. But I know in my heart you forgive me. I just have to find a way to forgive myself. Maybe then, your mom will see the changes in me, and be able to forgive me, too. But that's not going to happen if this divorce goes through. Daddy's not a bad guy. I do have a heart. That's why I need to find a way to spend more time with your mom, so she can see that I don't degrade women, anymore. I'm no longer like my father."

Steven's hand shuddered as he moved the flowers back to their original position. "No matter what happens between me and your mother, I will never stop coming to visit you." He leaned over and kissed the headstone. "Or stop loving you." Another tear fell as he slowly stood and walked away.

If things had turned out differently, she would be almost two years old, now. Would he have been a good father? Steven struggled with that question, daily. It may have taken some work, but he would have been there for whatever she needed. He would have tried his hardest to be all the things to her that his father wasn't to him. But none of that mattered now, so why keep thinking on it?

His hands shook as he pressed the remote to open his car door. He plopped down in the front seat of his car. His throat tightened. He was raised to be strong, not to show emotion, and crying was not included in that category. With a heavy heart, Steven drove out of the cemetery and down the street.

✄

Emily's heart raced as she searched through her closet. When Emily lived with Steven, she had a walk-in closet and her clothes were always out of order—like her life, back then. This closet was small, and her clothes were neatly arranged. She hoped her new life was the same.

Emily pulled out several suits and threw them on the bed. One by one, she held them up to her small frame while looking in a mirror. Which one would be appropriate to wear to court? Her hands shook as she picked up the black suit first from the bed, and held it up to her body. No, that one wouldn't do. It looked like it was more appropriate for a funeral than for a divorce court, even though it was the death of a marriage. Emily picked up the red suit and shook her head again. That one looked like it was for a party. Then, she reached for the white suit, but that one wasn't right either. She tossed all the clothes on her queen-size sleigh bed, before settling on the gray suit. Maybe this would be the one. Emily held it up in front of the dresser mirror, and the tightness in her chest lessened, a little. Yes. It looked like appropriate attire for court.

Her door buzzer went off, breaking her concentration. She wasn't expecting anyone, and Robert had his own key.

"I didn't expect to see you, tonight. Not that I'm not happy to see you, but I know you're usually tired after work," Emily rambled, as she closed her front door. Her eyes broadened, watching Monica walk past her and click the kitchen light on, making the white walls even brighter.

"I'm sorry, I know I should have called first, but I need to talk to you. I figured you would be home from work, by now. I was trying to catch you alone, before Robert got here." Monica threw her box-shaped purse on the kitchen chair.

"Robert's not stopping by tonight, I had some things I needed to take care of."

"Is everything okay?" Her eyebrow rose.

"Everything's fine." Emily shrugged. "Why wouldn't it be?"

"Well, you said Robert wasn't stopping by and—"

"I don't have to spend every night with Robert. He has his life, and I still have mine."

"I realize that. I put you two together, and I don't want anything to come between you two."

"Nothing's going to come between us. We're fine. In fact, if you follow me into the bedroom, I will show you why I needed some alone time tonight."

The apartment was small, and the bedroom was only a few feet down the hall. Emily glanced at the mountain of mail on the dining room table that was just outside the kitchen. She hadn't had time to get to it, and tonight would be no different. "Maybe you can help me decide," Emily continued.

"Decide what?" Monica followed behind her. "What's all this?" She looked down at the clothes sprawled all over the bedroom.

"I'm trying to find something presentable to wear to court, next week." Emily picked up the gray suit.

"Why are you doing this now?"

"It's better to start early. I don't want to be pressed for time when that day comes."

"No, that's not what I mean." Monica pried the suit from her sister's fingers. "What else is going on? I think this search for the perfect outfit to wear to court has a bigger meaning."

"You always blow everything out of proportion." Emily rolled her eyes. "Finding appropriate clothing doesn't have to mean anything else."

"Ems, I'm serious." Monica's expression was stern. "Your hands are shaking. Now sit down and tell me what's wrong." Monica sat down on the bed and patted the space beside her.

Emily, disgruntled, sat down beside her. "I'm going to talk to my lawyer in the morning. Cora wants to discuss some final things with me before next week. I guess it has me on edge, a little. It means the divorce is finally becoming a reality."

"I thought everything was already a reality."

"It was, but now it's even more of a reality than before."

"Ems, you still want the divorce, don't you?"

"Of course I do." Emily glowered at her sister before jumping up and walking back to her closet. How could Monica ask her such a thing? After everything she had been through, how could Monica think she was weak and would change her mind?

"If you have, there's nothing to be embarrassed about." Monica followed her to the closet.

"But I haven't," Emily said, still facing the closet. "Can we please talk about something else?"

"There's a question I want to ask you. And I don't want you to take it the wrong way."

"You know you can ask me anything." Emily turned toward her. "What is it?"

"If you really want this divorce, why don't you skip all the court proceedings? Instead of dragging this out, you could sign the papers and be done with it. Why do you even need to divide up possessions?"

Emily's jaw dropped. "Now you sound like Steven." As soon as Emily said the words, she wished she hadn't. But it was too late.

"Steven? When did you talk to him?"

"He came up to the school to see me."

"Why didn't you tell me?"

"I was going to tell you when I saw you at the hospital, but I didn't get a chance. Then, the more I thought about it, the more I wanted to forget it ever happened. I mentioned it to Robert, and I felt like I didn't need to talk about it anymore."

"Are you okay? Did Steven hurt you in any way?"

"No…no." Emily shook her head. "He didn't touch me; he wanted to talk. Well…"

"Well, what?"

"He did grab my elbow, but he wasn't trying to hurt me. He wanted me to listen to what he had to say."

"That doesn't matter." Monica glowered. "There is no excuse for him ever putting his hands on you."

"Don't you think I know that?"

"Sometimes, I'm not sure. You always make excuses for him. He's having an off day or he lost a case. Steven promises he won't do it again. And then, who's there for you after he shoves you into walls? Who did you talk to after you two got in those horrible arguments? And who did you move in with after he pushed you down the steps and you lost the baby." Monica held up her hands. "Your baby was stillborn because of Steven."

"I don't know why you're bringing all this up." Emily's eyes watered. "You know what a difficult subject this is for me. And you should know that I'm not going to run back to him because he's on this quest to win me over."

"I'm sorry. I know I shouldn't have brought up the baby. I worry so much about you when it comes to Steven."

"I know, since Mom died you feel like you have to take on this motherly role." Emily wiped a tear from her cheek. "And, I'm not negating everything you've done for me, but that was thirteen years ago. I'm thirty years old, and it's time to move past this. I'm fine. If you don't mind, I'd like to be alone."

"You sure you don't need to talk more?"

"Yes, I'm sure." Emily nodded.

"If you need me, for anything, call. But I'm sure you already know that."

"I do."

Her mouth dry, Emily walked Monica to the door and hugged her good-bye. Monica was only three years older but always thought she knew what was best. After Emily had left Steven, she got her own apartment. She had been so depressed over the way her marriage had turned out that it took her a while to find the energy to file for divorce. It had been a few months since she had served Steven with the papers. Emily needed to move on with her life with Robert.

Monica knew the pain Emily had endured and had helped her through all of it. So why would she bring up the baby, now? Monica knew Emily didn't like to talk about the loss of her baby. It had been almost two years, and the hurt was still there. Just thinking about it made her chest feel like it was caving in. Emily had spent a year in therapy. Counseling had helped the emotional pain lessen, but it would never go away for good. How could anyone ever get over the loss of a child?

She sat down on the sofa and let her unwanted tears flow. Trembling, Emily grabbed the pillow from the sofa and held it tightly, hoping if she held it tight enough, it would take away the aching in her heart. Maybe it would drown out all the pain, and any memories she had of that dreadful night. But a stupid pillow wasn't a replacement for a baby—her baby. Anger overtook her, making her throw the pillow across the room, shattering a glass on the coffee table along the way. The clinking of thousands of pieces of tiny glass hitting the tiled floor made her flinch, but she didn't care.

Every time Emily thought about that night, anger, hurt, and sadness overcame her. She clenched her fist, letting her nails dig into her skin. That was why she avoided parks and play areas—anywhere a mother would take a small child. It was too painful to see a baby with its mother. It was too painful to see the joy in a mother's eyes while holding her newborn. That's why she shut those feelings away and locked them up. Her little girl wasn't there for her to hold, and it wasn't fair.

She and Steven had been having issues, on and off, when she had become pregnant. Steven had gone on and on about how he wasn't ready to be a father. Emily had truly felt in her heart the baby could have been a new beginning for them. Instead, she had been nine months pregnant and arguing with Steven at the top of the steps. She should have just ignored him. She shouldn't have let him get to her. Steven had grabbed her arm to make her listen to what he had to say. He shook her and ended up pushing her down the marble stairway. But to this day, Steven claimed Emily ripped her arm away and slipped.

She stood from the sofa and wiped her face. If anyone saw the way she stumbled to the bathroom, they would have assumed she was drunk. Emily cringed, seeing how red and puffy her eyes were in the mirror.

Trying to shake the memories from her mind, she brushed her teeth. She needed to get ready for bed; but, all she could think about was how the doctor had walked into the room and explained that the fall had been too much on her body, and the baby was born with no signs of life. Monica had been by her side, but Steven had been nowhere to be found.

"*No more memories,*" Emily whispered. "*It hurts too much.*"

The tears continued to flow, stinging her eyes before falling into the sink.

CHAPTER FOUR

Emily was awakened by the rain, hitting the roof of her apartment. Rolling over, she noticed the clock flashed seven. Why hadn't the alarm gone off? Emily had been so busy dwelling on the loss of the baby that she must have forgotten to set it.

She had to be at her lawyer's office at nine a.m. Tired and groggy, Emily stumbled over to the window. The sky was still dark, and it was pouring down rain. Not just little sprinkles but an all-out downpour. It figured, this being D-day; the day she finished up the divorce paperwork. She picked up the pace and got ready.

Emily splatted down in the driver's seat and put the key in the ignition; but, when she turned the key, nothing happened. The car made a funny clicking sound, but the engine didn't roar and start, like usual. Her heart raced, faster, but she still tried not to panic.

Just take some deep breaths and try it again.

The second time she tried, the car still didn't start.

Could this day get any worse?

She got out of the car and walked to the front of her carport. Emily opened the hood and looked around like she knew what she was looking at. Of course, she didn't, but maybe she could tell if something had been tampered with. Emily could not. There was a loud bang as she slammed the hood back down. She climbed in the driver's seat to get out of the damp air and to figure out what happened.

Maybe she had left a light on and it drained her battery. Or, maybe Steven had messed with her car or had someone do it for him. He was always pulling crazy stunts, back in the day. Sometimes, Emily would see a strange car behind her, but she could never see the driver. The car would follow her for blocks before it would turn off. It was the same vehicle, every time. Then again, maybe this wasn't Steven's doing at all. Steven didn't cause her to oversleep, and he didn't cause the downpour of rain. He had no idea Emily had an appointment with Cora today. Even if he did know, what would he have to gain by tampering with her car? Why would he care if she was signing more papers today? Why was she being so paranoid? Emily was having the worse morning ever.

It was now 8:30 a.m., and there was no way she would make it on time. It was just an appointment. It could be rescheduled. But Emily had been all set to do this today, and she didn't want to reschedule. The most logical thing to do was call her lawyer's office to tell them she was running late; then, call a cab.

The dampness made it feel colder than it was. She shivered. November weather in Precone was sometimes unpredictable. It was not cold enough for snow, and that was a good thing. It would have been better to wait for the cab in her apartment. Emily pulled her jacket closer to her chest to gather in some warmth. Mud was everywhere and the last thing she wanted to do was fall in it, so Emily carefully made her way back to her apartment. She had left her umbrella in the car, leaving her head exposed to the elements. The rain felt cool as it hit her face and even cooler as the puddles splashed her feet.

She'd only made it to the outside of her door when the screeching cab pulled up, so Emily quickly turned and got inside. The brown eyed, dark haired gentleman stared at her. With a nice smile, he asked where she needed to go. Emily offered a friendly smile back as she explained the directions to him. He mumbled about what a crummy looking day it was, and she nodded in agreement. Turning to the window, Emily noticed an abundance of clouds. She blinked in amazement. How could the already dark sky become so much darker in a matter of minutes? The rain came down harder now than before she had stepped inside the cab.

Turning her head forward, Emily noticed a picture on the cab-driver's dashboard. She mustered up another small smile. No doubt, it was a picture of his family: a pretty woman, probably his wife; and two teenage girls, probably his children. If he had a picture of them on his dashboard, they were probably still happily married. There would be no happy family photos, not for her, not anymore, at least not with Steven.

Her earlier smile faded as quickly as it had appeared. A lump developed in her throat. No, it had nothing to do with wanting to have a life with Steven again. It had everything to do with never wanting to go through a divorce; and, never wanting to be in a position where she would have to obtain a lawyer to divide up possessions. But this was the right thing to do. Her eyes watered. Emily had spent far too many years suffering in silence, and those days were now over.

The driver explained, because of the rain, he was trying to drive safely and follow the speed limit. Emily tried wiping the moisture away from the foggy window, so she could see out. The dampness from her coat seeped through, making her quiver. She noticed the driver staring at her through the rearview mirror. Then, she saw him turn up the knob for the heat.

"*Thank you*," Emily mouthed. She welcomed the hush of the heating vents, ramping up higher.

She thanked and paid the driver, then exited the cab. Soaking and dripping wet, Emily ran up the steps of the building. She, apologetically, explained to the receptionist why she was late, even though she had already explained earlier, on the phone, when she had called. Kate, the older woman, slanted her eyes as if she didn't care. It was now ten a.m., and Emily was an hour late, so she would have to wait to be squeezed in. She could have gone to the ladies room to freshen up her appearance, but decided against that in case her name was called earlier than expected.

Her legs wobbled as she searched for a seat. Like one of her teenage students, Emily slouched down in her cushy chair and waited for the receptionist to call her name. All the while, Emily prayed her head would stop pounding like she had a hangover.

Her clothes were damp and wrinkled. Emily felt the gaze of a blonde haired woman sitting across from her, staring as if she was crazy. Never mind the woman, she sighed. She had bigger things to worry about, like proving to Monica and Steven she could move on. Emily would march right in to Cora's office, and announce she didn't want anything in the divorce, except for it to be over.

Her heart felt heavy and her head spun. Emily picked up a magazine from the green chair next to hers, hoping it would distract her from her flurry of thoughts; but, it didn't help, so she tossed it back in the chair. Emily's foot wouldn't stop twitching, so she glanced down at it, noticing the plush carpet was bluer than the sea and it matched the walls.

She stood when the receptionist called her name and dragged herself into the main office. Her feet felt like lead weights were holding them down. Her stockings squished in her shoes. Emily plopped down in the hard metal chair across from Cora's desk.

Cora was a small woman in her late fifties. She had black hair and brown eyes, reminding Emily of a judge on one of the television court shows. And today, Cora's black hair looked even blacker than usual. Emily sighed, remembering that she had put sunglasses on when she entered the building.

"Are you alright?" Cora asked.

"Yes, I'm fine," Emily said, ripping the sunglasses from her face. "Why?"

"First of all, you never wear sunglasses in my office. Second of all, now I see why—your eyes are all puffy. So once again, I ask are you alright?"

"Yes, I'm fine. I didn't have a very good night."

"Did your bad night have anything to do with the divorce?"

"Not really…I don't know." Emily shrugged her shoulders and

shifted in her seat. "Maybe…sort of." She crossed her legs. "I'm sorry, Cora. I'm not all here today."

"Would you like to postpone this appointment? We can reschedule, that's not a problem."

"No, I want to get this over with. You don't know what I went through to get here."

"Since you think you feel up to it, then we should get started. There are a few more documents that I need you to sign before next week."

"Cora," Emily's face dropped. "I think I've changed my mind."

"So, you don't want to go through with the divorce."

"No…no…that's not it." Emily shifted in her seat, again, and uncrossed her legs. "I want this to be over with, now. I'm tired of everyone saying I'm dragging this out because I don't really want it so…" Her thoughts drifted.

"So…" Cora waited for an answer. "Go on, Emily, finish what you're saying."

"I'm going to prove to everyone that I'm ready. I don't want to go to court. I don't need to divide up anything with Steven. I know if I choose not to, this could be over with now."

"Emily, are you sure?" Cora raised an eyebrow. "A divorce shouldn't be about proving anything to anyone. It should be about what you want to do, in your heart. Unless, you're trying to prove to yourself that you really want the divorce."

"No," Emily shook her head. "I want the divorce. I don't need to prove anything to myself."

"Then, I think you should stick with the original plan. I think you should go to court. You don't want to regret not dividing up possessions or not asking for spousal support, later. Once Steven has everything, there's no going back. You once told me, with all you went through in the marriage, you deserved to get something out of it. Even if that something is just a car, it's better than nothing."

"You're right, Cora." Emily frowned. "I would like my car back. The one I have now is old and barely runs. I purchased it, for five hundred dollars, after I moved out. It would be nice to have my

BMW back. Then, I wouldn't have to wonder if, or when, it will start. I had enough of that this morning."

"Alright then, let's start signing papers."

Emily's head was still spinning. She felt like she was at a car dealership, and Cora was a salesman delighted for her to sign on the dotted line. Emily knew Cora was a good lawyer. She also knew Cora had her best interest at heart.

Walking out of Cora's office, Emily felt like a weight had been lifted off her chest. Cora was right, this was her decision. If Emily wanted to fight for a car, she should fight for a car. If she wanted part of the properties they owned in Precone—or in Florida—or the money they had in the bank, why shouldn't she have it. While riding down in the elevator, Emily called for another cab; but, every company she called said there would be an hour, or more, wait. She could take the subway. Or, maybe Emily could catch up with Robert. He traveled around for his job, so maybe she could catch him in between sales meetings. Maybe he could come and pick her up. If he happened to be in the area, he could drop her off at home.

"Is everything alright?" Robert asked, on the other line.

"Yes, everything's fine. I finished my meeting with Cora, and I wondered, if you're not too busy, if you could pick me up."

"What happened to your car?"

"It died on me this morning. I had to take a cab. And now, every company I call is about an hour out."

"I just got out of a meeting. I'm about twenty minutes away from where you are. I'll swing by. And since you have the day off, we could stop for lunch, before I drop you home."

"That sounds wonderful." She smiled. "I'll see you when you get here."

Blinking, Emily felt the cold air hit her cheek as someone came around the revolving door. Her chattering teeth and her trembling body made her want for a warm fireplace. The damp air was nauseating. She could tell others felt the same as several people around her mumbled over the conditions of the day.

Her ears perked up, hearing the familiar beep of Robert's car horn. She watched him step out of his silver Chrysler and walk up to the revolving doors with an umbrella in hand. And Emily noticed Robert's smile brighten when he saw her. He was so thoughtful and loving. Steven would never have walked to her with an umbrella in hand. He would have just honked and waited for her to walk to the car. At least the man Steven had become, now, wouldn't proffer that nice a gesture toward her.

"I could have come to you," Emily said, grinning like it was the first time they had met.

"No, I wanted to bring you the umbrella," Robert said, smiling back.

"How did you know I didn't have mine?"

"I know you. I know how forgetful you are when you're in a hurry." He leaned in and kissed her forehead. "That's one of the things I love about you."

"You love my forgetfulness?" Her eyebrow rose.

"No, I love your quirky ways." He brushed a strand of hair out of her eyes. "Are you alright?"

"Why does everyone keep asking me that today?"

"Your eyes are red and puffy, and your clothes are damp, and…" He leaned in and kissed her cheek this time. "Shall I go on?" Robert smiled.

"No, you shall not." Emily gazed up at him.

"I think rather than us going to lunch now, I should drop you at home first." He grabbed her hand and led her through the revolving door. "I need to get you out of those wet clothes."

"What was that?" she said. She laughed, watching the difficulty he had opening the umbrella for her. And she laughed at the suggestive nature of his comment.

"You know what I mean." He smiled back. "I don't want you to get sick."

❧

Robert made his way around to his side of the vehicle. He closed the umbrella and sat down in the driver's seat. His chest rose, with pride, as he looked over at Emily. She gazed out the window at the rain. He didn't care if her hair was drenched and her eyes were swollen; to him, she was the most beautiful woman in the world. Tearing his gaze away from her, he checked his side mirrors, then put the car in gear.

"How did everything go with Cora?"

"Fine."

"Care to elaborate?" He watched as her puffy hazel eyes turned to look at him.

"I signed everything that needed to be signed. We're still going to court, next week, to finalize everything. And once that's over, I'll be a free woman." Emily leaned her head back into the seat.

"I can't wait until that day comes. The day when you'll be all mine." The rain was still coming down in buckets, making it hard to see out of the window. The wipers swished as Robert turned them up to the faster setting. "If Steven wasn't so stubborn, he would give you what you deserve. But he won't."

"And, that's okay. Everything will be hashed out soon, and then, it'll be over."

"Yes, it will." He gripped her hand. He always liked to hold her hand and drive with his other one. Surprisingly, he felt her pull away.

"What's wrong?"

"My hands are so rough and dry. I'm embarrassed to let you hold them."

"I don't mind."

"I know, but let me put some lotion on first." She searched around the vehicle, looking under the seat and turning to look in the back. "Where did you put that lotion I left in here?"

"The one for lotion emergencies?" He grinned.

"Yes, that's the one." Emily smiled back.

"I think I put it in the glove box."

Watching her lean over to open the glove box gave him a light-bulb moment. Stupidly, he had placed the engagement ring in the glove compartment, a few days prior, when he had decided against asking for her hand in marriage, and he had left her house, in frustration. Robert had several stops to make that day and had been afraid of losing the ring. Not wanting it to fall out of his pocket, he had decided to put it in the glove box. The ring had been in there for days, and he hadn't thought about it, until now.

His eyes bulged. Before he could open his mouth, Robert saw her rummaging through the glove box. "Emmie, your hands are fine. I don't think I put the lotion in there, after all." He tried to steer her attention back to him. His heart pounded, a mile a minute.

"It's right here, silly." Emily pulled out the lotion and closed the glove box. She squeezed a dime size portion into her palm, and rubbed her hands together.

His heartbeat slowed. He was relieved she didn't notice the ring box. He dodged a bullet. Robert meant for it to be an inaudible sigh, but somehow it became an audible sigh.

"Are you alright?" Emily turned to him.

"Yes, you know I'm always great when you're by my side."

"You say the sweetest things to me." She leaned over and tapped his nose. "I don't know what I would do without you."

"Let's pray you never have to find out. I hope to always be here for you, no matter what."

"I hope so, too." Emily leaned over to open the glove box, again.

"What are you doing?" he asked, panicking.

"I'm putting the lotion back where I found it. I may need it again, if I have another lotion emergency." She grinned. And then, Emily was suddenly quiet.

Robert saw her face drop, and he knew it was all over. Feeling like a robber caught with a wad of cash, he knew the jig was up.

"What's this?" she asked, clutching the box. The glove compartment banged as she slammed it closed.

He saw her hands shaking as she tried to open the box.

"Emmie, it's nothing…"

"Oh, it's something, alright." Her smile brightened. "Is this what I think it is?" Emily didn't wait for a response. She opened the box. Tears came to her eyes. "Robert, it's so beautiful." Emily gasped.

Not knowing how to respond, Robert remained quiet. They were approaching a yellow light, and with the rain pouring, he didn't think he should try to make it through the intersection.

"When were you going to give this to me?" Her smile faded. "I'm sorry if I ruined the surprise."

"No, Emmie, you didn't." He stopped at the red light.

They were at the four way intersection at Fifth and Trumble. There was uneasiness in Robert's chest because the intersection was busy. There were directional arrows for the turning lanes lit and traffic everywhere. But since the light was red, Robert turned back to her. "I was going to give you the ring, at dinner, the other night—"

"Why didn't you?" Emily questioned, while blinking away tears.

"I wanted to, but I didn't want you to feel rushed. I know you're not divorced yet. And I convinced myself you would have said no. You once said marriage frightened you because of everything you'd been through." He glanced at her. "I never want to frighten you."

"I know I said that, but I love you. I would never be afraid to marry you. I would have said yes." She put the ring on her finger and wiggled her hand around. "It's so beautiful," Emily said. "I just love it. So if you still want to marry me, I'm saying yes."

"Of course I still want to, but I think the ring may be a little too big. I was going to have it sized correctly." Robert looked back at the light. It was still red. He turned back to her. "I wanted us to go have it sized together."

"It's a little big, but I don't care because it's perfect." Emily twirled it around some more. The ring was 18kt white gold, and he saw the bright reflection of the round diamond in her eyes. "So, once again, yes, I will marry you."

"This isn't the way I wanted this moment to go. I wanted to be down on one knee," he said, grinning. "But I'm happy you said yes. I can't wait to be your husband."

"And, I can't wait to be—oh, gosh." She leaned over. "The ring slipped off. It fell on the floor."

"That's okay. We can find it later."

"No, it's not." Emily unfastened her seat belt. She leaned over and felt for it. "I don't want the diamond to get dirty."

"But you shouldn't have your seat belt off."

"We're stopped at a red light," she said, still searching for the ring. "It will only take a minute."

"Emily, I don't think this is a good idea." His tone was serious. Robert saw a green Escalade approaching in his rearview mirror. The roads were wet and slippery. The truck came on, quickly; it didn't look like it slowed down.

"See, I found it." Emily smiled as she sat up.

Robert's smile faded when he heard a deafening screech, like nails on a chalkboard. He felt a force hit the back of his car. It was followed by a big bang, like an explosion from the rear of his vehicle. The forced impact caused his car to skid beyond the red light, through the crosswalk, and into oncoming traffic. Robert's heart raced as his car stopped in the middle of the intersection, paralyzed and helpless to oncoming traffic. Suddenly, he felt a hit on his side of the vehicle. His window shattered. Glass fell on him. A piercing pain throbbed on his cheek. Robert's side air bag finally deployed, hitting him on the arm; but, his steering wheel air bag didn't deploy. Something wet was on his cheek—probably blood. Robert was dazed and confused as he tried wiping the wetness from his face.

His heart dropped into his stomach when he heard Emmie's bloodcurdling scream. At least her screams meant she was still alive. He turned to look at her, but his eyes widened, looking past her. Through the passenger window, he saw a white car coming toward them, charging toward Emily's side of the vehicle. His mind raced. He knew her seat belt was off. Why hadn't her air bag deployed? Everything started going in slow motion. Before he could help her, the car slammed into them. Her window shattered, and glass flew everywhere.

Robert saw a cut on her forehead. The first two blows had slammed her body around and into the dashboard. He felt helpless as he watched her fall from the dashboard back into the passenger seat. Like a rat caught in a trap, there was nothing he could do. He tried to call her name, but his breaths were slow and raspy; he couldn't speak. Her eyes shut and she became silent. Her body was lifeless as the shards of glass laid upon her. Blood gushed down her face.

Robert felt himself go in and out of consciousness. At times, he heard people outside of the car. He heard frantic calls for help and sirens in the distance. He heard yelling and crying. Robert's eyes opened again, and he saw Emily still lying motionless in her seat. He felt too weak to reach out and touch her. He couldn't tell if she was dead or alive.

Why hadn't he protected her? Why was the love of his life laying there dead to the world around her? He felt helpless. There was nothing he could do to save her. Why was he spared while she was hurt? Why didn't he have the strength to carry her out of the car?

Robert's eyes painfully, and slowly, opened. He blinked a couple of times, trying to figure out where he was. He finally made out that he was in a hospital. A nurse stood over him. He gazed up to see IV fluids being dripped into his veins. He felt pain coming from his face and from his left arm. None of that mattered. His heart raced faster, along with his memory. Where was Emily? He suddenly remembered the accident. Robert tried to sit up. The nurse wouldn't let him. She told him that he was too weak to move. In that moment, he couldn't care less about himself. He had to find Emily. He had to know if Emily was still alive. Feeling like a bird stuck in a cage, he tried moving, again. The nurse shouted at him and called someone else into the room. He made out a syringe. Someone mumbled this is for the pain. His eyelids became heavy, like a tiny person stood on them. And then, they closed.

CHAPTER FIVE

"David, where were you? You weren't answering your pager. I finally told them to call you overhead." Monica's hands trembled. She stood in the ER of Ceder Hospital.

The staff moved around like their feet were on fire. A red haired nurse tended to a man who screamed that his arm was broken. A white haired doctor jabbed a needle into someone's chest, right before the curtain whirled closed, for privacy. All the goings on made her shoulders tense.

"I'm sorry, but I'm here now. What's wrong?" David's voice cracked.

"Emily and Robert were in a car accident."

"Are they alright?"

"I don't really know. They saw I was Emily's next of kin, from a card in her wallet. So they called me in the pharmacy and asked me to come down. They haven't said much since I got here. They've just made me stand out here." Monica was in the ER hallway, just outside of the waiting room.

"Maybe I can find out something," he said, rushing past her into the trauma room.

Monica kept pacing. Her heart raced and her legs felt wobbly. If she lost Emily, or Robert, she didn't know what she would do. "*God, please let them be alright,*" she mumbled.

David's brown eyes watered. He kept scratching his hand over the one strand of gray hair that lay atop his dark head as he walked toward Monica. She took this as a sign that things weren't good.

"Robert's fine. He has a few bumps and bruises on his ribs and his arm. He's going to be okay. But…" He glanced down and back up at her.

"What about Emily?" A lone tear trickled down her cheek.

"Emily's not doing so well. She has severe head trauma. She's stable, for now. But they need to move her up to the ICU."

"When can we see her?" Tears flowed as her body continued to tremble.

"It will be a while before they get her settled upstairs. But we can go in to see Robert." He reached for her hand.

Monica was grateful that Robert wasn't lying unconscious as her parents had been. She was also grateful that Emily was stable enough to be moved to the ICU. That was a miracle in itself, a miracle her parents hadn't been fortunate enough to experience.

"Are you alright?" She blinked away tears. Remaining strong in front of Robert wasn't as easy as she hoped it would be. Noticing a cut near his cheek, and the bruises on his arm and face, made her tears surface.

"I'm fine." He tried to sit up more. "I need to know how Emmie is." He looked at David, and then back at Monica. "Have you seen her?"

Monica's voice quivered as she spoke, so David took over. "They wouldn't let us see her. They moved her upstairs, to the ICU."

"What does that mean? Is Emily going to be alright?" Robert asked.

"We don't really know anything, except she has a head injury," David said.

"This is my fault." Robert's eyes watered.

"This is no one's fault. It was a terrible accident." Monica tried to be reassuring.

"You can't blame yourself," David added.

Monica hated seeing the pained look on Robert's face, so she tried to be positive. "Em was stable enough to be moved upstairs. So that's a good thing." She mustered up a half smile.

"I was driving. This is on me."

"Robert, don't do that," Monica said, pleading with him.

"You have to leave now," said a red haired nurse as she walked into the room. "Mr. Johnson needs to rest."

"Robert, we'll be back to see you, later." Monica leaned over and kissed his cheek. "We're going to go up and see Ems now."

"Check with the desk when you come back." The nurse reached up and grabbed the IV bag. It was almost empty. She put a new one in its place. "Mr. Johnson will probably be moved to the observation floor. They will tell you what room."

"Thank you, very much," David said.

"You're welcome." The nurse smiled. "By the way, I know you two work here. I've seen you around. I'm sorry about your sister. I hope everything turns out for the best."

"Thank you…" Monica glanced down at her name badge. "Thank you, Nancy. And thank you for taking such good care of our friend, Robert." Monica smiled and left the room with David following behind her.

Monica hated going up to the floors where the air was cold and smelled of antiseptics. She shivered, walking inside with David close by. Her heartbeat was loud, like a drum solo, as Monica watched David walk up to the nurse's station. Hopefully, Emily was still stable and they could go in and see her, soon.

A gray haired nurse name Marge told them Emily was in room two. Marge said Dr. Washington was in with Emily, at the moment, so they would have to wait. David reassured Monica that Dr. Curtis Washington was a top neurosurgeon, one of the best at the hospital. How relieved she was that he would be the one taking care of Emily. Even though Monica felt a tiny bit better, she couldn't stop her heart from pounding in her ears. What if Emily didn't make it? What would she do without her sister?

"Dr. Washington said you can go in," Marge said. "He wants to speak to you."

After a few minutes, Dr. Washington came from behind the curtain and walked over to the door. He was a stocky, short man with gray hair and blue eyes. The doctor told them to come in, and then he explained what they would see. He didn't want the initial shock to be too much. The room was small—almost claustrophobic—and smelled clean like Lysol. Walking behind the curtain, they found Emily hooked up to life support machines. There were tubes in her nose and mouth. Her face and head looked swollen. There was an IV hooked up to her right arm. Her eyes were closed. She appeared dead.

"Emily's in a coma. She suffered severe head trauma, swelling in her brain. Her blood pressure is low. I don't believe in giving families false hope." Dr. Washington's face was stern. "And, in my opinion, if you talk to her, she probably won't even know you're here. There's not much we can do, except wait to see if the swelling in her brain goes down. Hopefully, the medicine will help lower her blood pressure, returning it to normal levels."

"But I don't understand why you're not doing surgery to relieve the pressure," Monica said. She tried to remain calm, but her tears wouldn't stop.

"Surgery doesn't always work in cases like this. I believe we should try other options, first. Surgery would be done if Emily had a hematoma on her brain, which she doesn't. That's one thing working in our favor," Dr. Washington said. "There's no need to shave her hair and cut her head open. It's not necessary, right now. I will let you have some alone time with her." He exited the room.

"He really needs to work on his bedside manner." Like a train stuck on the tracks, she was unmovable.

"Dr. Washington's not known for his sensitivity, but he's the best in his field. We're fortunate to have him on Emily's case. He knows what he's doing. We have to do what he says and wait."

"I know you're right." Her voice quivered. "I feel helpless. I feel like I need to be doing something to help her."

"You can start by turning around and looking at her." David took her by the shoulders and turned her in the direction of Emily's bed.

"I don't know if I can." Her eyes stung from crying. Monica leaned back into David's chest, needing him to take the weight of the world away.

He put his arm around her waist and held her tight, for a moment, before taking her hand and guiding her to Emily's bedside. "I want you to sit with your sister and talk to her."

"But Dr. Washington said Emily can't hear us," she said.

"That's one thing I don't agree with. I think patients in comas can hear us, sometimes." David wiped away a tear from her face. Then, he pushed the chair closer to Emily's bed and motioned for Monica to sit down. "I'll be right back. While I'm gone, I want you to talk to Em and to pray for her. I believe prayer helps. I really do." He leaned over and kissed her forehead.

Monica reached for Emily's hand. She couldn't believe a day ago she was talking to her, and now, here Emily was, in a coma, hanging on for dear life.

"Ems," she whispered. "Please, forgive me. I'm so sorry for bringing up the baby. And I'm sorry for ever doubting that you would go through with the divorce. You have to wake up. I don't know what I would do if you weren't here, anymore. You're my baby sister, and I love you more than anything. When Mom and Dad died, it was supposed to be you and me against the world. You can't leave me now. And you can't leave Robert either. You two are planning on starting a new life together. You have to make it through this. You're strong, you're a fighter. Please, make it through this."

Hunching over the bed, Monica prayed.

✄

"Could someone please tell me what room Emily Montgomery is in?" Robert stood at the nurse's station.

His clothes were tattered and ripped; and, he could barely stand, but he didn't care. His side hurt from the accident, but his chest hurt more, knowing the pain Emily was in.

"Only family is allowed in," a red haired nurse said.

"I am family. She's my fiancée," he said, loudly.

"Well, there are two people in with her already and—"

"I thought I heard your voice out here," Monica said, cutting off their conversation.

"Where is she? I need to see her." Robert rushed up to her.

"Why aren't you in the ER?"

"I couldn't lie there, anymore. Once they said they were moving me upstairs, I decided to check myself out. I told the nurse to give me my clothes, and I came straight here," he said, shakily.

"I don't think that was such a good idea. You're no good to Emily like this. She would want you to get the care you need."

"I'm going crazy. I need to see her." Robert brushed past her. "I'll be fine. I have a few bruised ribs. All I need is pain killers and an ice pack. I'll go see my regular doctor in a few days. Now, can you show me where she is?"

"Fine," Monica said, walking ahead of him. "I don't have the strength to argue with you. But before I take you in the room, I need to warn you."

"Warn me of what?" His brow furrowed, and his throat tightened.

"She's hooked up to a lot of monitors. She has tubes coming out of her nose, and her face is pretty swollen—"

"I don't care about that." Robert brushed past her, again. "I don't care what she looks like, I need to see her. Please."

Seeing Emily sent shivers up his spine. She was so pale and swollen. Her lips were black, and she looked weak and fragile. All the tubes and loud beeping machines, along with the ventilator helping her breathe, took his breath away. He wanted to touch her; but, she looked so delicate, he feared she might break. With his heart in his stomach, he sat down in the nearest chair beside her bed.

Robert was grateful that Monica and David had stepped away to give him more privacy. Like a faucet, more tears came, tears that made him flinch when they landed on the cheek that was cut in the accident. But his pain didn't matter; only hers did. Emily was so bruised. He noticed a pink and red mark, behind her ear, that looked more profound than the other bruises. This was wrong. She had done nothing to deserve this. This wasn't how their new life was supposed to begin.

His hand shook as he touched it to her face, hoping for a response; but, there was none. She was unresponsive and ice cold. He closed his eyes and prayed for some movement, even a blink of an eye, but there was nothing. The machines were keeping her with him, for now; but, how long would that last?

"Please, Emily," he whispered. "You have to fight to stay. You have to fight, for your family, for your friends, for yourself. I know I'm being selfish right now; but, most of all, you have to stay for us, for the life we are planning together." He held her hand up to his face. Her limp arm fell down, landing on the bed, in its original position.

Steven's steps were quick as he rushed off the elevator. He looked up at the dark walls to see the small signs that pointed him to the ICU. The lights were bright. He saw nurses, conversing behind a desk. No one paid him any attention. His chest constricted; he needed someone to tell him where Emily was.

"I need to see my wife." His voice was erratic. "Could you please tell me what room she's in? Her name's Emily—Emily Montgomery."

"Sir, there are three visitors already in with Mrs. Montgomery." One of the nurses—with the name tag Marge—finally looked up at him. "I'll have to ask someone to step out, so you can go in. I'll be right back."

"Excuse me, miss. How is Emily doing? The only information I received downstairs was that she was taken to the ICU." Steven needed some positive news.

"She's in a coma. She suffered severe head trauma in the accident. But the doctor will be back to give you an update, later." She smiled. "I'll be right back."

Steven paced back and forth. Emily's accident was hours earlier, and he'd heard about it on the news. His heart stopped when the news reporter named Emily as one of the victims. His wife hung on for dear life, and no one even bothered to call him. He should have been by her side from the moment she was brought in. None of that mattered. He was there now, and he would be there for anything Emily might need. He needed her to live. He needed to be close to her. That's what was important.

"Mr. Montgomery, you can go in now. A few of her visitors will be stepping out."

"Thank you." He nodded, grateful for the much needed alone time.

He walked into her room, panic-stricken at what he would find. He saw Monica, sitting there with a man he had only seen in photos, photos taken while he had Emily followed. He ignored them and turned his attention to Emily. He wanted to reach out and hold her hand, but seeing her like this paralyzed him.

All he had wanted, for months, was to be close to her. But now, something stopped him from touching her. He wanted to be close to her, but not like this, not when she was in this condition. What if he lost her for good? There would be no chance to win her back. He took a deep breath, and like a prisoner removing the chains from his legs, he walked toward the bed.

His legs wobbled beneath him as he gazed at her lifeless body. He felt weak and helpless. It was a feeling he wasn't used to and didn't welcome.

"Is there any way you two could give us some privacy?" He glared at Monica, and the man he knew to be Robert.

"No matter what you may think, you're not family anymore. After all the things you've done, you shouldn't even be in here." Robert stood.

"She's still my wife, and I have every right to be in here, more right than you." Steven glared. "You're just the *boyfriend*."

"This is not the time nor the place for this," Monica said, standing. "Emily's fighting for her life, and we need to keep the peace right now."

"Monica's right," Robert said. "We'll step into the hallway, but we're not going far. And I'm only doing this because I know you're not going to be levelheaded and step away. So out of respect for Emily and her recovery, I will. She needs quiet right now, and I want to make sure she gets that."

"How chivalrous." Steven glared while watching them leave the room.

In his heart, he knew they were right; Emily needed peace around her. But he also knew he needed them to go away, and the only way he could make that happen was by being rough.

He turned back to Emily, with a heavy heart, since she remained the same.

"Sweetheart, I'm so sorry this happened to you." He leaned over and stroked her forehead. "If there is anything I can do to make you better, I will. I need to see that precious smile of yours again, and I need to hear your laughter. I know I haven't seen that side of you in a long time because of the stupid things I've done. But I would do anything to even have you argue with me again. I need to see that fire in your eyes."

He knew he was being selfish, but he wanted her to fight; he needed her. He needed her in his life again.

"I need you to wake up, Emily, so I can make things right between us." He swallowed hard. "You have to."

He hoped his words would somehow change her condition. But

her body was still limp, and her expression was still slack and frozen. Not caring that there were tubes coming from every direction, he bent over and lightly laid his head on her chest. He wanted to feel her heart beating, to make sure she was still with him. And Steven needed to know Emily would never leave him again.

CHAPTER SIX

"How's she doing today?" Robert saw Monica standing outside of Emily's ICU room.

"I haven't seen her yet. The nurse has been in with her since I arrived, but I'm sure she's about the same," Monica said with a frown.

"Now, what's that look for?" Robert asked. "She's doing better. I mean, the color is coming back in her cheeks, and she's breathing on her own. Ever since Dr. Washington performed that ventriculostomy, two weeks ago, the pressure on her brain has significantly lessened. We have a lot to be thankful for."

"I know all of that."

"Then, what's the problem?" He unbuttoned his suit coat.

"It's hard to believe it's the middle of January and she's still in here." Monica blinked away tears. "It's been two months of torture. And I hoped, by now, she would have awakened. I know I'm being selfish, but it's been hard keeping a positive attitude."

"I know," Robert said. "Every day when I stop by, I hope that she'll be her old self again; but, it never happens."

"No." Monica shook her head. "She still has that same frozen look on her face, like she's dead to the world. I know she's getting better, but why hasn't she awakened yet? What if they're not telling us everything? What if she seems better but still never wakes up."

"Now you're being ridiculous. You can't think like that; you'll drive yourself crazy," Robert said, placing his hand on her shoulder. "I'm not giving up on her, and you shouldn't either. I'm sure she'll come back to us, any day now. We have to be patient and keep praying."

"Yes, but what if that's not enough?"

"It will be." He gave her shoulder another squeeze. "It has to be since this is my fault."

"You keep saying that. What does that even mean?"

"Nothing." He shook his head. "When can we see her? I decided to stop by on my lunch hour today. I don't have much time before my next meeting." He glanced at his watch.

"The nurse is cleaning her up. If she's not finished soon, I'll have to go as well. I need to get back down to the pharmacy. It's funny how I'm expected to continue on with life as usual when a loved one is in the hospital."

"I feel the same. All I want to do is stay by her bedside, watch over her, and make sure she's okay; but, I have to go back to my normal life." He put his hands in his pockets, then took them back out.

"It's hard to be normal without Emily."

"I know, but we have to be as normal as we can until this nightmare is over." There was anguish in the pit of his stomach, as much as he was trying to reassure Monica he was also trying to reassure himself. "I'm just happy you and David were able to talk her doctors into letting her stay here a little longer. I didn't want her to go to a long-term care facility. I know I'm being unrealistic, but I fear if she goes to one of those places, the hope of her waking up lessens. It seems like that would finalize that she's not going to get better. Besides, they've been giving her excellent care here, so why move her."

"I know that's the wrong attitude to have, but I kind of agree with you." Monica frowned. "I know it's selfish, but I know the staff here, and I like being able to come upstairs, any time I want, and visit with her. I like being close by, if anything happens. I also like knowing who is coming and going from her room."

"Like, Steven."

"Yes." Monica nodded. "I'm happy that he hasn't been around, lately."

"It is odd." Robert scratched the back of his neck. "At first, he was here every day, trying to visit with her and now…"

"He's nowhere to be found." Monica finished his sentence.

"Maybe he's forgotten about his quest to win her back and moved on to other things." He prayed that was true.

"One can only hope. Steven's the kind of guy who gets a thrill off the chase, and now that Emily's in a coma, there's no chase. She can't argue with him. So maybe there's no reason for him to linger."

Robert was silent. Even though he hoped that was the case, from all the stories he'd heard about Steven, he didn't think he was the kind of man who would give up so easily. Robert was curious as to when Steven would play his next hand.

"It doesn't look like the nurse will be finishing up any time soon." The curtain was still drawn around Emily's bed. "I have to go, but I'll be back later." He kissed Monica's forehead. "Call me if anything changes."

"You know I will." Monica gave a half smile.

He hated saying those five words. He didn't want to be called if anything changed. He wanted to be there to witness the changes. And if there were changes, he hoped they were good.

A physical therapist normally did range of motion exercises to keep Emily's muscles active and to preserve muscle tone and circulation. A respiratory therapist came in daily and provided breathing treatments, and tapped Emily on her back to promote movement of secretions in her lungs. Then, they did touch simulation, by using a variety of different textures—such as blankets or stuff animals or lotion—to see if it stimulated Emily. The nurses also performed smell simulation with perfumes or shampoos or different foods. They put a cotton swab up to Emily's lips with a sweet, salty or sour taste to see if she responded. These things were done daily. The only things Robert was allowed to do was read to her and talk to her. He also enjoyed caressing her hand. But no matter how small a part he played in her recovery, he was just happy to be near her.

❧

"Excuse me, Mrs. Wilson." Marge, the nurse, came from behind the curtain. "You can go in and visit with your sister, now."

"Thank you for taking such good care of her." Monica smiled. "I don't feel so bad leaving her, knowing that you're here. Any changes in her condition?" Monica's stomach clenched, waiting for Marge to answer.

"Well…" Marge paused. A smile appeared on her face. "Last night, Dr. Washington said we could completely take her off the ventilator. So when you go in, you'll notice it's gone."

"Oh, Marge, this is wonderful news." Monica beamed at the nurse.

"Yes, it is; but…"

"Oh no, what is it?" Her smile faded as quickly as it had appeared. "What's wrong?"

"The doctor wanted me to inform you that we still don't know the extent of the damage to her brain. And even though she may wake up soon, don't be alarmed if she's not exactly the same."

"I don't care if she's not the same. I'll be happy as long as she wakes up." Monica smiled. "I'm going to go in and read to her now."

The curtain swooshed as she ripped it back. Monica couldn't believe how much better Emily looked without the ventilator tube hanging from her mouth. Maybe it was her imagination, but the frozen expression seemed to be gone. Her heartbeats were erratic as she walked closer to the bed. She heard the faint sounds of Emily breathing again. It sounded tubular, like air being blown through a tube. And it reminded her of the soft breaths that came from a newborn.

It was wonderful and exciting. She sat down in the chair beside the bed, so she could take it all in. Everything was brighter now that Emily was on the road to recovery. The air in the room was lighter. The beeping noises had lessened. There was a speck of sunlight peering through the blinds. The red roses on the table beside her bed made the room smell like perfume. She grabbed some of the cards from the table. She had read them out loud before, but it wouldn't hurt to read them again.

"These are from some of your students. This one is from Joshua. It says *Mrs. Montgomery, get well soon. We miss you.*" She shifted in her chair and undid her coat. "This pink one, with the flowers on the front, is from Maggie. She says *I know you will make it through this because my father made it through his surgery. Please, get well soon and come back to work. We miss you.*"

Monica thought it was her imagination when she saw Emily's eyes blink. At first, she didn't think anything of it, since the doctors had said there were different levels of consciousness. Sometimes, a person who was unresponsive could still blink, but that didn't mean they were waking up. So Monica continued reading.

"This one is from Christina. She's another teacher at the school who you are really close to. Since only family is allowed in the ICU, she hasn't been to see you; but, as soon as you wake up and start doing better, she wants to come and visit. She says *Emily, you are truly missed. I love you so much. You have to wake up, so we can go…*" Monica's voice drifted off as she saw Emily's fingers move.

Monica's heart felt like it had burst out of her chest. She dropped the cards as she stood. It was as if Emily signaled her that she heard her reading. After a few more minutes, Emily's eyes stopped blinking; but, they completely opened and looked around, as if she was scoping out the room. Maybe Emily was trying to figure out where she was and who was talking to her.

Monica trembled. She took Emily's hand and softly spoke to her. She wasn't expecting Emily to speak, but she wanted some sign that maybe the nightmare was finally over.

"Emily, it's me Monica. If you can understand what I'm saying, squeeze my hand." To her surprise, she felt a gentle squeeze.

She didn't want to get excited, since—once again—this may be just a natural reflex. Even so, it was more response than she'd seen in weeks. Monica knew she should call for a doctor; but, she wanted to talk to Emily a little more, before a doctor came in and burst her bubble. A doctor would probably tell her it wasn't what she thought, or hoped, it was.

Swallowing hard, Monica leaned over Emily's body, wanting to look directly at her as she spoke. The grip on her hand continued, like she was holding on for dear life. The closer Monica got, the more she felt the warmness of Emily's breath, as she opened her mouth and tried to speak.

"M-Mon…Mon…Monica…"

Monica stood frozen, for a minute. This was a miracle. Emily spoke. This was what she had been praying for and excitement overcame her.

"Oh, my God, Emily, you're really awake." She felt Emily squeeze her hand, harder. "Can you understand me?" She felt another gentle squeeze. "I have to call a nurse." Her voice trembled. "But I don't want to let go of your hand. I don't want to leave you alone." Her eyes filled with tears.

Her first instinct was to run out of the room, screaming like a crazy person. But Monica remembered she could hit the red call button and a nurse would come. Her hands shook as she reached for the button and pressed it, hearing a beep.

"Is everything alright?" Marge entered the room.

"Emily spoke." Tears fell from Monica's eyes. "She even squeezed my hand, a little. I can't believe this is happening." Her smile widened from ear to ear.

"That's wonderful news." Monica saw excitement all over Marge's face. "I'll page Dr. Washington, right away."

"Could you also page my husband?" Monica's voice quivered.

"Yes, right after I page the doctor." Marge walked out of the room.

"Everything's going to be fine," Monica said, looking back at Emily. The grip on her hand was even stronger. "Don't you worry, Ems, you're awake now, so everything's okay again," she whispered, wanting with every fiber of her being to believe it was true.

Monica's tears blurred her eyesight, a little. But it still didn't stop her from seeing what was right in front of her. Her sister was alive, awake and talking. Emily's eyes were wide and looking around, in amazement. As far as Monica was concerned, everything was right with the world again.

"I heard the good news. How's our patient doing?" Dr. Washington walked into the room.

"She tried to speak, a little, but she stuttered and her speech was slow. She seems to be a little confused, but she does know who I am."

"That's understandable. Most patients who have been out as long as she has will be confused when they first wake up. If she knows who you are, I would say that's a good sign."

"Do you need me to leave the room?"

"No, actually I will just ask you to step back, a little, while I examine her. She seems to be more comfortable with you here, and I don't want to upset her."

"Ems, I'm just going to step over to that side of the room." Monica pointed, so she would understand. "This is Dr. Washington. He's going to examine you, but like I said, I'm not leaving. I'll be right here the whole time." Her voice trembled. She was relieved and scared at the same time. "I didn't get to explain to her where she is or what happened."

"That's fine. We don't want her to get overly excited. We'll see how much she already knows, and I'll fill in the blanks for her."

❧

"Hi Emily, I'm Dr. Washington, and I've been taking care of you.

I'm glad to see you're awake. I'm going to ask you a few questions. Do you understand what I'm saying?"

Emily's eyes widened and she slowly searched the room. She saw cards and flowers on the table nearby. Her heart fluttered like wings on a bird. Why couldn't she seem to calm down? Where was she? And what was this unfamiliar room she was in? Why was she hooked up to monitors? And why did she suddenly feel cold?

Emily's eyes focused in on Monica, standing farther back near the wall. The warmness of Monica's smile calmed her. She even found the strength to sit up more. Now that she felt more at ease, she could focus her attention on the doctor. She nodded—yes—to his question.

"Now, your sister said you were talking before I entered the room, can you talk to me? If you don't feel comfortable, you don't have to. But I would like to see how well your speech is."

Emily's mouth was dry as she tried to speak. "Y-yes."

"Good. That was very good. Do you know where you are?"

She looked around the room again. Her eyes settled back on the monitors she was hooked up to. Her throat tightened realizing where she was. "I t-think the—h-h-hospital."

"That's excellent. Now do you know what happened to bring you to the hospital?"

Emily shook her head from side to side. "N-no."

"Okay, that's fine. You're doing really well. You don't have to be frightened. You were in a car accident, and you've been in a coma. I'm going to examine you to see how your reflexes are. Is that alright with you? Do you feel up to that?"

She glanced Monica's way. She felt like a rope tightened around her neck. A car accident? Did she hit someone or did someone hit her? How long had she been in the hospital?

Monica stepped closer to the bed. "It's alright, Ems. I'll be right here."

Remembering he wanted her to speak, Emily slowly opened her mouth, and said, "Y-yes, that's fine."

The more Emily spoke, the more it seemed the stuttering was going away, although she still spoke slowly.

Dr. Washington took out a penlight. "Don't be alarmed, Emily. I'm just going to check your pupils." He shined the light into her eyes, and said this would enable him to measure her pupils and check her pupillary light reflex.

She blinked a few times. Having a light shined directly into her eyes wasn't the most comfortable feeling. She was glad when that was over.

Dr. Washington explained he would perform a neurological exam—a series of exams that would test her motor function, cranial nerves, coordination and gait her reflexes, and sensation. Those tests would be more extensive, so he asked Monica to leave the room while he performed them.

Watching her sister walk away wasn't as easy as Emily thought it would be. She was happy when the tests were done. The doctor explained that she had passed everything. Emily continued to listen as the doctor said he wanted her to have a CAT scan next. The nurse would come in and get her set up. Then, she would be transferred downstairs for that exam.

Emily tried to muster up a small, weak smile. She was happy she had passed the test. She guessed that was a good thing. But her mouth was dry. Everything was confusing and still a little scary. Did she really need more tests done, right now?

There were so many unanswered questions going through her mind. How long had she been lying there? What caused the car accident? She had always been an excellent driver; could the accident have been her fault? Her arms felt heavy, and her body felt weak. It felt like a block of cement weighed her down. The more Emily thought about things, the more her throat burned. Why hadn't Monica come back in the room yet? And where was Steven?

⁓

"I'm glad you're still here," Emily said. Her eyes were glassy as she focused in on Monica.

"Where else would I be? I told you I'd be here when you got back." Monica sat down.

"I know you did." Emily smiled and turned toward David.

He leaned in to give her a kiss on her forehead, and then sat down. "It's so good to see you awake and talking. I can't tell you how much we've missed you. How are you feeling?"

"I'm tired but I'm happy to see you. Thanks for being here."

"Like your sister said where else would we be? Besides I work upstairs, so I have to be here anyway. I just figured, you're here, I'm here, why not go down and visit for a while." He smiled. "But seriously, I was worried about you. I come down every chance I get."

"Thank you." She leaned over, to look past him, toward the door.

"Ems, are you okay? Are you looking for someone?" Monica saw Emily eyeing the door and figured she was looking for Robert. "Is there anything I can get for you?"

Emily's expression was wide-eyed. "Well, I was just wondering where Steven is. I thought he'd be here when I got back from my test."

Monica shot a quick look at David.

"Why would you be looking for Steven?" David asked.

"Because he's my husband, silly. I don't understand why he's not here."

"Ems, what about Robert?" Monica stood.

"Robert...who's Robert?" Emily's brow wrinkled, in confusion.

"Robert, your fi—"

"We should leave you alone for a while." David cut Monica off from completing her sentence. "You're probably tired. I'm sure you need some rest."

"Yes, I am a little tired." Her eyes looked heavy.

"We'll be right outside." Monica softly rubbed the top of Emily's hand.

Monica's stomach was in knots as she followed David to the door. "What's going on?" Her voice was panicky. "Why would she ask for Steven and not Robert?"

"I'm not sure." David shrugged. "It's understandable that she's a little confused. Just try and calm down. We'll find Dr. Washington and he can tell us what's going on."

"Is everything alright?" Marge walked up to them.

"Emily seems to be a little confused," David said.

"As far as I know everything was fine with her neurological exam," Marge said.

"What does a neurological exam include?" Monica asked.

"Dr. Washington checked her motor function, her reflexes, her coordination and her sensations," Marge answered. "He likes to perform the neurological exam and then he likes a neuropsychologist to come in after and perform an exam for mental status changes and to assess mood, personality and cognitive behavior along with memory and concentration."

"I guess that's who we need to talk to," David said.

"Do you know when they'll be getting here?" Monica asked.

"Actually she should be here any minute. Dr. Washington wanted me to page her after Emily was back from her CAT scan. In fact, there she is now."

A tall slender woman with dark, short hair and gray eyes and a white lab coat on walked up to Marge. She had received a page and was there to see the patient named Emily Montgomery.

The woman introduced herself to David and Monica as Dr. Wendy Robinson. She was going to ask Emily a series of questions. She had all of the necessary information she needed in Emily's chart and from the forms Monica filled out when Emily was admitted. She asked David and Monica to remain outside the door, and she would go over the results with them, later.

"What if something is seriously wrong with her memory?" Monica watched Dr. Robinson walk into the room.

"Now Monica," David put his arm around her. "Emily's alive

and she's awake. That's what really matters. She's confused, right now. I'm sure everything will be fine. Try not to worry."

"I'll try," Monica mumbled. But her stomach did flip-flops, and she had a bad feeling that she couldn't shake.

How could Emily not know who Robert was? Robert had mentioned to Monica that in the car ride before the accident Emily had found the ring and said yes to his proposal. So how could Emily not remember the man she was supposed to marry? How would Robert feel if he arrived and Emily looked right through him and asked for Steven?

❧

"Hi Emily, I'm Dr. Robinson, one of your doctors. It's very nice to meet you." She extended her hand.

"What happened to Dr. Washington? I thought he was my doctor."

"You have several doctors for different reasons. Dr. Washington is your neurosurgeon. I'm your neuropsychologist." She sat down in the chair beside Emily's bed.

"I don't understand what the difference is."

"Dr. Washington deals mostly with your nervous system which includes your brain and your spine, its structures and connections. This could include surgical or non-surgical procedures. My job is a little different. I deal with brain behavior relationships. I assess brain functioning. I deal with the mind and its changes, due to injury or trauma."

"So, you're saying there's something wrong with my brain because of the car accident."

"Well, something like that, but let's talk a little more before we jump to any conclusions. Now, I'm going to ask you a few questions. Answer as best as you can, alright?"

"Alright." She nodded. There were unwanted butterflies in her stomach.

"What is your full name?"

"Emily Ann Montgomery."

Dr. Robinson jotted down some notes on a pad. "What is your maiden name?"

She looked back at the doctor. "Emily Ann Davis."

"You're doing very well. Let's continue on. What year is it?"

Emily frowned. "I'm not sure. Is that a bad thing?"

"No, Emily, sometimes when people have been in an accident, and have had some sort of injury, they might not remember everything right away. That doesn't mean it won't come back in time. The year is 2016. Does that ring any bells?"

"No." Emily shook her head. "I'm sorry, that year doesn't mean anything to me." She fidgeted with her hands. "I don't understand why I can't remember."

"That's fine. There's no reason to get upset." Dr. Robinson leaned over and patted her hand. "Let's continue on with the next question. Who is the president of the United States?"

Emily closed her eyes. The unwanted butterflies continued to swarm. Why was she so nervous answering a few simple questions? And why didn't she know the answers? Feeling like she was on trial in a courtroom full of people and she didn't know what to say, she started to tremble. Why was this so difficult?

"I'm sorry. I don't know that either." Emily opened her eyes. "What's wrong with me?" She blinked away tears.

"You've had severe head trauma. That would make anybody a little confused. But like I said, it's okay if you don't remember everything."

"I don't want to do this anymore." Emily shifted. She felt like she was under water and couldn't breathe. "I'm tired of all these questions. When is Steven getting here?"

"I know answering questions can be tiring. We just need to go over a few more things. So who is Steven to you?"

"Steven's my husband."

"And how long have you been married?"

"For one year, but we have been together for two." She smiled.

"Are you two happy?"

"Yes, we're very happy. He's the love of my life." Her smile grew wider.

"Emily, where is your place of employment?"

"I used to work as a waitress but that was years ago. I no longer work—Steven doesn't want me to."

"I think that's all, for now." Dr. Robinson stood. "I don't want to exhaust you. We'll pick this back up, tomorrow. You get some rest now." She patted the top of her hand.

"Dr. Robinson, is it alright if my family comes back in?"

"Yes, it's fine. But I don't want them to stay too long. You've been through a great ordeal and you need rest."

"One more thing, doctor, could you check with the front desk and see why my husband isn't here yet? Maybe there's a mix up and they won't let him come up." Emily swallowed hard. "I can't understand why he isn't here to see me yet."

"Is everything alright with Emily?" Monica rushed up to Dr. Robinson.

"Physically, she seems fine; but, there are some things we need to discuss about her mental health. Why don't you two follow me down to my office. It's more private there."

Reaching the doctor's office, Monica smelled peppermint. The doctor probably used it to calm her patient's nerves. Maybe it would calm hers as well.

"Please, take a seat," Dr. Robinson said. There were two seats across from her desk. "Now, to begin, I want you to know that I informed the desk that Emily can't receive any visitors right now—no matter who it is."

"Is that necessary?" David asked.

"Yes, it is. Until we can assess her situation more, it is necessary."

"Does that include us?" Monica glanced at David.

"No, it doesn't include you two." Dr. Robinson moved her chair closer to her desk. "When I was with Emily, she asked for her husband, Steven. I see on the form you filled out Mrs. Wilson, that you checked the box marked single for Emily—instead of married—and you put yourself down as her next of kin. But just now, Emily seemed to think she was happily married. So I need you to clarify a few things for me. Is she married or isn't she?"

"Technically, she's still married. She's separated." Monica shifted in her chair. "She had a court date scheduled to finalize the divorce, but that never happened because of the accident. I didn't see any reason to put down Steven's name. I'm her next of kin, and that's why I wrote what I did on the form. To be frank, doctor, she's engaged to a nice man named Robert, now. Steven is basically out of the picture."

"And, under occupation, you wrote high school teacher," Dr. Robinson continued. "Emily is under the impression that she doesn't work—"

"I don't understand why she would say that." Monica chimed in. "This is very upsetting."

"Monica, let the doctor speak." David rubbed the top of her hand.

"I understand that it's upsetting." The doctor continued. "And now that I know a little more history, it helps in determining some things. I have to say, from talking to Emily, and seeing how much she needs her husband to visit—among other things—that she may have retrograde amnesia." The doctor clasped her hands together. "Let me explain what that is. It's a loss of access to events that happened, or information she may have learned, before the injury occurred. Most of the time, patients that suffer head trauma are more likely to lose recent memories that are closer to the traumatic incident than memories from the past." She glanced down at Emily's chart.

"Is this temporary or permanent?" Monica asked.

"All cases are different. No two subjects are just alike."

"And what does that mean?"

"In some cases like this, patients quickly regain memories from the past. And sometimes, they regain memories at a slower rate—meaning months or years. But in other cases, the patient never regains any memories from the past. We just don't know. It's basically a wait and see process."

"So, she could stay like this forever?" Monica asked.

"Yes, she could. But we have to remain positive and be happy that she woke up at all." Dr. Robinson smiled.

David changed his gentle rubbing of Monica's hand to a light squeezing. "Dr. Robinson's right, we have to remain positive. We should be glad that she's alive and that she remembers us. She could have forgotten everything."

Monica looked toward David. "I understand that." She turned back to face the doctor. "But what I don't understand is, out of all the times for her memory to go back to, why would Emily go back to when she and Steven were happy? Why wouldn't she go back to a time when Steven treated her badly, so she wouldn't be calling out for him, and wanting to still be with him? This doesn't make sense." Her head was spinning, like she was on a roller coaster and needed to get off.

"We, as doctors, don't know every single thing about the brain; so, maybe in your sister's case, she's also blocking out some things along with the retrograde amnesia. Maybe, she's repressing some of her memories because they are too painful to remember, and she wants to go back to a time when she was happy. Happier times are more palatable to the brain. Unfortunately, the happy times Emily remembers are with Steven, not Robert."

"Can we do something to make her remember? How about hypnotizing her?"

"No, no." Dr. Robinson shook her head. "All we can do is have faith and pray that, in time, her memory will come back. And hopefully, some of it will. But she may never get all of it back. In cases like this, we don't know."

"So, what do we do now?" David asked.

"The CAT scan did show some abnormalities in the brain, which I confirmed by talking to her. I'm going to talk to Dr. Washington about having an MRI scan done as well. Maybe it will show damage that the CAT scan didn't. I'll also keep working with her, with your help of course, to fill in some of the blanks in her life. By discussing these things with Emily, maybe more memories will come back to her. This is going to be a lengthy process, so we have to be up for it."

"I'm up for whatever it takes to get my sister back to her normal self," Monica said.

"That's good, Mrs. Wilson, because your sister's going to need you to be patient and understanding with her. One more thing I want to add. You may notice mood swings or childish behavior from your sister. That's also part of the trauma she suffered, so don't hold it against her. She may not realize what she's doing." Dr. Robinson stood and extended her hand to Monica. "You will make it through this. It's difficult, at first—extremely difficult—but hopefully, it will get better in time." She smiled.

"I hope you're right." Monica stood, trying to smile back; but, her head pounded and she really wanted to cry.

"I recommend that Emily have no visitors for the next few days, except for you two. I think unfamiliar visitors will upset her. So I'm sorry, but that includes Robert. When you speak to Emily over the next few days, be gentle. Try and stay on safe topics for now. If she brings up something that might upset her, explain to her that certain things shouldn't be discussed at this time because it might hinder her recovery, and the doctors need to assess her more fully before we delve into certain subjects. Hopefully, Emily will be alright with that explanation. In a few days, if she still doesn't remember, we'll proceed in helping her fill in the blanks. I'll be checking on her, frequently. There will also be a physical therapist checking in on her to get her muscles back in working order. She needs to get down to the business of walking again, and dressing herself, and, for that matter, brushing her teeth. If you need me, and I'm not around, then have me paged."

"We will and thank you," David said.

Monica turned to David. "What do we do if Steven shows up? She didn't mention anything about that."

"Don't worry about that, right now. We'll handle it, when the time comes."

⚜

Robert felt like he was walking on a cloud as he entered the ICU. Monica's message said it was good news. He assumed that Emily was awake and talking. But when he got to the ICU desk, they informed him that no one was allowed in Emily's room. Now, the cloud dissipated and a noose twisted around his neck.

He saw Monica and David, standing over near Emily's room. They looked engrossed in conversation. Maybe something bad had happened to her between the time Monica called him and the time he arrived at the hospital. As soon as Robert walked up to them, David excused himself—his pager had gone off and he was needed elsewhere in the hospital.

"Mon, what's going on? Why won't they let anyone in to see Emmie?"

Monica's eyes were sad. Robert's throat constricted. Her silence was deafening. All he heard was the loud chatter of nurses talking over by the desk, and a rapid response code called overhead.

"Let's go somewhere quiet, so we can talk," Monica said.

Robert followed behind her; his lungs burned like fire. Like a man on death row not knowing if this would be the last day of his life, he didn't know if his fiancée was lost to him or not. They stopped in the hallway outside of the ICU. The sunlight through the square-shaped window blinded his eyes.

"Monica, are you going to tell me what's going on? I'm starting to freak out." He moved in front of her, to block out the sun, and squeezed her elbow. "Did she take a turn for the worse? On the phone, you said it was good news. Did something bad happen before I got here?" His hands shook as he spoke.

"While you were gone, Ems woke up and we even talked, a little.

The nurse and the doctor came in to look at her, and they ended up taking her down for a CAT scan." She shifted her weight on her hip. "When Ems came back from the CAT scan, David was with me in the room. We talked to Emily and she seemed fine until…" Her eyes watered. "Until she asked where Steven was."

"Why would she ask for him? I don't understand."

"According to the doctors, she has retrograde amnesia; and, because of her head trauma, she's lost recent memories that are closer to the car accident than memories from the past. So what I'm trying to say is, we think her memory has gone back to the time she shared with Steven."

"You think?" His voice was loud.

"I know you're upset. It blows my mind that she thinks they're still happily married. It doesn't seem like she even remembers the bad times. The doctor said it could be due to the trauma that she's blocking out those bad times or repressing certain memories." Monica glanced at the floor. "I don't really understand it."

"Amnesia?" He took in a breath. "All this time, I was so worried about her waking up that nothing else even mattered. I told myself as long as she woke up I didn't care if she couldn't walk or she wasn't her old self. I would be there for whatever she needed. And now, she came back to us. She's alive, and I'm so relieved." His voice quivered. "I know this sounds selfish, and I don't mean to be, but what about me? Did she mention me at all?" He wiped his eyes.

"I'm sorry. She doesn't remember you. I mentioned you and her face went blank. She didn't know who I was talking about. The doctors said that this might be temporary. They don't know for sure."

"So, Emily can't remember me? She can't remember the love we shared?" Robert's fist clenched. He wanted to punch the nearest wall. "What about our plans? What about our future? How can this be happening?"

"Please, try and calm down. It may not be this way forever." She rubbed his shoulder.

"What are we supposed to do in the meantime?"

"We're supposed to pray and have faith that her memory will come back. Who knows, this time tomorrow, she may remember you."

"Can I see her?" His throat was tight so he undid his tie.

"I'm sorry. Dr. Robinson advised against that. We're supposed to give her time, not push her too much."

"But maybe, if I'm able to see her, it would spark a memory in her. This is ridiculous." He shook his head. "I'm her fiancé. I should be able to see her."

"I know, but give it a few days. Maybe she'll remember you on her own. And if not, I'm sure the doctor will let you see her, then. We need to wait."

"So, what am I supposed to do in the meantime? Hang around here, watching Steven visit her?"

"That's one good thing; I think Steven is on the list of people who can't visit her."

"You think? What does that mean?" His nostrils flared.

"Dr. Robinson didn't really clarify, but she did say David and I were the only ones who could see her. So I assumed Steven isn't allowed to see her, either."

"I hope you're right. However, if it turns out Steven is allowed to see Emily, then I'm going to see her, too. It's only fair."

"I know, you're right. I'm not disagreeing with you. But for right now, for Em's sake, we have to do as the doctors say. They know what's best."

CHAPTER SEVEN

"Sorry I'm late." Dr. Robinson walked into the room. "My prior meeting ran long. How is our patient doing today?"

"I'm okay," Emily said.

"Just okay?" Dr. Robinson patted the sheets over her leg.

"I would be better if someone could tell me what's going on. Why does it feel like I've been getting the runaround for the last few days? No one will answer my questions. No one will tell me why Steven hasn't come to see me yet."

"I know you have a lot of questions. That's the reason we're all here today. Do you remember a few days ago when you first woke up, and I asked you a few questions?"

"Yes. I remember."

"That's good. Today, we're going to discuss a few more things. Hopefully, we'll be able to address all of your unanswered questions. I will warn you that some of the things might be a little overwhelming. But I need you to try and listen, very carefully, and not get upset. Your sister and brother-in-law are here for moral support, and because they know your history better than I do."

Emily felt her eyes watering. Her stomach felt queasy.

"Is something wrong, Emily?" Dr. Robinson asked.

"You're scaring me." She wiped her hand across her eye.

"That's not my intention; but, we do need to get these things out in the open, so you can feel whole again."

"I would like that. I do feel like something's missing." Emily shook her head. "I feel like you're keeping something from me."

"When we spoke earlier, we discussed the year and who the president is—"

"Yes, I remember." Her face felt hot.

"Do you now know the year or who the president is?"

"No," she shook her head. "I still can't recall."

"That's fine, Emily. The year is 2016 and Barack Obama is the president of the United States. I realize a few days ago I told you the year and it didn't mean anything to you. What about now? Does hearing the year or the president's name help you remember anything?"

"No, it doesn't," she said. A long sigh followed.

"That's fine." Dr. Robinson crossed her legs. "What I gauged from our earlier conversation is that you can't remember certain things. I believe you have retrograde amnesia."

"What does that mean?" Emily felt frustrated, like someone stood on her chest and she couldn't breathe.

"It means you can't remember some things before the accident. Basically, your brain has taken you back to a time in which, I believe, you felt safe. You have blocked out recent events closest to the accident."

"What events? Is that why Steven hasn't come to visit me yet?" She rambled. The person standing on her chest became heavier. "I don't even know how old I am."

"First of all, you're thirty years old. Second, I know you said you don't work; but, you do. In fact, you're an English teacher. You have a classroom full of high school students. Your sister indicated this on the form she filled out when you arrived."

"But that's not possible. Steven never wanted me to work." Emily shook her head. "When I met him, I worked part-time as a waitress, and I was in college, taking courses toward a teaching degree. After we married, Steven said he never wanted me to work again. So I stopped working and dropped out of school. None of this makes any sense." She frowned.

"Why don't we let your sister explain things to you. She's been with you every day, and she knows what you've been through. I'll be right here, if you need anything."

Emily trembled. Why did everyone have such serious expressions on their faces? Why were they treating her like a fragile glass that could easily break?

"Emily, things have changed a little, since the time you remember. You and Steven have been married for six years."

Emily let out a small sigh.

"But you went through some difficult times, and now you two are separated."

Emily bit down on her lip.

"You haven't lived with him in a year and a half. You were in the process of divorcing him." Monica's voice was soft as she sat down on the edge of Emily's bed.

Emily's eyes felt like they were bulging out of her head. She wanted to scream. Maybe she should tell them to stop, but she needed to get through this, she needed to hear whatever else they had to say.

"Emily, if this gets to be too much for you, we can stop. We can always pick this up later," Dr. Robinson said.

"No. I want to hear all of it—tell me, please." Her lip trembled.

"Well," Monica continued, "After two years of marriage, you decided you wanted more. You said you didn't feel fulfilled, and you wanted to work again—"

"But I did feel fulfilled." Emily cut her off. "I helped out at the country club. We held fundraisers, we helped people."

"That was during your first year of marriage." Monica continued. "By your second year, you didn't want to do that anymore. You wanted to go back to school to finish your teaching degree. You only needed thirteen more credits. That's when a lot of your problems started. Steven wanted to control you; he didn't want you to finish school or to work. You did both anyway." Monica shifted on the bed and continued. "You two were also having some other problems, so you separated. During the time you and Steven were separated, you kept teaching since you loved your job. You also met, and fell in love with, someone new. His name is Robert. I introduced you two. He's a wonderful man, and he loves you very much."

"Emily, is anything coming back to you?" Dr. Robinson asked.

Emily shook her head no. Her eyes watered. She felt like she was locked in a jail cell, with no way out. She felt like someone told her she had committed a crime she knew she hadn't. Could she really be separated from Steven? Could she really be divorcing him? Could she really be engaged to someone named Robert? Why were they saying these things to her? Her heart dropped into her stomach and her ears felt like they were on fire. Even though her family was right in front of her, Emily felt alone. And she couldn't stop shaking.

"If I have this new life and I'm so happy, then where is this Robert person? Why isn't he here?" Her tears turned to anger. "I don't believe you." She shook her head. "Steven loves me. So what if he was a little controlling. I wouldn't divorce him for that."

"That's true—you wouldn't, but like I said earlier there were other problems." Monica's tone softened more.

"Well then, I need you to explain it to me. What were these other problems?"

Monica glanced at Dr. Robinson, who nodded for her to continue.

"Steven cheated on you several times. He started treating you poorly."

"I don't believe you," Emily blurted. Steven had promised her he would never act like his father, so that meant they were wrong. They had to be.

"Emily," David took over. "What your sister is trying to say is that Steven is not the nice man you remember. He hasn't always been so good to you. He's done some unspeakable things to you in the past, but you can't remember, right now."

Emily didn't know what to say. Her face felt like stone. The fire in her ears had now moved up to her brain, and she felt like she was about to explode.

"What are these unspeakable things? Just say it."

"He was verbally and physically abusive to you," Monica said.

"So, you're saying he hit me?" Her eyes widened.

"Not exactly. He's pushed you several times—into walls and down stairs. You had bruises on your back and on your side. No one would have ever known, unless you chose to tell them."

"So, I take it, I chose to tell you?"

"Not at first; but eventually, yes, you did confide in me."

Emily fell silent.

"And then, the last straw for you was when Steven pushed you down the stairs when you were nine months pregnant and you lost the baby."

Emily's eyes opened wider and her insides quivered.

"That's right Emily, you were pregnant." Monica continued. "It was a little girl."

"Why are you saying these things?" Tears were caught in her throat. "You're lying. Steven would never hurt me in that way, he would never do that to me." Her watery eyes leaked like a faucet.

"Ems, why would I lie to you? What would I have to gain by doing that?" Monica blinked. "You need to know that you had the baby, but she was stillborn—because of Steven."

"I don't want to talk about this anymore. I want you to leave." Emily feared their words were true. Yet, she couldn't wrap her mind around it. A time bomb ticked in her chest, and it would explode any minute. It was all too much. Emily needed to be alone.

"But Ems…"

"I mean it!" Emily glanced at Dr. Robinson. "Doctor, please make them leave. I don't want to talk about this anymore—please."

"Alright. I think it's best if we give Emily some time alone, so she can process everything. It's a lot of information, all at once. I think she needs to get some rest," Dr. Robinson said.

Emily rolled over and closed her eyes. She curled up in a ball as if they weren't in the room anymore. There were so many emotions running through her. Emily didn't know how to deal with them. She felt hurt and anger and loneliness. Emily was scared, and she felt betrayed. Darkness loomed over her and she couldn't breathe.

If the people she loved were saying these things about Steven, could they be true? And if that was the case, then was she in love with this Robert person who she couldn't remember?

"Could I see you two for a moment?" Dr. Robinson asked. She pointed to an out of the way spot near the corner.

"I don't think that went very well," Monica said. "But you deal with this all the time, so maybe I'm wrong."

"Everything that happened in that room was to be expected," Dr. Robinson said, placing her notebook in her white lab coat pocket. "Emily was told that the only life she remembers is not exactly like she knows it to be. I think we should leave her alone for a while. She has a lot to process. Maybe some of what we said will cause her memory to return. You two should go home and get some rest. I'll check on her, later; and let you know how she's doing in the morning. And as far as visitors go, I still think you two should be the only ones to see her until I've had a chance to assess her memory again. I'll leave instructions with her nurse. And Mrs. Wilson, don't look so down, your sister will be fine."

"I hope you're right," Monica said.

David watched the doctor walk away. "I'm sure things will look better in the morning, after we've had a good night's rest. Why don't we go home? I can follow you."

"I would love that, but Robert is stopping by tonight. I promised to let him know what's going on."

"Don't stay too long." He smiled. "And, tell Robert to hang in there."

"I will," she said.

Before she could take in a breath, she spotted Robert. Like a lion searching for its prey, he came right for her with fire in his eyes.

"What happened? Did everything go okay?"

"Emily listened to what we had to say, and naturally she was very upset and confused." She switched her purse to her other arm.

"That's understandable. When can I see her?" He talked fast.

"She still can't have any visitors, at least not right now. She doesn't remember her life with you, and the doctor wants us to give her more time to let it all sink in."

"How much time?" His voice got louder. "How long do you think that will take?"

"I'm not sure. Maybe seeing you before she's ready will scare her."

"I would *never* hurt her in any way."

"I didn't mean it like that."

"It's just…I feel if I could see her…maybe it would spark her memory…and then, this could all be over."

"I hope that happens, too. And I agree with you. After Dr. Robinson assesses Emily tomorrow, we'll see what she says. Ultimately, the decision is up to her."

"I realize that. I just want to see her." His eyes watered.

"I know, and I'm sorry." She took his hand and squeezed it. "I'm heading out now. Why don't you come, too? There's no sense in you hanging around here tonight."

"No, I think I'll stay here a little longer." He pulled his hand away.

"Robert, you're—"

"No, I'm not going to sneak in to see her. I want to sit in the waiting room for a while. It makes me feel closer to her."

"If you say so," she said, turning to walk away.

CHAPTER EIGHT

Robert was at the hospital as soon as visiting hours started the next morning. He took a personal day from work. He had to talk to Emmie. Now that she was awake, he had to be near her.

"Is Emily Montgomery able to have visitors now?" Robert was at the nurse's station.

He had on his blue suit and red tie. He wanted to look his best, if today was the first impression that Emmie would have of him. His stomach was in knots. He hoped the answer would be yes.

"As a matter-of-fact," the gray haired nurse said, "Dr. Robinson is coming out of her room, right now. You can ask her yourself."

He saw the tall, dark haired doctor walking his way. She stopped at the desk and spoke a few words to the nurses.

"Dr. Robinson, may I have a few words with you?" He stepped closer to her. "My name is Robert Johnson and I'm—"

"You're here to visit Emily."

"Is it that obvious?" He gave a half smile.

"I've seen you here with the Wilsons, so I know who you are."

"Then, I'm sure you know how determined I am to see her."

"Yes, I'm well aware." Dr. Robinson shifted her yellow files to her other arm. "I spoke with Emily this morning. She's calmed down quite a bit from yesterday. She would like visitors and that includes you. But you must be patient with her. She may exhibit mood swings and childlike behavior, at times. If you sense her getting upset, then change the subject or even step out of the room."

"I promise, I'll leave if she gets upset." He nodded. "But I'm praying that doesn't happen."

Robert's stomach knotted as he approached Emily's room. He had no idea what was about to happen. His palms were sweaty, and he swiped his hands together. It was so quiet, he heard his own footsteps, clacking against the concrete floors, as he entered Emily's room. It smelled of baby powder and clean linen. Emily sat quietly in bed in a hospital gown, looking toward the window.

"Emmie," he said softly, so as not to startle her. "I was told you could have visitors now. I hope it's okay that I'm here."

Emily followed his steps all the way to her bed. She stared at his kind face. He had a nice smile. It was friendly and inviting. And he had warm green eyes. Her white hospital gown paled in comparison to his dark blue suit.

"Y-you must be Robert." Her stomach felt queasy.

"Yes, I am. Robert Johnson." He extended his hand.

His hand felt warm and strong. "Why did you call me Emmie, just now?"

"That's my nickname for you."

"I'm sorry. I don't remember." She released his hand and stared down at the bed.

"I'm sorry, if I made you feel uncomfortable." His voice was shaky.

"You didn't." She glanced back up. "This is all so confusing. I wish I could remember you. But so far, I don't."

"It's only been a few minutes. If we talk for a while, maybe it will spark something. That's if you don't mind."

"No, I don't mind." Emily was nervous, but he seemed like a nice person. And if everyone kept saying he was her fiancé, then obviously she loved him. Even though her stomach cringed, she was sure she'd be fine spending time with him.

"I guess asking how you are is a stupid question." He glanced down and back up. "I mean, you're in the hospital with amnesia; so, how well could you be." He ran his hand through his hair. "I'm sorry. I'm rambling. Please, forgive me."

"You don't have to be sorry. I realize this is awkward for you as well as for me. And to answer your first question, I am a little tired."

"Would you like me to leave?"

"No, you're here already." She shrugged. "We might as well talk."

"I'd like that." He smiled. "And I promise, I won't stay too long."

"You don't have to be nervous." She felt bad for him. He was all over the place.

"Do you mind if I tell you about some of the things we used to do together?" He took out a handkerchief from the top pocket of his blue suit, and tried wiping the beads of sweat from his forehead. Finally sitting down, his gaze stopped on her again. "I won't stay too long. I know you need your rest."

"You know, you said that already." She grinned. He seemed so flustered, she didn't know how to help him. "But no," she continued.

"No, to what?" His eyebrow rose.

"No. I wouldn't mind if you told me some of the things we used to do." She gave a half smile.

"Well, we loved going to amusement parks—especially the ones in Chicago—and riding the roller coasters." His voice cracked. "Six Flags was one of our favorites. Now I know, some people think roller coasters are only for teenagers, but I don't agree. I think someone in their twenties or thirties can still enjoy going on a ride or two."

"I agree. I think it's for the young at heart. But I'm surprised you got me to go. I've never been one to ride roller coasters."

"I know. You weren't. That is, until you met me." He beamed.

"Really, that's hard for me to believe. Even Monica couldn't get me to ride. When we were young, she would call me chicken." She sat up from her slouch. "How were you able to accomplish what no one else could?"

"I took you to a park, probably on our fourth or fifth date, and talked you into getting on a roller coaster. You held on to my hand the entire time, and you screamed your head off. But when we got off that ride, you said you wanted to go again."

"You must have magical powers." She grinned. "Because I don't see how that's possible."

"No magical powers." He shifted in his chair. "It was all me. I knew you didn't like heights. And you didn't like rides that moved too fast. It makes you feel like you're not in control. So once I gained your trust—and you knew I wouldn't let you get hurt—it was easy for you to go with me. As long as you stayed by my side, you were fine."

"We sound like a nice couple." She felt a little misty eyed.

"We are." His smile faded.

"Can you answer a question for me?"

"Anything."

"I've been told I was in a car accident, but I don't know how it happened. I am curious."

"You have a right to know." He swallowed hard. "It was a rainy day, and we were together. I drove. A car hit us from behind and pushed us into oncoming traffic."

"That sounds horrible." She blinked. "But you are alright?"

"Yes, I'm fine."

"What else did we do together?" She smiled. Suddenly, she wanted to know more about him and their relationship. He was so easy to talk to.

"We went to museums and concerts. We also took ballroom dancing classes." His gaze never left hers. We'd drive to Chicago and visit the art museums and the Shedd Aquarium."

She felt all the affection Robert had for her in his warm smile and in the way he spoke.

"I've always had two left feet."

"Not anymore." His chest puffed up. "Now, you're a better dancer than I am."

"I can't wait to hear how that happened. How did you get me to ballroom dance?"

Her anxiousness and nervousness went away. Emily still didn't know him. But she saw why she would have wanted to date him. She also saw why she would have been attracted to him. Just from the few brief minutes they had spent together, she felt giddy like a schoolgirl on her first date.

As he continued telling her stories, her tiredness vanished. She suddenly had an abundance of energy. She enjoyed her time with him. The only problem was after all the stories Robert told, Emily still didn't remember him. Nothing resurfaced, nothing at all.

The next morning, Emily was awakened by Marge's voice, announcing it was time to get up. The blinds clattered, and the sunlight poured into the room. Marge took her vitals, gave her a sponge bath, and made sure she had something to eat.

"Your physical therapist, Pete, will be here soon to take you down for therapy," Marge said, with a smile. "Pete did your range of motion exercises to keep your muscles active while you were in the coma. But you need more than that. We need to get you walking again. Pete's going to help you get back on your feet, so you can get out of here."

"I'd like that, but I'm a little nervous." She rubbed her eyes. The light stung them. "What if I'm not able to keep up?"

"Pete's a professional. He won't push you, if he feels you can't handle it. But I know, you'll be fine."

Emily tried to think positively, but a butterfly roamed around in her chest. This was all new to her, and she wished Steven was there, with her. He hadn't been there since she woke up, so maybe that was a sign that everything Monica had said was true. Robert, on the other hand, had been there with his nice smile and kind eyes. He said all the right things to make her comfortable, and she wouldn't mind seeing him again.

"Hello, Emily. I'm Pete Mossly." A tall, thin man with sandy hair and dark eyes walked into the room. "I'm going to help you get into this wheelchair, and then I'll take you down to therapy."

"I'm surprised the transporters aren't wheeling me down, like they did for my other tests."

"You'll find that I like to do things myself. I want us to get started on time. Sometimes, that doesn't happen, if you're waiting on transport." Pete smiled and put his arm around Emily's waist, to help her out of bed.

Everything looked different in the hallway. She was too out of it the other day to notice, but the walls were dark and drab; and, the smell of mildew and medicine lingered in the air. Some nurses look exhausted, while others looked well rested. She'd been in a hospital before, but this time felt different. She'd been dead to the world for months; so, maybe that was it, maybe that's why everything felt brand new.

All of the physical therapy equipment surrounding her was a little overwhelming. The odor in this room wasn't much better than the hallway. A musty smell replaced the medicinal smell. At least the yellow walls were brighter than the darkness of the hallway.

Emily was anxious, nervous and excited, all at the same time; and, her heartbeat increased. She wanted to get back to normal. What if she didn't have the strength to walk again? What if she felt weak and tired forever? What if her body refused to cooperate with her? Emily had to remind herself to remain strong. Her mind wasn't all there, but at least she could get her body back in working order.

Pete explained that while she was in a coma he came in and worked her muscles. He moved her arms and legs around while she slept. He reassured Emily that she would be fine, once she got back in the groove of things.

She felt exhausted, already; and they hadn't even started yet. Just getting in the wheelchair and riding down the hallway had basically done her in. But she didn't want Pete to know that. He was so excited about getting her up and moving again. Emily shared his excitement but was a little overwhelmed.

Pete dimmed the lights a little, since he didn't want the bright lights to give Emily a headache. She wanted to shout out how much she enjoyed the light. The light made her feel alive again, the light meant she was awake.

"Alright, Emily," Pete said. He stood near her side, holding out his hands. "I want you to stand. You can hold on to the walker, at first, to maintain your balance. Once you're walking, a little better, you won't need the walker as much. Don't be afraid. I'm right here to catch you, if you fall."

Fear prickled inside of her. She had to find a way to calm down. She stood, and her legs wobbled beneath her. She almost tipped over before she could even grab on to the walker. Pete caught her and helped her stand again.

"Take your time and don't push yourself," he said. "Only stand, and don't think of anything else."

Like a newborn learning to crawl, and then stand and walk, she did as he asked. She stood and took a few deep breaths. She grabbed the walker and placed one foot in front of the other. Emily walked, slowly. Her heartrate decreased since she trusted him and knew he would catch her if she fell.

He helped her stretch, and then they worked on strength and endurance.

"I think that's enough, for today," he said. "I don't want to tire you out. We'll pick this back up, tomorrow." He helped her back into the wheelchair.

"Once we're through this phase, we can move on to coordination, balance and weight lifting."

Her first day had been productive, and Emily was proud of what she had accomplished. Pretty soon, she'd be able to bathe herself, walk again, and go to the bathroom on her own. Then, maybe she could go home. But where exactly would home be?

∽

"I see we had the same idea," Robert said. He saw Monica standing in front of Emily's room. He was on his lunch break; she probably was, too.

"Yes." Monica smiled.

"Why are you looking at me like that?"

"I heard about your visit with Emily yesterday; and I have to say, I'm glad that things went so well."

"Did she tell you that?" His heart raced at the thought.

"Well, when I visited with her last night, Emily mentioned it. She wasn't mad. She enjoyed your time together, and she told me she wouldn't hate it if you visited again."

"I'm happy to hear that." He thought he'd made some positive progress with Emily, but hearing Monica made it all more real. "I know she still doesn't remember me." His voice quivered. "But I got her to smile. And I'm hoping the more time I spend with her, the more she'll remember. I know somewhere, deep down inside, she loves me. And I know, I can't give up on her."

"You're not going to lose her. I know things will work out," Monica said.

"Why are you out here?"

"She's down in physical therapy, so I was…" Her voice drifted off.

"What's wrong?"

"Steven's here," Monica whispered. "I hoped we would get more alone time with Ems before he showed up."

"I hoped he wouldn't show up at all." Robert's jaw clenched, in anger.

Robert turned to see Steven walking toward them, wearing a tan suit and carrying a vase filled with flowers. It felt like a thousand tiny needles were being jabbed into his spine; Robert flinched.

"I just finished speaking to Dr. Robinson," Steven said, with a sly grin on his face. "It's such good news about our girl." He looked like he'd won a million dollars.

"Steven, Emily isn't here at the moment," Monica quickly said.

"I know, she's down in PT." His eyes brightened. "I can't believe she woke up." He shook his head, in amazement. "I'm so relieved. I can't wait to see her."

"What's the rush? You haven't been around for weeks." The sight of Steven being so smug made Robert cringe.

"I don't think that's any of your concern." Steven stepped closer to Robert. "I'm here now."

"Steven, I think we should talk before you see her," Monica chimed in. "There are some things we need to get straight."

"Dr. Robinson said she'll probably be moved out of the ICU soon." He continued on ignoring Monica. "I'm so sorry I wasn't here, but an emergency came up. I hated missing her first words."

"Steven, if you spoke to Dr. Robinson, then you know the situation. I don't want you to try and take advantage of it. It's not fair if you do that. Besides, she could get her memory back at any moment," Monica said.

"I hate that you still think so little of me. I wish you would give me a chance. I love your sister. All I want to do is make it up to her. This is my chance to do that." His tone was serious, and his eyes were meek.

Feeling like the referee in a boxing match, Robert stepped between them. "You're talking about Emily like I'm not even here."

"Nothing against you man, but she's legally my wife. I have a right to try and make things right with her."

"She's with me now." Robert's face felt hot. "She doesn't want you anymore."

"Why don't we let her be the judge of that?" Steven stepped even closer to Robert and switched the vase to the opposite hand. "Emily's the only one who can decide who she wants to be with."

"Steven, you know that's not fair. You know, as well as I do,

Emily cannot fairly pick between you two, not in the condition she's in," Monica said.

"If you think I'm going to give up because she doesn't remember me, you're wrong. This is a tiny setback, but it won't be this way forever," Robert chimed in.

"I think you're kidding yourself. But whatever," Steven said, shrugging. "It's not my business or my problem. Now, I'm going in to wait for my wife." He brushed past them.

"This is insane." Robert's fist clenched. "Are we going to let him go into Emmie's room after he's been absent for weeks?"

"We have to be smart about this. We can't make a scene right in the middle of the hallway."

"I realize that but—"

"Hello, you two."

Robert heard Emily's soft voice, and the screeching of the wheels on her chair, as she came toward them.

❧

Robert was back. He looked so handsome in his gray suit and black coat. Seeing his warm eyes and kind face sent a shiver up her spine.

"It's nice to see you again." She glanced past Monica to Robert.

"Are you talking to both of us, or only Robert?" Monica smiled, stepping closer to the wheelchair.

"Both of you." Emily grinned back. Her stomach felt warm; she knew they noticed her gaze on Robert.

"It's nice seeing you again, too." Robert stepped closer.

"I need to get Emily into her room, now. She had a very productive day and she needs to rest," Pete said. "As soon as I get her safely into her bed, I'll leave you alone, so you can visit with her." He pushed the wheelchair through the door.

"Can I help in any way?" Steven asked, in a low voice. He stepped in front of her wheelchair.

"Steven, you're here." Emily's eyes widened. She felt giddy, like it was her wedding day and her fiancé stood at the altar.

"It's hard to believe you're sitting up and staring at me with those beautiful hazel eyes." He leaned down on one knee by the wheelchair. Their gazes met. "You don't know how hard I prayed you would wake up and come back to me." He leaned into her and softly kissed her on the lips. "I'm sorry I wasn't here when you woke up. I hope you'll forgive me for that."

His touch was just like she remembered. His brown eyes were soft, and she believed his words were true.

"That's okay," she said, smiling. "You're here now and that's what matters."

Realizing Pete still stood behind her wheelchair, and Robert and Monica were standing in the doorway, she apologized.

With Pete's help, Emily climbed into bed. She already felt sore. Lying in the bed felt wonderful, like lying in a bed of soft roses. Her eyes felt heavy and she felt weak, but that didn't stop her from noticing the wonderful aroma in the room. There was a beautiful arrangement of yellow, pink and purple flowers in a glass vase. She was certain Steven had brought them.

"Thanks for looking out for my girl." Steven held his hand out to Pete.

"No problem. That's what I'm here for. Emily is a wonderful person. It's not hard spending time with her." He released the hand-shake. "Unlike some of my patients, she's a breath of fresh air. Emily really tried hard today, even though she was tired. With progress like that, she'll be out of here in no time." He turned to leave the room. "See you tomorrow, Emily." He waved.

"Bye." She waved back. "He's a nice man." Emily glanced around the room and all eyes were on her.

"He seems to be." Steven plopped down on the bed in front of her blocking her view. He made himself comfortable. "But enough talk about him, it's time I hear about you. I missed you." He stroked her hair.

"I missed you, too, but we're being rude. You haven't

acknowledged my other visitors, Monica and R-Robert." Her voice was shaky.

The man she was supposed to marry and the man she was married to were both staring at her. She had no idea how to respond. A lump developed in her throat.

"I spoke to them, before you got here." Steven glanced over at them. "And, I'm not trying to be rude, but they've had all this time with you and I've had so little. I want to know how you're doing."

"Whose fault is that?" Robert stepped closer to the bed.

Emily saw his kind face hardened, and she had no idea how to make the situation better. Her head spun.

"I know this is awkward, for everyone; but, if you don't mind, I'd like to spend some time alone with Steven."

She saw the disappointment on Monica and Robert's faces; but, she felt it was best, for now. She needed to ask Steven some questions.

"If that's what you feel is best." Monica patted the blankets over her leg. "I have to get back to work."

"So do I." Robert's serious tone softened. "However, I want you to know I don't like leaving you alone with him, and I will be back."

"I believe you." She gave a half smile.

The covers bunched as Steven moved closer to her on the bed. "I can understand if you're upset because I wasn't here when you woke up—"

"Steven," she tried to cut in.

"And, I know your sister probably told you I've been missing in action for quite a while before that. I'm sorry about that." He rubbed her chin. "An emergency came up that I needed to take care of. I know that's no excuse. I guess part of the reason is because it was hard for me, seeing you barely hanging on. It hurt watching you lay so still and silent. It bothered me that Robert was here. He and your sister acted like I didn't have a right to sit with you." His hand moved from her chin to her cheek. He gently stroked it. "I believe they were even trying to have me banned from seeing you."

"I'm sure it wasn't like that."

"But it was." He nodded. "So, I stayed away. Even though I wasn't around much, I checked on you constantly, and I called your doctors every day."

"I'm not upset because you weren't here when I woke up." She cleared her throat. "Although, I did wonder where you were, and I was confused about what was so important it would cause you to stay away. That's not the problem," she said. Then, she took in a deep breath.

"Maybe you should rest. I know you've had a long day, and I don't want to make it even longer." He stood.

"No," she said, grabbing his hand. "I need to say this. Monica and David said some terrible things about you, horrible things, things you supposedly did that I can't remember..." She hesitated. "We're separated and going through a divorce." Anxiety curled up in her stomach just saying the words. "And, I'm in love with Robert now."

"Yes, Em, I'm not exactly sure on everything they told you, but most of it is true. We went through some rough times, because of me; but, I've been trying to make it up to you over the last few years. I wanted to start our marriage over, but Monica introduced you to Robert, and you decided you'd rather be with him."

Her heart dropped into her stomach. She remained silent, shifting on the bed because she didn't know how to respond.

"I really believe that you wanted to try again, to make our relationship work; but, you were too afraid, and once Robert came along, he kind of destroyed us."

"How could he destroy us?" She bit down on her lip. "Monica said I gave you several chances, so why would you think he was part of my final decision?"

He walked toward the window. "He was safe and new and you rebounded with him. Since he was around, you didn't feel the need to give me that one last chance—even though I know you wanted to."

"I told you all of this?" Her stomach felt like a ball bounced around inside it.

"No. I felt it when I was around you." He turned to her. "The last few times that I came to see you to discuss things, you trembled. And it wasn't because you were afraid I'd hurt you. It was because you knew you still had feelings for me. Instead of going with those feelings, you couldn't—or wouldn't—because you were in too deep with Robert. I saw all of this in your eyes. That's why I know we can still work, if you give me a chance. Please." He sat back on the bed.

"Why did you cheat on me and shove me around? I need to understand." Her voice cracked.

"After we were first married, you were so happy being a home-maker. Then, suddenly, one day, you weren't happy with that any-more." He shifted his weight. "It's no excuse, but I felt like you were distancing yourself from me when you wanted to finish your college degree and start teaching. I felt like I was losing you. That's when I started cheating. I felt that was the way to get the attention that I deserved—the attention that you weren't giving me."

"So, I made you cheat." She rolled her eyes.

"No, that's not what I'm saying at all. I realize this is on me. I felt insecure, like I wasn't satisfying you, and I wasn't man enough to keep you happy. My ego deflated, and I used other woman to inflate it again. I was so angry with the way our marriage was turning out that I took it out on you. At that time, I felt it was your fault since you weren't there for me all the time, like I was used to. So I shoved you and pushed you—just like my father did to women—because you weren't doing what I needed you to do," he said, softly. There was sadness in his eyes. "I was jealous of your career, and I'm sorry."

"You let your father's traits seep in." She touched his face. "You promised you would never do that."

"I know, and all this time, I've been telling you that I'm sorry and I'll never do it again."

He seemed so sincere. She didn't know what to make of it.

"I need time for all of this to sink in," she said, turning away and pulling the blankets up to her neck. "I need to rest."

"Do you mind if I stay and watch you sleep?"

"It's fine," she said.

Maybe Emily should have made Steven leave, so she could be alone with her thoughts, but he looked so distraught. What was the harm in letting him sit there?

⬥

"What will it be?" Chuck, the bartender, asked.

"Just a beer." Robert sat down on the bar stool. "You know what? Make it two." He held up two fingers.

He shouldn't be drinking. But what was the harm in a few beers? After the day he had, why shouldn't he drink to take the edge off?

The smell of liquor and cigarette smoke wafted in the air. It was dark and dank. A couple of guys got loud over in the corner. There were a couple of guys playing darts near the back where the pool tables were. He ignored all of that. It was none of his concern. He had his own problems.

Robert drank, on occasion, like most people. But that had all come to an end after he'd witnessed a drunk driver hit a little girl. He had to give a statement to the police, and he had to testify in court. The little girl had died. It was horrible.

That's how he'd met Kelly, his former fiancée. The little girl was her sister. He had met and befriended the family, after testifying in court. That was years ago, when he was in his early twenties, but it still haunted him. What caused someone to drink so much they'd risk someone else's life? He promised himself he would never turn out like that, no matter what the circumstances.

"You doing okay, man?" Chuck asked.

"I think I'm going to call a friend for a ride."

"You've only had like two drinks. If you're feeling tipsy already, then you're a lightweight," he chuckled.

"I'm not used to drinking." Robert shrugged. "Is it okay if I leave my car here until tomorrow?"

"It's fine with me." The glasses clanked as Chuck gathered up the ones in front of Robert.

Robert saw his reflection in the glass, and he let out a small sigh. It may sound crazy, but he knew it was for the best. At least it would make him feel better.

"Thanks for coming to get me, Monica." Robert laid his head back on the seat in Monica's blue Acura and closed his eyes.

"It's fine. If you don't mind me asking, how did you end up here?"

Robert opened his eyes. He rolled down the window. The car began to smell like a pool hall. "I went to visit with Emmie after work, but when I looked in her room she was asleep and Steven was sitting in the chair reading the paper. It burns me up that he sits there like he belongs there." He hit the button and the window squealed as it rolled down more.

"I know, I feel the same way." Monica shook her head. "I witnessed the same thing when I went to visit, and we exchanged a few words. He acts like he's done nothing wrong."

"All of this reminds me of Kelly."

"How so?"

"Kelly was the first girl I ever loved. But when it came time to commit to her, I couldn't do it." He shifted under his seat belt. "I did love her. I guess, I felt part of the reason I was with her was to help her through her little sister's death. I knew she needed someone; I was that someone," he said, sighing and closing his eyes. "So, once I realized that, I knew I couldn't marry her. I didn't want to end up in an unhappy marriage where we fought all the time, like my parents."

"What does that have to do with Ems?"

"This time I was ready to commit. I thought we could be happy. And now that I'm ready, look at what's happened." He frowned. "She may never remember me."

"You don't know that, and even if she doesn't," Monica paused and turned down the radio. "I know my sister. She's not going to toss you aside because she can't remember you. She knows you were once important to her and that means something to her."

"Did you see her eyes light up when she saw Steven?" The radio button squished as he pushed the volume down arrow. He still heard the loud music; it sounded like a rock concert.

"Yes, I did. I also saw her eyes light up when she saw you waiting outside of her room."

"I'm not giving up on her." Robert shook his head. "Tonight was a minor setback. I plan on being there for whatever she might need, no matter what Steven pulls."

He closed his eyes and laid back onto the headrest again. He knew what he shared with Emily was real, and one day she'd see that, too.

CHAPTER NINE

"You know it's been almost two weeks, and we never finished our conversation." Steven sat in the chair next to Emily's bed. "Are you upset with me?"

"What gave you that impression? I haven't pushed you away or told you not to visit me." She sat up straighter. Her gown choked her, so she pulled it away from her neck.

"I realize that." He leaned forward. "But things have been awkward between us, and I don't know where I stand."

"I don't know what you want me to say."

She knew he was right. Her physical health was getting better. She'd been well enough to be moved to the observation floor. But her mind and her heart weren't any better, and she'd been having mood swings. She still couldn't remember everything. Her chest felt like fire because her heart still loved him but her head didn't know if she could trust him.

"Sweetheart, you're going to be released soon, and I need to know if you plan on coming home with me."

Emily grabbed a few of the cards from her students off the nearby table and started thumbing through them. She wasn't sure where she would live, and she didn't want to think about it right now.

"You can't deny that I've been a gentleman." He brushed his

hand through his hair. "When Robert comes to visit, I leave the room and let you two spend time together. Do you know how much that hurts me? Yet, I continue to do it because I want you to see how sorry I am."

"I know you've been trying, Steven, and I appreciate it. But everything is so confusing right now. I don't know what to think or how to feel. You've slacked off work and let colleagues take over your cases. You're here all the time being so loving and doing and saying all the right things. But—"

"But," Steven said, cutting her off. "You still don't know if you can come home with me and give me another chance. You'd rather be with a man you can't even remember."

"Don't put words in my mouth. I didn't say I wanted to be with Robert. All I want, right now, is to get back on my feet, so I can get out of here and regain my life."

"And what life is that? You can't go back to teaching," he said, sitting down on the bed. "At least, not right now."

"Are you happy about that?" she snapped.

"Why would I be?" He stroked her cheek. "I realize now how much your career means to you, and I would never try and keep you from it."

Her eyebrow rose.

"Why are you looking at me like that?"

"I don't know. I guess I'm surprised to hear you say that—especially since you never wanted me to teach in the first place."

"We already discussed my reasons." His nostrils flared. "I felt like I was losing you to your career. But now, I see that because a woman wants to work, it doesn't take away from the marriage. Sometimes, it enriches it."

"That's right. It makes her feel respected and worthy." She blinked. Sunlight barreled through the window, making the room much brighter than she would have liked. "Not to mention, it helps to have two incomes."

She didn't know where all of this anger came from since she did remember being happy staying home, being a wife, and working on fundraisers at the country club. But if sometime during her life she had changed and grown, then what was wrong with that?

"I agree." He leaned in and kissed her cheek.

Once again, he said all the right things, and Emily didn't know what to make of it. This was the side she knew, the loving and caring side of him. The other side, the one that Monica had spoken of, she couldn't remember. Could she trust this new Steven and go home with him? Should she try to build a life with him, starting over? Her focus should be on getting healthy and strong, but she also needed to figure out where she belonged.

"Am I interrupting something?" Robert walked in.

He was a welcome distraction from her incessant thoughts.

"I'll make myself scarce," Steven said, exiting the room.

"He's getting good at that," Robert said.

"Yes, it's nice of him to give us privacy."

"That's one way to look at it."

"What's another?"

"I know you think he's being kind, but I think he's overbearing. He's always hovering over you, like an eagle ready to pounce."

"I don't think it's that bad. He's a little overprotective because he cares. I know he does, I can feel it." She saw his eyes sadden at her words. "I'm sorry. I know you don't see him that way."

"You didn't used to, either."

"I know but he's apologized over and over. I feel it's time to move on. It's good for my recovery to dwell on happier things." She shifted on the bed. "What else do you like to wear?" she asked, trying to change the subject. "I only see you in suits."

"You don't like my blue suit." He smiled, glancing down and back up.

"No, you always look nice in your suits, but that's all I ever see you in."

"That's because I always come straight from work."

"Well, one of these days, I'd like to see you in casual clothes, like blue jeans or khakis."

"And one of these days, I'd like to see you without that hospital gown on." His face reddened. "I didn't mean naked." He fumbled over his words. "I meant street clothes."

"I know what you meant. You're cute when you get flustered like that," she said, with a giggle.

Being with him was light and easy. It was like meeting someone new, yet feeling like you've known them all your life.

"So, you think I'm cute." He smiled. "You've never said that before."

"I know, I sound like a schoolgirl. So I'll change that to 'I think you're very handsome'."

"I think you're beautiful." His gaze was strong. "Once you get out of here, I'd be happy to take you out on a date. Then, you'll see me in regular clothes."

She wanted to say she'd like that, too, but she didn't. She remained quiet and smiled. Every time Robert was around, her heartbeats were erratic. It was best not to say anything at all, until Emily was certain what she wanted to do.

❧

"Thanks for meeting me here." Robert stood in front of Dr. Robinson's office. "Since you're considered the next of kin, I think she'll take this better coming from you. I may come off as the jealous boyfriend."

"No, I think you look like the concerned fiancé," Monica said. "I agree with everything you're doing."

"Thanks for the support." He rapped his knuckles on the office door.

"Right on time," Dr. Robinson said, opening her office door. "Please take a seat." She pointed at the seats in front of her desk. "How can I help you?"

"We know Emily's getting better, and it's wonderful." Robert sniffed at the fruity perfume scent in the air. "When I visited her yesterday, she was in such a good mood. It looks like she'll be released soon. You mentioned that she was doing so well she won't have to spend time in a rehabilitation hospital. So I was concerned whose care she will be released into."

"What he's trying to say, in a nice way, is we don't want her being released into Steven's care," Monica clarified.

"I know we touched on this issue, a little, when Emily first woke up; but, everything happened so fast that we didn't really delve into it." Dr. Robinson clasped her hands together on her desk. "I know you're concerned about your sister's well-being and safety. I am as well."

"When Emily was first brought into the hospital we tried to keep the peace." Monica crossed her legs. "We were only concerned with her waking up from the coma. And Steven disappeared for a long period of time, so we didn't worry much about him."

"To be frank, we hoped he was never coming back." Robert shifted his weight. "Now that he's resurfaced and has been spending so much time with her, I feel like we need to bring up the abuse issue again."

"In my sessions with Emily, I have asked her if she feels safe around Steven. Her response to me was yes."

"How can she know that when she can't even remember the abuse?" Monica asked.

"Apparently, he's been honest with her and explained to her all the ways he has harmed her. So she does believe it happened, but she said he promises he's changed."

"How can Emily believe that?" Robert asked, rubbing his forehead in frustration.

"In my estimation, I think she's struggling with this. In her eyes, Emily remembers all the good times and love she shares with Steven; but, she also knows he's hurt her in ways she could never have imagined. Emily wants to believe in the man she remembers and that Steven can be that man again."

"That's all well and good for now, when they're in the hospital," Monica said. "What about when he gets her home alone? Then, the real Steven could start to show."

"First of all, I think you're jumping to conclusions. No one has said that Emily will go home with Steven. That's Emily's decision."

"Since she is, or was, estranged from Steven, and I'm the next of kin, shouldn't I make the decision about where she will go?" Monica's eyes widened.

"That would only be if Emily wasn't fit to make her own decisions and—"

"I don't think she is." Monica cut Dr. Robinson off.

"I was going to say that's not the case."

The phone on the desk blared like a car alarm, making Robert cringe.

"Sorry about that. I'll let it go to voice mail." She straightened some papers on her desk. "Emily is in her right mind. Her memory is just impaired. Is there any record of this abuse? Any evidence, like pictures of the bruises or any police reports filed?"

"No." Monica's face dropped. "She never filed a police report. I didn't find out about the abuse until it was already happening; and by that time, she was embarrassed and didn't want anyone else to know." Monica bit her lip. "David and I tried to talk her into filing but she refused. She wanted to act like it never happened."

"What about her lawyer? When Emily filed for a divorce, did she cite abuse as the reason for the divorce?"

"No, she put down irreconcilable differences because she was embarrassed that she'd let herself be treated that way for so long."

"I told her I wished she hadn't done that." Robert's chest felt heavy. "There's nothing we can do about it now."

"Robert's right." Dr. Robinson nodded. "Unfortunately, if there's no documented evidence of abuse, and Emily doesn't remember it right now, it would be your word against Steven's."

"But Steven admits to it." Robert leaned forward.

"Yes. He makes light of it, saying it was only a few pushes here and there. If he's as savvy a lawyer as you say he is, then there's no way he'll put that down in writing to incriminate himself. Besides, that's not the bigger issue here. We're forgetting that Emily is the one who gets to decide. She may decide to go home with you, Mrs. Wilson."

The circular clock on the wall ticked like a time bomb, reminding Robert that his dreams were about to explode. This meeting wasn't going his way.

"Let's remember this may all be a moot point. Emily may not want to go home with him," Dr. Robinson said, standing. "I'll speak with her again, and if she does, I'll pass this along to a case manager who can arrange for a social worker to make regular visits to the house, to make sure she's doing well. I have another appointment I have to get to." She extended her hand. "If you have any more questions, my door is always open."

"Thanks for your time," Robert said.

"Yes, thank you," Monica added.

Robert knew Steven hoped to take Emily home. The doctor was right, this was Emily's decision. Hopefully, Robert had spent enough time with her that she'd want to get to know him better. Maybe Emily wouldn't want to go with Steven.

The buzzing coming from his pocket made Steven's whole leg shake. He hated to leave Emily alone, but it would do him some good to stretch his legs a bit. His eyes narrowed as he tried to find a quiet place to talk. Several nurses were chatting in one area, and some doctors were talking in another. Visitors were crying in the hallway. There was a loud television in the waiting room, along with some woman's high-pitched laughter. The smell of antiseptic and cleaner spray mixed together in the air.

Maybe the old wing of the hospital would have less people in it. But he couldn't find a place to talk there either, and the creaking floors just annoyed him. He found himself outside, where the wind was loud and strong, whipping right through his bones, like he stood naked in a tunnel.

In his rush to leave Emily's room, Steven had forgotten his coat and his car keys. Shivering, he found his gray Cadillac XTS and leaned on it to make his phone call. His fingers shook as he took his cell phone from his pocket and hit number two on his speed dial.

"Hello, Mitch." Steven's voice trembled from the cold air. "I'm returning your call."

"I've called you several times, man."

"I know. I'm sorry about that. I have a lot on my mind these days."

"I realize that, and I hate to bother you, but this is important. It's so important that I have to talk to you in person."

"Where are you?" Steven's eyes widened.

"I'm parked in the last row in back."

Turning, he saw Mitch parking a ways down. Still shivering from the cold made him put a pep in his step; he picked up the pace.

"Why are you standing out here without a coat on? It's cold." Mitch shuddered. His window was rolled down halfway and he leaned in over it.

"I realize that, but I forgot my coat and keys upstairs, and I didn't feel like going back up to get them."

"I'm surprised your car is even in the main parking lot. Don't you usually used the valet service?" he asked.

"Don't even bring that up. You know valeting is a sore subject around here."

"Yes, I know. In fact that's why I'm here."

"Can I get in your car and talk?" He put his hands in his pocket. Like a swimmer in freezing water, he shook from the cold.

"I would advise against that. My car reeks of cigarette smoke. I know how you hate to get that smell on your fancy suits," he said, adding a laugh as he glanced at Steven's gray pin-striped suit.

"That's a nasty habit. I thought you stopped smoking." Steven's hands tingled, like he was holding ice. He rubbed them together, hoping to generate some heat. It wasn't working. He tried blowing on them; nothing but cold puffs of air came from his mouth. He glared at Mitch, who sat in his warm vehicle. He still hadn't received his answer.

"I did stop, and then I started back." Mitch shrugged.

Steven stepped back from the car, a little. The smoke barreling out of the window stung his eyes.

"Say what you need to say, so I can get back inside."

"Like I said earlier, sorry to bother you, but I can never get in touch with you anymore. It's like you've been avoiding my calls. I need to tell you that Robert and Emily's car accident wasn't my doing."

"What on earth are you talking about?" Steven narrowed his eyes. "Why would you say such a thing?"

"Remember the envelope full of money you gave me? The one you gave me to give to Jerome?"

"I'm fully aware of the envelope, and what I told you to use it for." Steven swayed from side to side, hoping it would help create some heat. The cold still rippled through his body.

"You were supposed to use it to stir into Robert's past—any dirt you could find would suffice—not try to kill him in a car accident."

"I know, but I told Jerome to be creative in his efforts to get dirt. Part of stirring involves a bit of following. Jerome did follow him that day. But he didn't harm Robert in any way." Mitch's dark eyes shifted. "Sometimes that brother of mine goes off and takes matters into his own hands. I just wanted to keep you informed."

"Good to know." Steven's shoulders shook. "Sorry I didn't return your calls. The police said the driver who caused the accident had brake failure, and the wet pavement only made it worse. No charges were filed against the driver. So you can stop worrying. I need to get back inside." He rubbed his hands together. He knew his face was red. His cheeks were going numb.

"One more thing." Mitch held up his finger.

"What is it?" Steven asked, frowning. He was getting annoyed.

Mitch was one of his very best friends, but his fingers were numb and his toes felt like he stood in a block of ice. He needed to get back inside before he froze to death.

"I would understand if you needed the money back from Jerome." Mitch shrugged. "He hasn't found out anything yet, and I know you need the money."

"I'm fine. If I'd known you would get all sappy on me, I would've never confided in you about my money situation." Steven flinched. "He can keep it. Tell him to keep digging." He turned to walk away. "Emily may be back with me now, but who knows what the future might bring."

⤚

Emily was bored. She was tired of watching the news, there was nothing but the same sad stories. Some poor woman was kidnapped. Someone was shot at a club last night. Some unfortunate child had been abused. The news sure hadn't changed much since she'd been in a coma, but everything else had. She had a whole new life that she couldn't remember.

She was restless and kept shifting her weight in bed. Steven had stepped out to take a call. This was a good time to go for a walk. Being confined to the bed drove her crazy. She gathered herself and shakily climbed out of bed.

Every step she took felt wonderful and would have been even better if she didn't have to drag the IV pole along with her. It was awkward and, in the way, just plain hard to pull. It felt as if she had a third arm. She wished she could disconnect it. But she hadn't been drinking as much as the nurses would have liked, and the IV fluids helped with that. And then, there was the drafty, drab hospital gown. If only she could wear some regular clothes that covered her backside.

Now that she was out and about, she noticed every little thing. She was used to the flowery aroma that came from her room. That was now replaced by the smell of medicine. She didn't care. It felt good to stretch her legs.

There were nurses going over charts with doctors. And other nurses were talking at the nurse's station. No one told her to get back to her room. That was all Emily cared about. She was finally out and about, like a convict escaping from prison.

The television played in one of the larger waiting rooms. Her favorite movie was on; her smile expanded from ear to ear. The waiting room had four rows of cloth chairs with hardwood legs and two long, black, cushioned sofas on each side. She was about to venture inside the waiting room when she felt a warm hand on her shoulder. Her insides quivered when she saw Robert standing in front of her. Her legs wobbled beneath her. His presence unnerved her. Emily felt like she was losing her balance. The next thing she knew, Robert's strong hand reached out and grabbed her arm.

"You okay?" he asked. His hand let go of her arm, his arm went around her waist.

"Yes, you startled me, a little bit." She knew he only put his arm around her waist to keep her steady, but a tingle still developed in her spine. "I wasn't expecting anyone to come up behind me."

"I'm sorry about that. I didn't mean to scare you." His arm gripped her tighter. "I didn't expect to see you out of bed—and by yourself."

"I...I know." She felt uncomfortable, a good uncomfortable. "I was going stir-crazy in that bed. I needed to go for a walk."

"I'm surprised they let you walk around by yourself."

"I'm not supposed to." Emily shrugged. "But I'm feeling much better, so I thought I'd push myself. I have to, if I want to leave here soon." She noticed the brightness in his eyes dimmed. Maybe he was worried that she was pushing herself too hard. "Why are you here?" she asked, already knowing the answer; she wanted to hear him say it.

"I'm here to see you. And I can't say that I'm disappointed to find you out here. It's nice to see you in a setting other than your hospital room."

"I agree."

"Shhhh," came a voice from the waiting room.

"I guess we're talking too loud." Robert gazed at her.

"I guess we are." Emily smiled. Her eyes lifted to his. "Robert, you can let go of me now. I think I'm okay."

"Sorry." He took his arm from her waist. "You feel so natural in my arms."

"Thanks for stopping my fall," she said, trying to make him feel better. She saw the embarrassment on his face. His cheeks were red. She knew he meant no harm. He innocently held her, probably the way he used to.

After what seemed like minutes of gazing into his eyes, Emily felt a cold rush in her chest. Feeling a little weak, she shifted her weight to her other leg, and moved the IV pole into her other hand.

"Are you sure you're alright?" Robert had a look of concern on his face.

"I feel a little light-headed."

"Maybe I should get you to your room."

"No, no." She shook her head. "I was hoping we could talk a bit." She tried to reassure him. "I'll be fine."

"Well, let's go over here." He pointed to the window along the long hallway. "Maybe you can lean on the ledge, for support. I don't want you to fall."

"That sounds like a good idea," she said, grinning. She couldn't help notice he had a grip on her elbow, keeping her balanced. His other hand grasped her IV pole, helping push it. His touch made a warm feeling appear in her stomach.

"Were you going to sit in the waiting room?" Robert asked, once they reached the window.

"As a matter-of-fact, I was," Emily said, still grinning. "I wanted to watch my favorite movie, *The Wizard*—"

"*Of Oz.*" He finished her sentence. "You love that movie so much."

"I keep forgetting how well you know me." Her face flushed.

"Yes, I do." His tone was strong, and his gaze overtook hers.

There was an awkward pause. They both turned to face the window. It was too dark out to see anything, so the awkwardness continued.

"You look nice." She turned back to him. "I know I said I wanted to see you in something else, but I didn't expect it to happen so soon." She cleared her throat. He had on blue jeans and a nice shirt under his black coat. "I like that color brown on you. It offsets your green eyes nicely."

"Thank you. This was one of your favorite shirts—well, it used to be." He looked down and then back at her. "In fact you helped me pick it out."

"Really." Emily beamed. "I wish I could remember."

"I wish you could, too," he said, sighing. His eyes saddened and he looked away.

"I want you to know that I enjoy your visits and hearing about our life together." Her voice was soft and her gaze remained back on the window.

"I'm happy to hear my efforts haven't been in vain. Sometimes, I feel like giving up." He turned to her. "Because it hurts so much when you look at me with that blank stare, because you can't recall the things I'm reminiscing about." His eyes watered. "I shouldn't have said that." He blinked. "I guess that makes me less of a man, admitting my true feelings."

"No." She reached for his hand. "It makes you more of a man because you did." She smiled and tenderly squeezed his hand. She felt him gently squeeze back.

Their eyes remained locked on each other. The same tingling in her spine that she felt earlier returned. Only now it felt even stronger. Holding his hand made her feel like a newlywed on her honeymoon. If she felt this way without even remembering him, what will happen when she did? Was their love stronger than the love she remembered sharing with Steven? The thought made her pull her hand away.

"Did I do something wrong?"

"No, you're fine. I guess I don't know what to say to you." Emily slowly turned away from Robert and her tone became softer. "I know you're the man I was supposed to marry, but I'm sorry. I still don't remember you. I don't know if I ever will."

"It was more than that." He turned her chin back to face him. "I was the man you were going to have a family with, grow old with." His tone was serious. His eyes continued to water.

She felt like a dagger had pierced her heart. His words were lovely and genuine and true. Emily clearly hurt him, and she didn't know how to make it better. She had no idea how to make his pain go away. She stepped closer to him. Touching her hand to his face was all she could think to do. She rubbed his cheek with her thumb and felt her eyes watering along with his. As Emily felt their gazes strengthen, she took her hand away and stepped back.

"I'm making you upset. Maybe I should go now."

"No, please don't go…" Robert paused. "Just stay with me for a few more minutes." His voice trembled. "Emmie, are you really considering going home with him?"

"I haven't made up my mind yet." She blinked.

"I worry about you being alone with him."

"I'm a big girl. I'm not going to let him hurt me."

"I know you believe that, but I don't trust him with you. You can't remember everything he's done and I don't care if he's changed, I need to be there to protect you."

"That's sweet but I can take care of myself. It'll be okay." Her jaw tightened, she was reassuring herself as much as she was trying to reassure him.

CHAPTER TEN

"I thought we could have a chat." Dr. Robinson sat down in the chair next to Emily's bedside. "Are you up for that?"

"Yes." Emily gave an odd half smile.

"I have good news, and I hope you consider it good as well. I spoke to Dr. Washington and to Pete, your physical therapist. We feel you're progressing so well that you're well enough to leave the hospital."

"That's great."

"Do you feel ready for that?"

"Yes, I do. At least, I think so." Her stomach felt hollow; she still didn't know where she belonged.

"Well that's good news, then. You'll still see me for your regular checkups. You'll also still have regular visits with Dr. Washington and Pete. That will be done on an outpatient basis, probably once a week, until you're fully recovered."

"Where will I reside?"

"Where would you like to reside?"

"The last home I remember is the one I shared with Steven. We were happy there." She shifted on the bed.

"Are you saying you want to go back there? I know the history between you and Steven. You don't have to stay there, if you don't want to."

"I don't have a problem staying there. It will be familiar. But I guess I might be a little scared." She glanced down at the sheets on her bed.

"What exactly would you be scared of?"

"That's a poor choice of words. I meant to say I'm nervous."

"Why are you nervous?

"It's been over a year since I lived with Steven; but, in my mind it's like it was yesterday, since I can't remember those years in the middle. After being told the things he's done to me, it will be kind of awkward or uncomfortable." She shrugged. "A part of me thinks, if he has changed, I would like a life with him. And I would like to go home with him to see how things will be with him. But the other part of me thinks I shouldn't give up on finding out what Robert means to me."

"What do you mean?"

"I feel something for him." She paused and fussed with her fingers. "Every time he's around me, something feels comfortable and familiar about him. A part of me wants to keep exploring that. If I go home with Steven that may never happen."

"It's only natural that you would feel something for him. Just because you have amnesia doesn't make the feelings you shared for him any less real. I believe those feelings are buried deep down inside and that's what you're feeling when you're around him.

"Since you're having such a hard time, maybe you should stay at a neutral place, at first, like your sister's house."

"You mean stay with Monica and David?"

"Yes, how does that sound?"

"I don't think they have enough room for me." She shifted on the bed. "They're living with David's parents while their new house is being built."

"Where did you hear this? This is the first I'm hearing of this."

"Last night, David came to visit with me. We got to talking about things, and he said he and Monica were having a house built. They'd put their condo up for sale, and they received an offer earlier than expected, so they had to move in with his parents until their house is ready."

"I'm sorry, Emily, I didn't know that. Monica never mentioned it."

"She never mentioned it to me, either." Emily gulped down some juice from the tray on her table. Her mouth was dry. "When she's here she never discusses herself. She only wants to talk about how I'm doing."

"That's understandable, she's worried about you." The doctor wrote something down on her pad. "Does that factor into your decision of who to go home with?"

"Maybe, a little." She shrugged. "I've met David's parents, once or twice. They are nice people, but I don't want to intrude; I don't want to be in the way. David said it would be fine to stay with them, but I still feel like that's not his call to make. It's his parents' call. Their home is not that big, and I don't think there's enough room for me. Of course, David said they'd manage."

Her mouth was still dry, like she was lost in a desert, so she sipped more juice.

"I've been told that I have my own apartment." The plastic cup thumped as she put it down. "Maybe I could stay there until I figure everything out."

"I don't think that's such a good idea. Once you're released, you'll be on restrictions—driving will be one of them. I think you need people around. You shouldn't be alone."

"I feel like I don't know who I am or where I fit in. If I go home with Steven, it hurts Robert. If I don't, it hurts Steven. He's been trying so hard to make things right between us."

Dr. Robinson stood and placed her hand on Emily's shoulder.

"I know this is hard. Everything doesn't have to be decided today. We'll take this one day at a time. Remember, never let anyone pressure you into doing something you don't want to do. Alright?" She handed Emily a tissue.

"Okay." Emily dabbed at the wetness on her cheeks.

She felt helpless, like a fish out of water, and she couldn't breathe.

❧

"Emily, I have a surprise for you." Steven walked in smiling. "Are you alright? You look upset." He opened the blinds to let more sun in.

"I'm okay." She sat up straighter in the bed. "Dr. Robinson was just here. But we can discuss that later. What's the surprise?" She wiped her tear stained face.

"You have a few visitors; but, if you don't feel up to it, I can ask them to come back another time."

"No, I feel fine."

She was curious who the visitors could be. Since she'd been moved out of the ICU, Emily was allowed more visitors. She hoped someone she knew besides Monica, Robert or David would come to visit. Not that she wasn't happy to see them. Maybe someone new would help spark her memory. Steven had called the school and had the office convey to her class to stay away until she felt better. Monica kept saying it was because he didn't want her memory to return, so she would stay with him.

"I'm going to leave so you can have some privacy," Steven said, walking out of the room.

"Hello, Emily." A tall, slender woman with blonde hair and blue eyes walked near her bed. "I'm Christina Hart. I teach at the school with you."

"I recognize that name." Emily bit down on her lip. "I received a card from you. My sister told me that we were close. I teach English and you teach—"

"Math," Christina said, finishing her sentence.

"Yes." Emily nodded. "You teach math," she added, smiling.

"I know you don't remember me, Mrs. Montgomery. I'm Maggie, one of your students."

"Maggie," Emily said, repeating her name. "That's such a pretty name for a beautiful young lady." Emily loved her curly red hair and her green eyes. "I remember your card, it was pink with a flower on it. Thank you for sending it."

"You always had a way of doing that," Maggie said.

"Did I say something wrong?" Emily asked.

"No, that's not what I meant." Maggie swung her brown purse over her shoulder. "You always knew how to make each of your students feel special. Well, especially me." She glanced at the floor.

"I take it we were close." Emily's eyes shifted to hers.

"Maggie is one of your favorite students." Christina said. "I know we teachers are not supposed to have favorites, but sometimes we do."

"May I ask why I took such a special liking to you?"

"I reminded you of yourself when you were young."

"How so?" Emily was intrigued by the conversation. Her heavy chest feeling from earlier, now felt light like a feather.

"You said you were shy, like me, and you were into your studies instead of boys."

"Yes, boys should come later. It's important to graduate from high school first." Emily smiled. "I didn't go on my first date until I was already out of school."

"You always said that, too." Maggie grinned. "I'm so happy your better now. I wish your memory would return, so you could teach our class again. Everyone misses you. Mr. Nathan has taken over. It's not the same."

"I don't know who Mr. Nathan is, but I'm sure he's a fine teacher. Maybe not as good as me," she said, letting out a small giggle. "I'm sure he does okay."

"It's good you're laughing," Christina said, rubbing the top of Emily's hand. "Seriously though, we miss you. I need my friend back." Her eyes watered.

"I hope to be back, one day. I really do." Emily felt close to them. She blinked the haze from her eyes.

"We should go now," Christina said. "We know you need to rest."

"This was so nice. I hope we can do it again." Emily waved and watched them leave the room.

"I hope that went well," Steven said, walking back in the room. He took off his black suit jacket and threw it in the chair.

"It was very nice. Did you arrange all of that?" She placed a strand of hair behind her ear.

"As a matter-of-fact, I did. I called the school office and told them that you were better and could have visitors again. I gave the office my cell phone number and asked potential visitors to call me first, since I wanted to make sure you were having a good day." He sat down on her bed. "Your friend, Christina, wanted to come with the young lady, Maggie."

"I thought you and Christina didn't get along very well." Her eyebrow rose. "Or, that's what I've been told."

"You were told right." He brushed her cheek. "We didn't always get along. But this is different. You're sick. You need your family and friends around you. Besides, Christina and I may have our differences, but we both still love you, and that's all that matters."

"I can't believe you did that." She leaned in and kissed his cheek. "That was so sweet of you." She blinked. "I'm not going to forget this." She hugged him tightly around his neck.

He wasn't trying to keep her isolated. He did want her to remember. From everything Emily had witnessed, he had changed.

CHAPTER ELEVEN

"What's going on?" Robert noticed Monica standing outside of Emily's room with a long face.

"It looks like Emily's gone."

"What do you mean?"

"The nurse said her husband wanted her discharged, so she's gone." Monica looked brokenhearted. "So, I had Dr. Robinson paged, to see if she knew anything about it."

"Well, what did she say?" His heartbeats hammered in his chest. He needed answers.

"She had planned for Emily to be here for a few more days, but she said Steven *and* Emily decided, together, that she should go home today."

"I don't believe this." Robert shook his head. "How could he just swoop in and take her without telling any of us? Is it because he's still legally her husband?"

"No, I don't think that's it. Dr. Robinson said Emily insisted on going home today. The doctor wanted to call me first, but Emily didn't want you, or me, to know about it. She probably feared we'd talk her out of it," Monica said, pacing back and forth. "This was her choice." Her black heels tapped on the concrete floors.

"It still feels like they just sneaked off." Robert felt like he stood under an abandoned building that had caved in.

"The last time I spoke with her, she was undecided on what to do. I felt like she was leaning toward coming home with me and David."

"I felt she was going in that direction, too—especially after yesterday." He took in a deep breath. "I can't believe Emmie would do something like this."

Seeing the blank stare on Monica's face, he elaborated. "Yesterday, I found Emily alone in the hallway and we talked and held hands. I felt like I was getting through to her." He massaged the back of his neck. "I practically begged her not to go home with him. I really thought she wouldn't. I guess I was wrong."

"This is Steven's doing. I know he has something up his sleeve." Monica narrowed her eyes.

"We can't even call Emily because her cell phone was destroyed in the car accident. I should go over there and break the door down."

"That would just give Steven a chance to make you look like the bad guy. I still have Steven's home number," Monica said. "I have to go back to work, but as soon as I get off, I'll call and let you know what happens. It's going to be okay." She squeezed Robert's hand.

"I know it is," he said, trying to reassuring himself as Monica walked away.

The hallway seemed longer, and darker, than normal. The beeping sounds were louder than usual. Every smell made his stomach nauseous. He felt like he was on an elevator, stuck between two floors, with no way out. The woman he loved had just gone home with someone else.

Emily couldn't believe she now sat in the passenger seat of Steven's car. Arranging for Christina and Maggie to come and visit showed her his loving side, the side she remembered and knew was still in there. He had said he loved her, and if she would give him a chance, he would prove it to her. Steven had asked her to trust him and to come home with him. If Emily felt uncomfortable or unsafe in any way, she could leave and go stay with her sister. He wouldn't stand in her way. Emily's nerves were tingling, thinking of the hurt Monica and Robert must have felt when they found out she had left. But she tried not to dwell on that and to just enjoy the drive.

The hospital was only twenty minutes from their home, so they didn't have far to go. Emily wished the ride was longer since it was nice being out and about. Everything felt brand new. Since her accident and her time in the hospital she hadn't been outside much, except for a few walks with her physical therapist. It seemed like she hadn't rode in a car in decades.

There was a hissing sound as Steven rolled down the windows. The air smelled fresh. The sky looked clear. There were streetlights and storefronts and other cars. She felt like a puppy as the wind swooshed across her face.

She saw the car wash Steven took their vehicles to. They past the flower shop where he always bought her roses. Next to it was the brick market, her favorite grocery store where Anita, their maid, shopped. There were also some unfamiliar places, like the Starbucks where the donut shop used to be, and a new hi-rise where a parking lot used to be.

Steven grabbed her hand and pulled it to his lips. He would always do that when they first married. His touch sent a shiver up Emily's spine. The nervousness she felt when they left the hospital intensified.

They pulled up in the driveway of their house. It was as big as she remembered. In her mind, she had always lived there; but, in reality, she hadn't lived there in a year and a half. Just thinking about it made her head spin. She jumped when Steven opened her door.

"Are you alright?" He reached for her hand. "Your face is flushed."

"I'm fine." She gave a half smile.

"Do the clothes I bought you fit alright?" His eyebrows rose in question.

She knew he was trying to figure out what was wrong. She tried to act normal. "Yes, they fit fine. Anita did a good job picking them out."

She had on thick jeans and a red, knit turtleneck underneath her coat.

"Once you're all settled, we can have dinner. I'm sure you're hungry."

"I'd like that." She smiled, holding on to his hand. "Why didn't you park in the garage?" Her attention turned to the five car garage that was attached to the house.

"I usually keep this car parked outside."

"Alright." She found that a bit odd. When they were first married he had said all their cars should be parked in the garage. Cars were kept up better if they were out of the snow and the cold. But that was a long time ago she had to keep telling herself. Even though, to her, only a year had gone by.

"In case you're wondering, your BMW is parked in the garage," he said, helping her up the front steps. "I was angry when you left me. You had to go and buy that old car, and I'm sorry about that."

"You don't have to keep apologizing."

"It's hard not to. I'll try to stop, since we're starting over."

"Okay. By the way, where is my other car—the old one you're talking about?"

"It's still parked near your apartment. Why do you ask?"

"Just curious." She shrugged. "That's all."

"You no longer need it now that you have the BMW back. Maybe I'll try and sell it. But we can discuss that later. Right now, I want to get you in the house."

Steven opened the front door and Emily stood frozen. Everything was familiar but also strange.

"Is Anita here?" she asked.

"No, I sent her home after she cooked dinner. Don't worry, you'll see her soon." The door slammed behind them. "You're not afraid to be alone with me, are you?" His eyes narrowed.

"N-no." Emily's voice quivered. "Why would you think that?"

"Because you're trembling," he said, touching the small of her back.

"I'm fine." She stepped away from Steven. "What did she make?" Emily asked, changing the subject.

There was a wonderful aroma in the air. It smelled like baked bread and tomato sauce. She hoped it was lobster ravioli, one of her favorites. She headed for the kitchen.

Steven grabbed her arm. "Wait a minute, I thought we'd go upstairs first and get you settled before we eat."

"You mean to the bedroom?" She frowned.

"Yes, to our bedroom. Is anything wrong with that?" His jaw clenched at her reaction.

"No, I guess not." The earlier tightness she felt in her chest remained.

Her heart beat more fiercely than she would have liked. Emily couldn't seem to steady herself. She stepped inside the master bedroom, to finding it filled with red roses.

"What's wrong?" Steven asked. She knew he'd noticed her somber look.

"Nothing." She shrugged, glancing around the room. "The room is just as lovely as I remembered. And the roses are a nice touch. Where will you be sleeping?" she innocently asked.

He gave her a strange look. "In here with you, of course. I wasn't expecting us to be intimate. But it's been such a long time, and I want to be close to you. Is there anything wrong with me just lying next to you?"

She glanced at the floor and then back at him. "No, that's not a problem."

"Obviously, it is or you wouldn't have mentioned it." He sounded hurt.

"It's just, we haven't been together for a while now. I thought we could sleep in separate rooms until I feel more comfortable." Her voice was shaky.

"The last thing you remembered was us still being together and happy. So in your mind, no time had passed. And you said, instead of dwelling on things you can't remember, you'd give us a chance."

"That's what I thought I wanted, too; but, now that I'm here, everything is confusing."

"I think your making too much of this." He angrily brushed his hands through his hair. "You were fine when we left the hospital, but now that we're home, it's an entirely different story."

"Don't do that." She shook her head. "I'm going through a lot right now, and I have every right to change my mind. Now that I'm here, I feel a little nervous." She wrung her hands. "We were getting a divorce. I was engaged to someone else. Now, all of a sudden, I'm here trying to make this work. I woke up from the coma thinking I was twenty-five when I'm really thirty. It's a lot to get adjusted to."

"I'm sorry. I don't want to argue your first night here. But I would like you to give us a chance, like you said you would. That's all I ask. I'm going downstairs to set the table for dinner."

Feeling like she'd been knocked over by a ton of bricks, Emily sat down on the bed. Maybe he was right to be upset. All she could remember was her love for Steven, and the life they shared together. But now that she was here, she felt strange. Her chest felt heavy. She hadn't felt this way in the hospital. Maybe it was because in the hospital other people were always around. Now, it was just the two of them, and it would take some getting used to.

Emily picked up a picture that Steven had on his bedside table, a picture of happier times. It was their wedding day photo. Could they ever be that way again?

Steven stormed into the kitchen, like a bolt of lightning followed behind him. He felt like fire came from his ears as he started slamming any drawer he could reach. He turned his anger on the refrigerator. It thumped as he flung the door against the wall. He grabbed a dark beer.

"This homecoming is not at all like I pictured it," he said, grumbling under his breath.

He slammed the refrigerator closed.

He didn't want to show anger in front of Emily; but now that he was alone, he could slam as many things as he needed to until he calmed down.

His phone buzzed in his suit coat pocket.

"Mitch," Steven answered. "What do you need?"

"You sound upset," Mitch said. "I got your text saying Emily left the hospital with you. I thought that would be good news. Did something else happen?"

"I thought once I got Emily home, we'd fall back in place—to that happy time. I'm not naïve. I knew it would take a little bit of time, but for some reason she's too nervous to relax in her own home. So at this rate, she'll never get there." He plopped down at the kitchen table and nursed his beer.

"I still don't know how you got her to agree to go home with you in the first place."

"I saw her and Robert in the hallway holding hands, which I took to mean they were becoming closer. I had to think of a way to get her on my side. So I called the school office and told them she could have visitors."

He gulped down some beer. The bottle clanked, landing back on the granite tabletop.

"It didn't matter who came as long as someone did. And I lucked out because one of her good friends, Christina, and one of her students, Maggie, came to the hospital and that did the trick. She was so ecstatic that I had gone to all that trouble that she agreed to give me another chance. It also helped that she found out her sister is living with her in-laws, and they don't have room for her. It was news to me, but it might have pushed her decision right over the edge. But what good is all of that, if we get home and she can't be herself."

"You know I'm always honest with you. I think things will get better between you two. You have to give it some time."

"When did you become a marriage counselor?" Steven said, with a chuckle.

"Look man, I've been following the saga of your lives ever since you first met. So believe me when I say, I know no matter what you've done you do love her, in your own way."

"Thanks for that. I appreciate it." Steven calmed down a bit. "You know, I'm not always a patient man," he said, then took another swig of beer. "But I'm going to try to be."

"By the way, I don't have any news yet on that project…"

"It's okay, we don't have to discuss that right now. I need to set the table and get back upstairs to my wife. Talk to you later," he said, disconnecting the call.

The plates and glasses clanked against the table. He decided to use the good china. He hoped this first dinner would go well with Emily, the first of many more to come. He knew how easily things could go wrong. Steven had a way of messing things up even when he didn't want to. Sometimes, he was selfish and let his temper get the best of him. He had tried hard to change, but sometimes, he felt himself slipping back to old habits. That couldn't happen, not this time.

His mother had died from breast cancer when he was a little boy. After she had passed away, he had to raise himself because his father fell apart; he couldn't keep a job, and he started bringing home one woman after another. His father had become an alcoholic and took out his anger on Steven by hitting him.

He never wanted to be disrespected like that again. So he went to college and found a good job. Steven wanted money and power, so he'd never feel like that abused little boy again. His father had passed away, from a heart attack, when Steven was twenty. He chose not to attend the funeral. Steven wanted to forget that part of his life ever existed. But sometimes, when things weren't going his way, he saw traces of his father that he didn't like. Traits that weren't so easy to escape, no matter how hard he tried.

The calmness he'd felt after talking to Mitch faded, and his leg twitched. He wiped his sweaty palms on his dress pants. Steven took in a deep breath and slowly turned the knob. Entering the room, he found Emily with red eyes holding their wedding photo in her hands.

He took the photo out of her hands, and sat down next to her.

"I'm sorry." He wrapped his arm around her waist and leaned into her. "I was so excited to have you home. I expected everything to be like it was before. I wanted everything to magically fall into place." He turned her face toward his. "I didn't mean to put pressure on you. I know it's a lot for you to take in."

"Yes, it is." Her eyes watered.

"Once again, I'm sorry." He wiped a tear from her cheek. "It's my fault for expecting too much, too soon. I have no problem sleeping in the guest bedroom."

Leaning in, he kissed her cheek than moved to her mouth. He didn't want to force things, or make her uncomfortable. But he hoped she wouldn't pull away. Surprisingly, he felt her move closer to him, like she welcomed his embrace. His pulse increased when he heard her softly moan. Moving his fingers under her sweater, he caressed her stomach. No matter how much he wanted to be with her, the little voice in his head told him this was too much, that he took it too far. Somehow, he knew if he didn't stop himself, she would do it for him.

"I can't do this," Emily said, pulling away. "I got caught up in the moment. It was like when we first started dating, but I can't. It's wrong."

"I wish you wouldn't say things like that. It's not wrong." He shook his head. "We are married." He rubbed his hand over his face. "I'm going to sleep in the guest bedroom tonight, to give you a little space. I want you to feel comfortable here."

"Thank you. That means more than you know," she said, smiling.

He took her hand. They made their way downstairs to dinner. They reminisced about the past, the good parts of the past. Those were the only parts Emily could remember. Steven hoped it stayed that way.

✍

Emily walked downstairs the next morning to the smell of bacon and eggs wafting in the air. Steven stood at the stove with a Kiss The Cook apron on.

"How did you sleep?" he asked, with a smile.

"Good. The bed here is much softer than the one in the hospital." She unloosened the tie on her bathrobe, a little, and sat down at the table.

"Well, I should hope so." Steven placed two pieces of bacon on her plate.

"I expected to find Anita down here cooking." She poured herself a glass of orange juice from the pitcher sitting on the table. It sounded like a faucet flowing as it sloshed into her glass.

"No, I gave her the day off, so we could spend some time alone." He put a spoonful of eggs on her plate. "I hope that's alright with you?"

"It's fine."

She had never known Steven to cook breakfast before, or any meal for that matter. This was a welcome surprise, and a nice gesture.

"I thought we could also go to the humane society and look for a cat," he said, sitting down across from her. "I know you always wanted another American shorthair." He poured himself some orange juice. "It's better to get one from the humane society rather than a pet store. The ones from the humane society have been hurt and abandoned and they need homes."

Her eyes widened, but she remained quiet and let him continue to talk.

"I know your cat died when you were eleven years old, and your parents said you were irresponsible because you weren't watching him when he ran out in the street. You said you would get another one when you were older." He gulped down a mouthful of juice. "Do you remember?"

"Yes, I told you that story when we were dating. I'm surprised *you* remember." The sunlight from the kitchen window blinded her. The wooden legs of the black vinyl chairs squeaked as she scooted over.

"I remember everything you tell me." His eyes softened.

"Since we're speaking of things we remember, I recall you're allergic to cats. That's why we didn't have one. Besides that you don't even like cats."

"I realize that. I've done research, and I can take medication to help with the allergy. I can take shots and use antihistamine. That should help, along with a humidifier."

"You'd go through all of that so I could have a cat again?"

"For you, yes. I want you to feel safe here. If a cat will do that, then I'm willing to try."

"I don't want you doing crazy things to win me over. All I want is to see how we interact with each other in our day-to-day, normal lives."

"It's not crazy," he said, shifting in his chair. "Besides, I was already doing this before your car accident. You don't remember. When we were separated, and I begged you to come back to me, I went out and bought a gray-and-white cat. I came to your apartment with him, but you refused to open the door and look at him. You told me to take the cat back to wherever I found him. You said a cat wasn't going to make up for all the hurt I put you through."

"That really happened?"

"Yes, it did."

"What happened to the cat?" she asked, then put a spoonful of eggs in her mouth.

"I wanted him to have a good home, so I ended up giving him to my friend, Mitch. You remember him, right?"

"He's your old friend from law school."

"Yes. He ended up giving it to his sister."

"Well, his sister can keep the cat. I'm sure she's attached to him by now. And I don't want you pumping yourself full of medication to make me happy. Is this how it's going to be?" she asked, standing.

"What do you mean?"

"You going above and beyond to get me to stay here." Her plate clanked as she put it in the sink.

"I didn't think that was what I was doing." His eyebrow rose as he stood. "I was making a nice gesture, but apparently you think I'm playing games to keep you here. Can you blame me, if I was?" He wiped his mouth with the napkin. "You're here with me now, but who knows when you'll up and decide you don't want to be here anymore. I fear the day when you'll walk out of here and go to Robert."

"I don't need any grand gestures." The water flowed like a river as she ran it in the sink. "I only want you to act normal. That way, I can get to know you again, not the man I remember from five years ago. I need to know the man you are right now." She turned off the faucet.

"That's all I want, too." He walked to her. "I know you agreed to give us some time to see how this goes. When—if—your memory returns, I hope you choose to stay with me." He touched her face. "I need this to be forever." He leaned in and kissed her lips.

His touch was gentle and caring, and it made her hands tremble. He was a human being who had feelings and felt pain. And no matter what he'd done in the past, she knew he could be that sweet man she knew when they first married.

⁓

"Are you ready for this?" Monica asked Robert.

"Of course, I'm ready. I was ready to come last night after

you said the phone just rang and rang; but, you wouldn't let me," he replied.

He pulled the collar of his coat closer to his neck. The wind roared and the air chilled.

"I know, but it was late, and I didn't want to upset Emily. I didn't think he'd harm her on her first night home," Monica said. She rang the doorbell and they heard chimes playing, then she rapped on the front door. "I always hated this house. It's like a mansion. No one needs to live in a house this big." She rang the doorbell and rapped on the door again.

"They should be up." Robert glanced at his watch. "It's eleven a.m. on a Saturday."

The door whizzed open and Steven stood there in beige khakis and a light blue shirt. He looked annoyed.

"I'm surprised to see you here." His voice was rough.

"Why are you surprised?" Monica said. "Emily is my sister. I haven't seen her since you stole her from the hospital yesterday."

"Stole?" he growled. "Your sister chose to come home with me. So I think stole is a poor word choice."

"It doesn't matter." She shook her head.

"Can you move aside so we can see her?" Robert said.

"Does Emily know you were coming?" He remained in the doorway.

"Is there a problem?" Robert asked.

"Emily needs her rest. Maybe you could come back another day."

"So, you're not going to let us in to see her." Robert clenched his fist.

"This time your observation would be correct."

"This is insane." Monica rolled her eyes. "And, the exact reason why I didn't want her coming home with you."

"You two are ridiculous." He shook his head. "She can't come to the door. She's not even here."

"Where else would she be?" Robert asked. Steven was giving them the run around. "She just got out of the hospital yesterday.

Emily shouldn't be traipsing around on her own. She's not supposed to drive."

"Since you won't get off my doorstep," Steven said, stepping aside, "why don't you come in and wait."

They walked past the foyer. Robert's eyes broadened. He had never been in Emily's former home before and his mouth went dry. The rooms were large and extravagant. There were fancy paintings on the walls that probably cost more than his entire year's salary. The colors were bright, and the furniture looked like it was right out of an antique, French furniture store. The Emily he knew never cared for luxury like this.

"You can sit down and wait." He pointed at the gray-and-white, rectangular, silk sofa in the living room.

The sofa matched the gray walls, and there was a bronze statue of a lion near the stone fireplace.

"Steven, did I hear you talking to someone?" Emily walked into the room, wearing a long black wool coat with matching shiny rubber black boots.

"You have guests. I told them you weren't here, but they didn't believe me."

"I was outside," Emily said, unbuttoning her coat. A cashmere sweater and black jeans were underneath. "I was looking at the plants in the greenhouse."

"So, technically, you weren't here." Steven had a sly grin on his face. "And, I wasn't sure when you were coming back in."

Robert's jaw tightened. Steven was already playing games and he didn't like it. It was as if Steven knew he had the upper hand in the situation and used it to his advantage. No, he hadn't lied since Emily wasn't there. And of course, Steven had to let him and Monica in, which made him out to be a nice guy—in Emily's eyes, that is.

"Robert, aren't you going to sit down?" Emily pointed to the sofa. Seeing him again made her knees weak.

"Yes, sorry," he said, sitting down next to Monica.

"It's good to see you two." Emily smiled. "I thought you might be mad at me for leaving the hospital like I did." She sat down across from them on the gray-and-white love seat.

"We're not mad, just concerned." Monica shifted her weight. "Are you sure you're doing the right thing?"

"I'm sure your guests don't want me around, so I'll let you have your privacy," Steven said. "I need to make a call anyway."

"Did he pressure you?" Robert's eyes were sincere. "In the hospital, it felt like you were leaning toward going home with Monica."

"I was leaning that way until David told me you were living with your in-laws. There's no room for me there. You should have told me, Monica."

"I didn't because I knew you'd feel that way. We could have always made room for you. It wasn't a big deal. David could have slept on the sofa, and you could have slept in the second bedroom with me."

"That's what I didn't want." Emily shook her head. "I don't belong there."

"You belong here?" Robert's voice was loud. His eyes widened.

"That's not what I'm saying."

"Then, what are you saying?" Monica pressed.

"I'm sorry, Robert." She blinked. "Steven's been nothing but kind and considerate toward me, and I want to see where this will lead. We are still married."

"You've only been here one night. You have no idea what will happen tomorrow or the next day," Robert said.

"No, I don't, but I owe it to myself to find out. This is the only life I know. And now that I'm home, everything's just like I remember. I'm not being naïve. I feel I need to pursue this."

"And where does that leave me?" Robert's eyes softened.

"I don't want to hurt you but—"

"Don't even say it." Robert moved to sit down next to Emily.

"I know my Emmie is in here, somewhere." He touched her chin. "And, I know she's going to come back to me."

"Robert…"

"I thought our time together in the hospital meant as much to you as it did to me."

"It did." Her mouth dropped. "It still does."

"Then how can you give up on us and let me go so easily? How can you throw it all away?"

"You think this is easy for me?" she asked. "It meant the world to me that you opened your heart and shared your feelings with me." Her heart thumped in her ears.

"But not enough to keep getting to know me better?"

"How can I do that while I'm living with Steven? It wouldn't be right to date you while I'm married to someone else."

"This marriage isn't real." He took in a breath. "That is, unless you want it to be. And you do. That's what you've been saying since we got here. But I've been refusing to hear it."

The pain in his eyes made her stomach ache. It was like Monica was no longer in the room. All she wanted to do was hold him.

"Sorry to interrupt." Steven walked back in the room. "I promised Emily we'd go shopping for a new cell phone and some other things that she needs."

"We should go." Monica stood.

"Yes, I think it's time." Robert shook his head.

"Promise me you'll call me with your new number," Monica said, walking toward the door. "And, if Steven touches you in any inappropriate way."

"I will, I promise." Emily waved.

Monica smiled back at her. Robert no longer looked her way. He headed for the door without saying goodbye. Could she blame him? This was an awkward situation, and she had probably made it even worse.

CHAPTER TWELVE

Emily shivered in the cold. Her wool winter coat wasn't as warm as she would have liked. But she didn't care, it felt good to finally be out of the house. The sun shining down on her face made her heart expand, and the air was brisk and clean. A few weeks had passed since she'd returned home with Steven. She had only been out of the house a few times since then.

Steven had taken her for her weekly visits to the hospital. He scheduled her appointments with Dr. Robinson and Pete, her therapist, for the same day. She would have preferred them on different days, so she'd be able to get out of the house more than once a week. Since she was still on driving restrictions, someone still had to drive her where she needed to go. Steven had apologized for not being more flexible. This was more convenient for him, for his schedule, since he had to drive her. Now that Steven was busy with a new case, and Anita drove her, Emily would make sure to schedule her own appointments on the days she wanted to.

She hit the up button for the elevator and waited. Emily took great pleasure in the hustle and bustle of everyday life at the hospital. People conversing and laughing, it was all so wonderful. It was nice to hear other voices for a change. The only thing that bothered her was the babies crying, which could be heard quite often. The sound made her cringe and think about things she didn't want to, things she'd rather not dwell on. A vibration in her purse made her flinch. She was glad for the distraction from her thoughts of the baby Monica told her she had lost. Steven's name popped up on her phone's screen.

"Hello." Emily moved off to the side so she could talk. There were other people around, and she didn't want to be rude.

"Hey, babe. I was just checking on you. Are you at the hospital yet?"

"Yes. My session with Dr. Robinson will be starting soon." She continued. "Aren't you working?" Her voice rose an octave.

"Are you alright?" he asked.

She knew he picked up on her strangeness.

"I'm fine," she said, even though it felt like a heavy hand was on her chest.

"Don't push the driving issue with Pete. I know you feel like you're ready. Pete knows best. If he says you're not ready, then you're not ready."

"But I am ready. I know my own body." She was getting annoyed.

"Remember what I said, Emily. I have to go." He abruptly hung up the call.

She heard someone talking to him in the background. Emily sighed. She felt bad but she was happy their call was interrupted. Steven had been overprotective the last few days, which was cute yet also annoying. It started to feel like Steven was her parole officer, she wore an ankle monitor, and he had to know where she was at all times of the day.

❧

"Is your wife alright?" Leonard asked. He was another defense attorney at Steven's firm.

"Yes, she's fine." Steven put his phone on vibrate, and placed it back in his suit jacket.

"If you need to take off more time to be with her, I can gladly take the lead on this case." His amber eyes squinted as he chuckled, and he brushed a hand through his red hair.

"I'm good. I can handle it." Steven plopped down at his desk across from Leonard.

"You know I won the last two cases we tried and—"

"I know where this is going." Steven cut him off. "I know you've been on a roll while I was distracted with my wife's accident."

"Look, Steven." Leonard held up his hands. "Don't get defensive. I understand you had to take care of Emily."

"That's not what I was going to say." Steven shook his head. "I was saying I know you've won the last two cases, and I lost my last two. But before that, I was on a winning streak. It's just…" His heart dropped and so did his voice. "I was separated from my wife and my mind wasn't on my work. I was distracted and—"

"You don't have to go into all of that. I know you and your wife were estranged."

Steven could tell he made Leonard uncomfortable. That wasn't his intention. He just felt he needed to explain. He didn't like failure. So he needed his co-workers to understand his circumstances.

"That's over with now. I'm back on track and ready to get to work." His stomach bounced around, and he didn't like or welcome that feeling.

"You don't have to say another word." Leonard sipped a cup of coffee that was on the desk. "We're good. Let's get to work."

"Fine with me." Steven was happy to change the subject. They were starting a new case and he was happy to delve into it.

He defended a husband accused of murdering his wife. They were in a bad marriage, and her body was found dismembered in her bath tub. According to witness reports, the husband abused his wife on several occasions. She had been to the hospital several times with severely broken bones and bruises on her body. The husband admitted to abusing his wife, on occasion. But he claimed he wasn't guilty of her murder. Supposedly, he had a solid alibi for the time of the murder. He was with his new girlfriend. Would his new girlfriend's testimony hold up in court? That remained to be seen. It seemed like it would be an open and shut case, if the jury believed the new girlfriend. The guy's actual guilt or innocence wasn't up to Steven. His job was to defend his client, no matter what.

The whole case made Steven shudder. He had handled plenty of cases like this one before. But for some reason, this one bothered him. Maybe since he was starting over with Emily, and he knew he had treated her badly as well. Shaking his head, he took in a deep breath. Maybe he should let Leonard handle this case, and he'd take lead on the next one. No, he needed this win. He needed it more than anyone knew.

❧

"Nice to see you again, Emily. Please take a seat," Dr. Robinson said.

Emily sat down and unbuttoned her coat. She welcomed the heat in the room and the smell of peppermint in the air.

"Mrs. Hopkins, your social worker reports you're doing well readjusting to your life with Steven. Would you agree with her?"

"Yes." Emily nodded, and then remained quiet.

"So have there been any changes since I saw you last week?" Dr. Robinson sat down behind her desk. "Any flashes of memory?"

"No, nothing like that." Emily shook her head. "Does that normally happen?"

"It depends. With some patients they may see tiny flashes, and then eventually their entire memory returns, and with others a certain event may trigger their entire memory to come barreling back at once."

"And some people may never remember, right?" Emily squirmed in her chair.

"Yes, that may happen also. Is that what you want, Emily, not to remember your former life?"

"Why would you ask me that? That would make me crazy, wouldn't it?" she asked.

"No, it wouldn't make you crazy. It would make you afraid of the unknown. The last time you were here, you said things were going well with Steven, you said you two were becoming closer, and it was like when you were first married. So maybe you don't want to remember because that would force all the bad memories of him to resurface, and then this life you've restarted wouldn't be safe or simple anymore." Dr. Robinson wrote some notes down on her pad.

"It's not like that. I want to remember my life. But I can say, I don't want to see him that way in memories or up close in real life. So maybe remembering does scare me a little."

"That's understandable. You seem a little on edge. Is anything else wrong?"

"Things had been going well," Emily said, fidgeting with her hands. "It's just the last few days, since Steven found out I might start driving again, he's been acting differently."

"How so?" Dr. Robinson's eyebrow rose.

"He's been overprotective, which was cute at first…" She paused to gather her thoughts.

"And now?"

"Well, for instance today." She frowned. "He called me three times after he left the house for work this morning. Then, he called me when I was on my way here, and he called again before I entered your office. That's a total of five times, and it's not even afternoon yet."

"It sounds like now that you're going to be more mobile, more independent, he's worried."

"What would he have to worry about?'

"Maybe he thinks since you won't be glued to the house anymore, where he can keep tabs on you, he'll lose you."

"You might be right." She shrugged. "But if he doesn't trust me, this is never going to work."

An uneasy feeling grew in her stomach, and Emily wished it would go away.

❦

Her sessions with Dr. Robinson, and then Pete, had gone better than expected. Pete even told her she could drive again. Feeling like she'd won a million dollars, she poured out of the elevator and headed for Monica's office.

The pharmacy door dinged, letting the employees know someone had walked inside. Emily's eyes bulged, everything looked different. She hadn't been there in a long time, in her mind that is. She was sure she had been there in the last year or so, but of course she couldn't remember. The dirty yellow plastered walls had been painted a cheery rose color. The wood counter and metal chairs were in a different order. But the smell of medicine was still clearly in the air, and the room still seemed small and claustrophobic.

"Can I help you?" she heard a voice say.

Emily saw a small framed woman who looked to be in her twenties. She had dark brown eyes and golden hair. Her name tag read Veronica.

"I'm sorry." Emily stepped closer to the counter. "Is Monica Wilson here?"

"Can I ask who wants to see her?"

"I'm her sister, Emily."

"Emily! You're the sister she talks so much about." Veronica's smile was warm and inviting. "I'm glad to see you're out of the hospital and doing much better."

"Thank you." Emily smiled back.

"We haven't met." She held out her hand. "I'm Veronica. I haven't worked here for that long."

"Nice to meet you." Emily extended her hand.

"Your sister's on her break. Just go on back." She pointed her finger to the area behind the shelves of medicine. "I'm sure she won't mind."

"Thank you."

Emily saw Monica sitting at a small table. She sipped a bottle of water.

"Sit down." Monica waved her hand at the seat across from

her. "Is Steven lurking around somewhere? I know he takes you for your appointments."

"No, he's at work. He doesn't take me for all my appointments. Anita takes me to a lot of them. In fact, she dropped me off today."

"She sure does a lot of extra things a maid wouldn't normally do." The paper crinkled as Monica unwrapped a granola bar.

"I know. I think Steven's paying her extra to drive me around. Even if he didn't, she wouldn't mind, she's like family." The smell of peanuts wafted up Emily's nose. Her stomach growled. She didn't have lunch.

"Would you like some?" The bar snapped as Monica broke it in half.

"Thank you." Emily stuffed the bar in her mouth, chewed quickly, and swallowed. "I have good news. Pete said I could drive again."

"Are you sure Steven will let you out of his sight?" Monica put her elbows on the table and clasped her hands. "The way I see it, he's threatened by your independence. So now that you'll be driving and spreading your wings, don't be surprised if you see a side of him you don't like."

Monica's words echoed Dr. Robinson's, except in a harsher tone.

"He has been a little overprotective lately." She cleared her throat. Maybe she shouldn't have said it out loud, but it was too late to take it back now.

"And that doesn't bother you?"

"Yes, a little." She shifted in her seat. "I may have amnesia, but I'm not naive. Some people might say that's sweet."

"Yes. And some would call it crazy," Monica snapped.

"The point is, we have discussed some things. I'm not living in a dream world and not wondering why he's done the things he's done. I know that he felt insecure. I know he has issues from his youth that he has a hard time dealing with—"

"And that makes it all better?"

"No, that's not what I'm saying. It doesn't make it better, but at least I know what caused it. And we're willing to work on the issues and start over."

"I was hoping this was a phase you were going through, that you weren't really going to waste time starting over with him," Monica said, unclasping her hands. "Don't you ever worry that he may show that evil side of himself again? I mean, he's already starting with the overprotective stuff, which means the other stuff can't be far behind."

"It doesn't mean that." She had never thought of it that way. Could Monica be right? He'd been kind and sweet, but if he felt like she didn't need him anymore, would the affairs and the abuse come next? Would all the things she couldn't and didn't want to remember start again? And then, there was the baby she lost…

"Ems, where did you go?" Monica tapped her hand.

"I didn't come here to talk about Steven. I want to ask a favor." She swallowed hard; she wanted to change the subject. "Since I'm driving again, I hoped I could meet you one day next week. You could take me to my old apartment. Dr. Robinson said it would be good for me to familiarize myself with things from my past. Then, maybe, my memory would return."

"Would things from the past include Robert?" Monica gulped down the rest of her water. "Have you spoken with him lately?"

"No, I haven't." She looked down. "Not since the day he left my house with you."

"I gave him your new number. He said he was going to call. I'm surprised he hasn't. " Monica stood. "Do you ever even think about him?"

"I do, sometimes." She twisted her hands. "I care about how he's doing. Thinking about him makes me feel nervous."

"I'm glad you feel something for him." The water swished as Monica washed her hands in the sink. "I'm not trying to make you feel bad, but he's hurting."

"I'm sorry for that."

"None of this is your fault." She leaned in to hug her. "I thought you should know. Call me later," she said, while walking to the counter to take over for Veronica.

"I will." Emily walked out of the pharmacy door.

There was a loud commotion coming from the lobby. Emily's attention turned and she saw a news crew standing around with several nurses. There were also small kids wearing hospital gowns. Obviously, they were from the pediatric floor. There were a lot of men taking pictures with them, but she wasn't sure who they were.

Some of the older kids were giggling and some were crying. The smaller kids looked excited but tired. Some were still rubbing the sleep out of their eyes. Then, there was the clattering of people clapping. The snapping of cameras taking pictures reminded her of picture day back when she was in school. Emily wasn't sure what was happening. But whatever it was, it seemed like it was good exposure for the hospital.

"Wonderful isn't it?" a deep voice whispered in her ear.

She shivered hearing the familiar sexy voice. Turning, Emily found Robert standing beside her. Her heart dropped. He was so handsome. Robert had on a black, pin-striped suit and he held his gray coat in his hands. He looked like he could be on the cover of the magazine as the sexiest man of the year. He smelled sharp and clean, like soap mixed with sandalwood.

"Y-Yes it is."

"I'm sorry. I didn't mean to startle you."

"No, I'm fine. You didn't startle me—not at all," she said, trying to keep her composure, even though she was shaken.

"Why are you here, in the hospital?" His gaze was on her. "Is everything okay? You're not having a setback, are you?"

"No…no." Emily shook her head. "Nothing like that. I'm here for my regular checkup with my doctors."

"How are you doing? I hope I'm not prying."

"N-no, you're not prying."

He was so close, if she moved an inch to the right their noses could touch. Maybe it was her imagination, but she stepped back anyway.

"I'm doing well." Their gazes met. "What are you doing here? Are you alright?"

"Funny, I'm also here for my regular checkup. My doctor is on-site today, so I'm seeing him here."

"What does that mean?"

"When we were in the car accident, I hurt a few things."

"Like what?" Her voice was soft.

"Just my arm and my ribs. The air bag got me," he said, smiling. "It's no big deal."

"I never knew that. It is a big deal. That's nothing to play with. Are your ribs alright?" She reached out to touch him. It felt natural, like she was supposed to. Her fingers felt his ribs like she knew what she was doing. "Is this where it hurts?"

"It does when you push it like that." He flinched.

"What am I doing?" Her voice went even higher. "I'm sorry." She moved her hand, but he gripped it with his.

"It's okay if you rub it like this." He placed his hand over hers and gently showed her how to rub. "It's a little tender."

"Shouldn't it be better by now?"

"It normally takes three to six weeks but—"

"It's been months," she said, cutting him off.

"I haven't exactly been following doctor's orders. I like to work out and lift weights. My doctor told me not to overdo it; sometimes, I go a little overboard, and that doesn't bode well for my ribcage."

"You need to take better care of yourself." Realizing she was still holding on to him made her fingers tingle.

His hand was soft and warm. She looked up into his eyes. Coming to her senses she pulled away. "Sorry, I shouldn't be touching you. I don't know what's wrong with me." She turned away.

"Nothing's wrong with you." He smiled. "You're perfectly fine."

"Thank you." Her voice trembled. She couldn't muster up anything else to say.

"It's nice. They do this every year." He leaned his shoulder into hers.

"What exactly is it?" She glanced at him, then quickly glanced away.

"They have some of the big name athletes come up to the hospital and take pictures with the sick kids. They bring the kids downstairs to the lobby."

"Wouldn't it be better to have them stay in their rooms?"

"I guess it causes a lot of commotion, and it's not fair for some of the sicker kids—who aren't allowed visitors right now—to hear the other kids having a good time when they can't."

"That seems fair."

"Yes, it is. Also I think it would cause too much commotion to have the news crews go upstairs to the pediatric unit."

"You sure know a lot about this." Her eyes lifted to his.

"You used to know a lot about it, too." He continued staring at her. "Your sister and brother-in-law work here. They used to tell us about all of the hospital functions."

"Yes," she said. Her smile grew wider. "I guess they did. I can't remember." She playfully tapped the top of her head.

"Now it's my turn to get on you."

"Care to elaborate?" She frowned.

"Earlier you said my ribs were nothing to play with. Your amnesia is nothing to joke about. Especially…" His voice drifted off.

"Especially what?"

"Can we go somewhere and talk for a few?"

"Sure," Emily said. She didn't know if it was a good idea, but Robert was hurting because of her. She felt she owed him the courtesy of listening to what he had to say.

They walked around the hospital, trying to find a quiet place. Of course, there were none. A few minutes turned into almost an hour. They seemed to walk everywhere. The more they walked, the hotter she became. Feeling sweat bead on her brow, she unbuttoned her coat.

They were walking around a hospital filled with sick sad people, a hospital filled with stinky smells and horrible food. None of that mattered. Her heart hammered in her chest, and her skin prickled with goose bumps. Her insides tingled like ice had touched her skin. Talking to Robert was like conversing with an old friend she hadn't seen in years. He was so easy to talk to; the conversation flowed naturally. After all of the walking and talking, she was certain he still hadn't told her what he really wanted to say.

They somehow ended up in the gift shop. It was beautiful. The lights were bright and the air smelled like jasmine. There were rows of magazines and candy, along with a cooler filled with beverages. She tried to distract herself because he stood so close. Her tiny efforts weren't working. She heard Robert clear his throat. His voice quivered and Emily heard him quietly say the accident was his fault.

"What was that?" she asked, not understanding his words. "What are you saying?" She turned to him.

"It's my fault I lost you. It's my fault you can't remember me. And it's my fault that we're not together now."

His sad gaze unnerved her. She still didn't understand.

"I guess this is my punishment."

"I don't understand where this is coming from." Turning to him, Emily touched her hand to Robert's face. "You shouldn't say things like that."

"It's true." His voice shook.

Their stares were broken when Emily noticed the girl behind the counter staring at them. "Here." She took his hand. "We need to find a quieter place to talk."

They ended up in the cafeteria, where the smell of meatloaf and something with tomatoes, like spaghetti, wafted around. Some people were loudly talking while others looked distraught. There were about thirty round, wooden tables around the room, and ten rectangular, wooden tables with matching chairs in the middle of the room. It wasn't quiet, but at least they could sit down and talk at a table. Like normal people, they could carry on a conversation and not be stared at.

"Now what were you trying to tell me?" Emily stared right at him. Robert looked broken. His shoulders slouched. His face looked even gloomier than before. Placing her hand on top of his, she spoke, "It's okay. Whatever you need to tell me, just say it." Every time Emily touched him, a tingle went up her spine. But that wasn't important now. What mattered was whatever he was trying to say to her.

He opened his mouth and started speaking.

"I never told you this before, but the day of the accident, you found the engagement ring I was going to give you. It fell under the car seat, so you took off your seat belt to get it. The accident happened then. And it's my fault."

"How can you say that?"

"I should have never let you take off your seat belt, especially when it was raining outside and anything could happen."

"You can't blame yourself for my actions," Emily said. "I'm a grown woman. I should have known better than to take off my seat belt."

"That's not everything."

"What else is there?"

"The air bags in my car weren't working properly. That's why it took my side so long to deploy, and your air bag didn't deploy at all. The red warning light had been on for weeks. I knew there was something wrong with the air bags. But I was so busy with work that I kept putting off going to get it checked out. I was careless. Now do you understand why this is my fault?"

Her heart sank into her stomach.

"No matter what you say, Robert, this was not your fault." She squeezed his hand. "You're a good man."

A vibration came from her coat pocket, her cell phone rang. Emily needed to answer it, but she couldn't take her eyes off Robert's face. Her main concern right now was making sure Robert understood that he'd done nothing wrong. Ten minutes later, Emily noticed a small smile appear on his face. She longed to stay and talk more. But once again, the cell phone in her pocket buzzed.

"I don't want to leave. I have to." She squeezed his hand. Every time she touched him her heart rate increased. "Someone's picking me up. They're probably waiting for me in the lobby." She stood. "I wish we had more time."

"We can." He stood. "I mean, maybe." He blinked a couple of times. "We could meet, sometimes, to talk." He gave a half smile.

"I'd like that," she said, smiling back. "But now, I really have to go." She grasped her small clutch purse. "Take care of yourself."

"You do the same," he replied.

The heels of her boots clicked on the concrete floors of the cafeteria.

"Excuse me," she said, trying to make it through the still crowded lobby.

Feeling the heat from someone's breath on the back of her neck made her cringe. And even though she had spent the better part of the last few hours locked in a conversation with her former fiancé, nothing had changed. The revolving doors were still making the swooshing sound. People were still coming and going. Laughter was still heard all around. The hustle and bustle of the hospital was still there, and Emily still couldn't remember Robert.

The car ride home in Anita's black Honda was a quiet one. Seeing Robert had brought up a whole list of questions she had buried deep down. She hit the button for the window, and it swirled as it inched down. The cold air was much needed. She wanted to ask Anita a certain question for weeks, but she didn't because she was afraid of what the answer would be; or maybe because things had been good, and she didn't want to disrupt them. But now that they were alone, it was the perfect time to ask her.

"Did you ever hear Steven and me arguing?" she asked Anita. "I know you don't live with us. But you were in the house with us enough that you may have heard something?"

"Yes, I heard arguing every once in a while. All couples fight, here and there." The engine roared as Anita pulled up in the driveway. "I'm going in to finish the laundry. Are you coming?"

"I'm going to sit here for a few minutes, if you don't mind."

"I don't mind at all. But it's cold out, don't sit too long." The door thumped behind her.

She always wondered if Anita knew about the abuse, and if she did why she hadn't called the police. Anita had just confirmed she only heard arguing here and there. Emily heard piercing laughter, from a child, breaking her concentration. She peered out the opened window. It looked like her neighbors were just arriving home. She didn't know them. Or, she didn't remember them. They looked happy.

Emily watched as the father took his daughter, who looked to be four years old, from her car seat. The little girl giggled as he lifted her above his shoulders. The little girl had on a pink coat and a hood over her head. Emily couldn't see her hair but was sure the girl had pigtails. Every little girl has pigtails. She blinked, knowing that her little girl would have had pigtails by now. A tear graced her cheek. Why was she so upset? She didn't even remember her pregnancy, or losing her baby. She tried not to think about the baby. Yes, thoughts crept in, here and there, but she shook them off. This was the first time Emily had let herself really think about the baby and shed tears over her loss.

CHAPTER THIRTEEN

"Everything has been going good, up until today," Steven said.

"Why, what's happening today?" Mitch was on the other end of the line.

"Emily's made a decision that I don't agree with." Steven's voice was rough.

"Don't tell me she wants the cat now. I can find a gray-and-white cat somewhere and bring it to you if—"

"This has nothing to do with the cat," Steven said, cutting him off. "Look, she's coming so I have to go."

"I'll be in a meeting until noon. If you need me leave a message."

"Okay," Steven said, hanging up the call. He turned toward Emily who walked toward him. "Why do you have to do this?"

"I'm not doing anything." Emily buttoned up her long white wool coat. "Why are you making such a big deal out of this?" She put her gray cable-knit beret over her long hair.

"I don't think you're ready to drive yet." He reached for her arm.

"Pete said I am." She pulled away and snatched her purse from the living room table.

"I don't care what Pete said. Maybe we should get a second opinion."

"Steven, I know my own body, and I know I'm ready to drive." She walked to the door that connected the house to the garage.

"Besides, when I went out with Anita the other day, she let me drive on the way back. She said I did an excellent job." Emily leaned over and kissed his cheek. "Now stop worrying." She turned the knob and walked into the garage.

"I don't know why you need to go to your old apartment, anyway. Your life is here with me now." He followed behind her. The garage was freezing. Not having a coat on, he shivered.

"I realize my life is here. I'm going to get some of my clothes."

"I can buy you everything you need."

"I want to see the clothes I used to wear." She walked to her car. "Besides, it will be nice to see where I used to live."

"Honey, are you sure?" He playfully grabbed at the belt on the back of her coat. He hoped to divert her attention from the missing fifth car. Every time he had drove her somewhere, he had a vehicle already parked outside, so she wouldn't have had any reason to go near the garage. "Why do you have to pick up Monica, anyway? She should have come to you. Do you even know how to get to David's parent's house?"

"Monica gave me the directions. I'm sure I can find it." She tilted her head to the side, glancing at him. "Don't you have some work to do?"

"Aren't we in a mood today?"

"I'm not in a mood. I'm trying to get out of here."

"I understand that, but promise me you'll be careful."

"I promise, now stop stalling. I have to go." She turned back around to head for her car. Suddenly, she stopped in her tracks. "Steven, where's the Audi?"

"It's in the shop. It needed to have some work done," he said. He couldn't tell her the truth, at least not right now.

"Alright then." Her midnight blue BMW beeped when she hit the key alarm. "I won't be gone too long." She adjusted her mirrors, then hit the remote for the garage door. It squeaked as it rose. "Bye."

Once the squeaky garage door came back down, he stood there with a knot in his stomach. He felt like punching something. But what good would that do? It wouldn't bring Emily back. It wouldn't keep her safe and sound in the house. And it wouldn't keep her there under his watchful eye. He had to learn to let her go. How could he?

He didn't want her to drive by herself. He also didn't want her to go back to her apartment. What if being there sparked some kind of memory? He didn't want to share with her the real reason the car wasn't there, so he lied—just like he had lied about buying her a cat and bringing it to her apartment.

He needed to make an urgent call.

"Jerome, I need you to do me a favor."

He normally let Mitch call his own brother. That way, his hands stayed clean. But Mitch was in a meeting and Steven didn't have time to wait. He was trying to change but today wasn't a good day.

Steven needed to know if somehow Robert was going to end up in the picture. Monica could have invited him to meet up with her and Emily. He didn't put anything past her. He needed to calm down, and the only way he knew how was to remain in control. And the only way he could remain in control was by knowing who Emily was meeting with. Steven couldn't lose Emily, not after he had just gotten her back.

David's parent's house wasn't too far from Emily's home with Steven. Her hands trembled as she rounded the corner. Emily couldn't believe she was finally on her own. It was wonderful, but a little scary. She tried not to dwell on the fact that a car was what caused her to lose her memory in the first place.

Leaning over, Emily changed the radio station to something mellow, so she could relax. Then, she sat back up to keep her eyes on the road. Pulling up in the driveway was a piece of cake. As long as she didn't have to parallel park, she was good. Parallel parking had never been her strong suit, and even if she had some memory loss, she was sure things hadn't changed.

"I haven't seen this car in over a year. I was so used to seeing you in your old Ford," Monica said. The door thumped behind her. "How are you doing?"

"I'm good." Emily smiled. "It feels wonderful driving again."

"I'm sure it does." Monica clicked in her seat belt. "I'm surprised Steven let you go."

"There was no way he could stop me. I know you don't think so, Monica, but I do make my own decisions."

"Just like the decision you made to let him back in your bed."

"He's been so patient that I felt it was time. We haven't made love yet, if that's what you're worried about."

Emily noticed Monica didn't respond. Instead, she directed her on which way to go to get to her apartment on the south side of Precone; Emily's home with Steven was on the north side of Precone. They were about an hour's drive away from each other.

"There's the Mexican restaurant that you, David, Robert and I went to," Monica announced, pointing at a brown building with red trim. "We had some good times there."

"Did we go there often?"

"Maybe twice a month," Monica said. "Robert's favorite food is Mexican."

"I didn't know that." Emily shook her head. "I know Steven's favorite is Italian but…" Her voice drifted off.

"But what, Ems?"

"We never discussed our favorite foods when he visited in the hospital," Emily said, softly.

"I don't know if you realize it, but your family, your workplace and Robert are all on the north side of town. And you lived way over here on the south side of town," Monica said, putting emphasis on the way over part.

"I did notice that." Emily bit her lip. "Let me stop you before you explain why." Emily gripped the steering wheel. "I take it I was trying to get far away from Steven."

"That's correct."

Emily sighed and kept driving.

"Here we are." Monica took off her seat belt. "You ready to go in?"

"I guess…I'm a little nervous." Emily took off her seat belt and started fidgeting with her purse. She peeked up at the tan apartment building through the front window of the car.

"What's the matter?"

"Nothing." Emily frowned.

"Then, why is your face all scrunched up?"

"This is where I lived, where I slept, and where…where I spent time with Robert. You know I told you over the phone—"

"How you liked seeing him at the hospital the other day." Monica finished her sentence.

"Yes, it's so confusing. Steven's been trying, and I don't know if it's fair to him, feeling this way. But then again, I can't help the way I feel. Robert was my fiancé." She took in a breath. "Sometimes, I feel like this is all too much for me."

"I thought Dr. Robinson was helping you with that."

"She is, but it's a lot to work through, and it takes time. I sometimes feel like my head is going to explode; I'm married to Steven, so I need to make things work with him. I need to get Robert out of my head." Her eyes lowered. "Maybe I shouldn't even go in to see my apartment."

"Now you're being ridiculous. Everything's going to be fine. You have to stop worrying so much." Monica brushed a strand of hair out of her sister's eye. "We're going in to look around, that's all. It doesn't have to be that big of a deal."

"Alright," she said. Her stomach was in knots as she reached for the door handle.

"There's your old, green Ford over there." Monica pointed. "Do you want to go and look at it?"

"No, I think the apartment is all I can handle right now."

Emily's apartment had its own front door. There were three external steps that led up to the tan front door. It was attached to a row of other apartments that looked exactly the same. When they reached the door of the apartment, Monica used her key to open it.

"Is that my key you're using?"

"No, it's mine. I had a spare, for emergencies. But when you were in the car accident, they gave me all of your belongings when I arrived at the hospital; so, I have your personal key also. Would you like it back?" Monica asked as they walked up the steps to the second floor.

"No." Emily shrugged. "I don't know why I'd need it."

"Maybe, after you get tired of being with Steven, you'll need a place to hide out."

"That's not funny."

"Who's trying to be funny?" Monica asked, as they reached the top step that led directly into the living room.

"I'm surprised they didn't throw my things out of here." She tried to change the subject. "I haven't been here in months. I'm sure the rent hasn't been paid."

"It's been paid." Monica nodded. "Robert's been paying it."

"I thought we didn't live together."

"You didn't." Monica unzipped her coat, and proceeded to throw it on the living room chair, along with her small square-shaped purse.

"Why would he pay my rent for me, then?" Emily's fingers shook as she tried to unbutton her wool coat. Suddenly, she wished her coat wasn't so long. It felt like there were a million buttons to unlatch. Emily didn't understand why a man she couldn't remember would be paying her rent.

"Robert was worried they would kick you out of here. You didn't have a lease. You were on a month to month basis, and he made sure it was paid. If your memory came back, he wanted you to have a home to come back to."

"Seriously?" She finally managed to unlatch the last button on her coat.

"Seriously." Monica snatched Emily's purse out of her hand.

Then, she helped her pull her coat and beret off. "He would even come over, water the plants, and open the windows to air out the place." She threw Emily's things on top of hers. "He never stopped praying that you would get better. He always had hope. Robert told me coming here made him feel close to you since you two spent so much time here together. Even when you woke up and wanted to be with Steven, Robert still came here to feel close to you."

Emily couldn't stop trembling. Her thoughts were all over the place as she scanned the living room. The furniture was a caramel brown color. The sofa was circular and had hardwood legs with a matching love seat. It looked soft like faux suede.

"It's small," was all she managed to say. She knew it sounded shallow, but she tried not to think about Robert. Those were the first words that came to mind.

"Yes, it is. That didn't matter to you. You always loved this place. You said you didn't need all that extra fancy stuff that you had at Steven's. Nice, small and homey was all you needed."

Emily didn't respond. The smell of apple and cinnamon wafted in the air. She saw an air freshener plugged into the wall outlet. Apparently, Robert kept the place smelling wonderful as well as everything else.

Sighing, she walked straight out of the living room and into the dining area. There was a long wooden chest in the corner that housed tons of framed photos. She saw pictures of herself and Monica together. There were some pictures of the two of them with David. The majority of the pictures seemed to be of her and Robert. She couldn't believe there were so many.

Her face felt flushed. Emily forgot Monica was in the room as she picked up each one and looked it over. Her fingers slowly traced over Robert's face. It was as if he stood right in front of her. She was embarrassed at the tingling feeling she got just looking at his photos. She had heard all the stories, and Monica had even brought a few pictures to the hospital for her to look at. But the pictures she brought to the hospital were plain photos of them standing together that looked like they were taken at a studio. These photos were different. They were action shots of them at different places, doing things together. Suddenly, looking at the pictures made everything complete. Emily and Robert had a real life together, and here were the pictures to prove it.

"We look so happy." There was a lump in her throat.

"That's because you were." She placed her hand on Emily's shoulder. "It's the happiest I've ever seen you."

"I wish I could remember," she said, while blinking away tears. Emily reached for a photo album she saw laying near the framed pictures. She started thumbing through them.

"Why didn't you bring any of these photo albums to the hospital?"

"I did bring some."

"Not these photos. These really show our life together."

"I guess I figured the ones I had from my house would be enough. I never thought to come over here and take your pictures. Besides, Steven cautioned me not to bombard you with too many photos."

"Why would he do that?" She closed the album and turned to Monica.

"I've said this before, and I'll keep saying it, he doesn't want your memory to return. If it did, you may go back to Robert. He doesn't want that. I believe he'd do anything to keep you from remembering."

"You don't know that."

"No, I can't say for sure. But that's what I believe in my heart."

"I don't want to talk about this anymore. Can I see the bedroom now?" Feeling like she was on a Ferris wheel, her head started to spin.

"Sure, Ems. It's your apartment. You can go anywhere you'd like."

Monica led her down a hallway to the master bedroom. Emily glowered.

"What's that look for?" Monica asked.

"Oh, nothing. It's really white in here is all, but the furniture is nice. I'm glad I have such good taste," she said, letting out a small giggle.

"I did help you pick some of it out. So don't give yourself all the credit," Monica said, as she laughed with her.

"I guess we should both get the credit."

"Yes, we should. Wait until you see the bedroom."

Emily's face brightened as she looked at the dresser and the queen-size bed. The furniture in the bedroom was black and beautiful. The bed had four posts and looked to be metal. The dresser was made of wood.

"These colors aren't anything like the colors I have at the house with Steven." Emily wanted Monica to realize that she had noticed.

"That was the point. You didn't want anything to remind you of your former life."

"I guess that makes sense," she said, sighing. The carpet bunched as Emily walked over to the closet and opened the door. She took out some of the clothes and made another face.

"What's wrong this time?" Monica walked over to her and started helping her take out the clothes.

"These look different than the clothes I normally wear."

"You mean the ones you used to wear."

"What's the difference?"

"These are your normal clothes, Ems, not those flashy, designer clothes Steven used to buy for you. Do you understand?"

"Yes and no. I guess, I decided I didn't want to wear brand-name clothes anymore."

"Yes, you said you didn't need clothes like that anymore—and you couldn't afford them on a teacher's salary."

"That's right," she said, walking away from the clothes and the closet. "I'm a teacher now. It all seems so surreal. It's hard for me to wrap my head around it."

"There's a picture of you and your tenth grade class over on the dresser. Take a look at it. You took it at the beginning of the school year. It's a little different from the one I brought up to the hospital." Monica reached up into the closet and grabbed a bundle of clothes.

Emily's hands shook as she picked up the picture of her class. She wished she could remember, but just like in the hospital, she still couldn't. There was another picture of her and Robert, as if there weren't enough of them in the dining room. They were at Six Flags Great America. Emily's fingers trembled as she stared at it. She remembered Robert telling her the story when she first woke up in the hospital.

"Alright, I'm done. I think I packed everything." Monica searched in the closet one more time. "I have your shoes and purses. And I have all your clothes. I have to clear out the bathroom and we'll be all done."

"I'm sorry," she said, placing the photo back down. "I'm supposed to be helping you. I got so mesmerized, staring at all the photos." She plopped down on the bed. The mattress bounced as she settled her weight. "Everything is so unclear. I wish everything would go back to normal."

Monica sat down next to her and rubbed her arm. "You have to take it one day at a time."

"I know that's what everyone keeps telling me," she said, sighing.

"Why don't we go in the kitchen? Maybe we can find some bottles of water in the refrigerator."

"Yes, that sounds good. And that's the one room I haven't seen yet," she said, smiling a little.

"Steven bought you those?" Monica asked, eyeing Emily's velvet jogging pants.

"Yes."

"They must be designer."

"Don't start." She pulled on Monica's arm.

"We were going to the kitchen, remember?"

"Yes, I remember. I have to get something off my chest, and then I will leave it alone."

"Go ahead." She had a feeling she wasn't going to like whatever Monica had to say.

"I feel sad for you. It took all you had to get away from him, and now you're right back where you started." Her eyes watered.

"Please, Monica. Steven's different now. If you give him a chance, maybe you'd see him the way I see him."

"I don't think that'll ever happen." Monica shook her head.

"If I start to have a bad feeling or get a sign that I shouldn't be living with him anymore, I will leave." She squeezed Monica's shoulder. "And if that happens, you'll be the first person I call. Now, can we go get that water?" She pulled on Monica's arm again.

From the look on Monica's face, she could tell that she didn't believe her. And maybe Monica wouldn't be her first call, but she did know if she didn't want to stay with Steven anymore no one would be able to stop her from leaving—not even Steven.

Emily led Monica into the kitchen. The place wasn't that big, so she already knew her way around. Robert had done a good job of cleaning everything out. There was no water in the fridge. They were so tired they both plopped down in the hard kitchen chairs.

Emily scanned the entire room. There was a small glass oval-shaped coffeepot and a metal blender over in the corner. She couldn't believe this was her home. She heard a rattling. Monica's eyes shifted to Emily's, so she must have heard it, too. It sounded like keys jingling in the front door. They both stood and walked toward the living room to find Robert at the top of the steps.

Emily noticed Robert's eyes on her, and she couldn't take her eyes off him, either.

"Hi, Emmie," he said, nervously throwing his hand up. "I'm sorry if I startled you."

"I didn't know you were coming by today," Monica said.

Emily was a little suspicious. Maybe Monica had set this whole thing up to put her and Robert together.

"The key was in my pocket from the last time I was here." He seemed anxious. He dangled the key around. "And, since I was in the area, I decided why not stop by." He still fidgeted with the key. He kept glancing over at Emily.

"Why were you in the area?" Emily asked. "You live way across town. We all do." She shrugged. "This place is way out of your way."

"To be honest," he glanced down and then back at her. "I usually stop by, at least once a week, to check on the place. I hate to admit it, but it helps me feel closer to you."

Her nerves tingled, hearing his lovely words. Monica had told her the same thing earlier. Hearing it come straight from Robert's mouth made a shiver go up her spine. She smiled and her stomach felt like butterflies were jumping around.

"I know you used to drive a blue BMW, so I knew that was your car out front. I wanted to see you." His face was somber. "I realize you have your own life now." He shook his head and glanced down. "I guess I shouldn't have come up. I'm being selfish, putting you in this situation. I know it's awkward."

"No, it's fine." Emily stepped toward him. "I'm always happy to see you. In no way do I think you're selfish."

"I'm going to leave you two alone." Monica swiftly announced. "I think Robert has something to tell you."

Before Emily could stop Monica, she quickly exited down the hallway. She heard a thump as the bedroom door slammed closed. The breeze from Monica's speedy exit made a chill fall over the room.

"She couldn't get out of here fast enough." Emily turned back to Robert.

"Yes," he shrugged. "I guess she feels we should talk." His eyes were soft. "Would you like to sit down?" He waved his hand toward the sofa. He plopped down first and she sat down beside him.

Emily watched him unbutton his long cashmere coat. The smell of his cologne engulfed her. It smelled wonderful, like a clean manly aquatic smell. Maybe she should have sat across from him on the love seat. Being so close to him made her mouth dry.

It was eerily quiet for a few minutes as if they didn't know what to say. Emily blinked a few times. The sunlight pierced through the living room blinds, so she shifted her weight on the sofa. She wanted to look at Robert's face without the sun blocking her view. Underneath his coat he wore a cotton T-shirt that clung to his chest, her eyes drank in his muscular tone. If she stared any harder, she'd burn a hole right through his chest.

"You sure kept this place homey." She tried to break the silence. "You even kept plates and cups in the kitchen cabinets."

"Yes, that's the feel I wanted it to have when—or if—you returned home." His eyes found hers.

"You did an excellent job." The way Robert stared at Emily made her stomach flip-flop. "What did you want to talk about?" She shifted on the sofa again. "I'm sure it has nothing to do with the plates." She gave an awkward smile.

"No, it doesn't." Robert nervously placed his hand next to hers on the sofa. "I'm glad you like everything. That means my efforts weren't in vain."

"No, they weren't." Emily innocently placed her hand over his on the sofa cushion. "Don't ever think that." Noticing what she'd done, Emily took her hand away. She always seemed to find herself touching him. It was all innocent. But even so, Emily felt comfortable doing it.

"What Monica felt I needed to tell you was…" He cleared his throat. Emily knew as well as Robert did they needed to get back to the matter at hand. "I sometimes go to a bar near my house, to relieve my stress. I'm meeting a friend there after I leave here."

Emily didn't know why but her heart dropped. Could this so called friend be a woman? Why did it bother her so much? She had Steven. Robert had no one. She should be happy he was getting on with his life without her. But Emily wasn't, and her stomach felt like it had dropped into her knees.

"It's a guy friend from work," Robert continued.

Was he clarifying for her benefit? Maybe he'd noticed the panic-stricken look on her face. Maybe that's why he felt the need to say it was a guy. Even so, Emily did feel better. Her heart steadied to a normal pace.

"A guy friend," Emily repeated, while brushing a strand of hair behind her ear. She suddenly felt calm.

"Yes. Anyway, Monica thinks I drink too much. I can understand her point since I quit drinking for a long time." He shrugged. "So now, drinking a beer—here and there—seems like a lot." He walked over to the window. "What she doesn't understand is I don't always go to drink. Sometimes I play pool or darts." He peered through the blinds. "I need something to take the edge off."

"When did this start?" She stood but remained in front of the sofa.

"After the car accident." He looked back at her and then away.

"Robert, I'm sorry." She walked toward him.

She knew he tried to downplay it, and maybe he didn't have as many drinks as Monica thought. But whatever he was doing, it was out of character. Apparently, Monica thought so and now so did Emily.

"This is my fault," she said, softly.

"No, it's not." He shook his head, turning toward her. "This is why I didn't want you to know. I knew you would blame yourself. You shouldn't. I'm a grown man." He took in a breath. "I know right from wrong."

"I know you do." She put her hand to his face. "Sometimes the lines get a little blurred. We all fall sometimes, we all need a little help picking ourselves back up." Her hand trembled.

His gaze was overpowering hers. For a brief moment, Emily wanted to lean in and kiss him. Not knowing where this sudden urge came from, she stepped back.

"Why don't we meet sometime?" she suggested. "We could meet here and get reacquainted." Emily wanted to take back the words as soon as she said them. Instead, she added, "Maybe if we talked more it would help my memories return. And you wouldn't go to the bar to drink, or play pool, or whatever you were doing as often."

"What about Steven?"

"I'll find a way to work around him." Her voice quivered. The tiny voice inside Emily kept asking her what she was doing. It was as if a little angel was on one shoulder saying stop it. And on the other shoulder was a tiny devil telling her to continue.

"Are you sure?"

"Yes, I'm sure." Emily really wasn't sure. Why was she saying things she probably shouldn't?

"I don't want you getting into any trouble with Steven." Robert stepped closer to her.

"Trouble," her voice was high-pitched. "I'm a grown woman. I won't get into any trouble."

Emily tried to act tough but deep down she knew Robert was right. This was going to cause trouble in her marriage. But she also felt the need to help Robert make it through his tough time. After all, it was her fault he was having this problem.

"What days are good for us to meet? When can you get away?" Robert was eager.

Emily couldn't disappoint him. She felt like she was having an affair, and she was deciding when and how she could deceive Steven.

"I-I'm not s-sure," Emily stuttered.

"Ems, it's almost four." Monica came around the corner. "I didn't realize it was so late. I better get you home. Or, you can get me home, since you're driving."

"I didn't realize the time." Emily, grateful for the save, turned toward her sister. Feeling Robert's glare she turned back to him. "I-I'll call y-you…"

"Wait a minute." Monica's mouth dropped. "What's going on between you two?"

"Nothing," Emily mumbled. "I know Monica gave you my number. I don't have yours. When Steven got me a new phone, they restored my contacts, but he deleted your information before he gave it to me."

"It's understandable." Robert shrugged. "I probably would have done the same."

She shakily typed his number into her phone and made sure the phone was locked with a password, just in case someone's prying eyes glanced at her phone.

"So, what was that exchange I saw between you two," Monica prodded, with a smile, on the car ride home.

"We agreed to meet to get to know each other. What can it hurt? Maybe it will help my memory return." She tried to reassure herself, but her stomach felt unsteady.

"What brought on this big change?"

"He's such a kind man with a gentle soul, and it breaks my heart that he spends his time at a bar because of everything that happened between us."

"I think it's a good idea. What will you tell Steven?"

"I'll cross that bridge when I come to it." She sounded tough but felt sick, like she was in a race car with no brakes and heading for possible disaster.

Who knew going to her old apartment would put things into perspective? Emily's life with Robert was real. Seeing the pictures, the furniture, and even the coffeepot made it a reality. It was so much more definite when it was right in front of her, instead of being told to her in stories. The attraction Emily felt toward Robert was real.

"Hi, Richard." Steven plopped down in the cushioned chair across from his accountant's desk. "Sorry I'm so late."

"I've been trying to get you in here for weeks," Richard scolded, while adjusting his glasses. The light in the room made his brown eyes appear brighter than normal as he slanted them in Steven's direction. "We need to discuss your finances." He scratched the small bald spot at the front of his head. "If you don't want to let go of the house, then you'll have to cut back elsewhere."

"You dive right in don't you?" Steven frowned.

"Look Steven, I've been handling your affairs for years, so there's no need for us to make small talk. We need to get to the matter at hand." He took a sip of his coffee. "There's no sense in beating around the bush—"

"Alright, alright." Steven held his hands up. "You can cut the comedy act. I see your point."

"We discussed this the last time you were here; there's no way around it." Richard leaned forward, his face stern. "If you want to live comfortably, or at the standard you're used to…" His eyes narrowed. "Then, you need to do as I asked the last time we talked."

"I already have." Steven shifted in his seat. "I found buyers for the two condos, and I flew down to Florida right away, before they changed their minds. I accepted their offer." Squirming a bit, he shifted again and placed his right foot on top of his left knee. "That was the only reason I left Emily's side while she was in the hospital."

He had hated to leave Emily alone in the hospital for as long. But he had to get to Florida and accept the offer before the buyers changed their minds. Yes, his real estate agent could have handled everything. But those properties were special to him. He and Emily had shared some wonderful times there. The baby they never had was conceived during one of their vacations there. Steven's throat constricted at the thought of having given them up, but he knew it had to be done.

"That may not be enough. You need to cut out some other things as well." Richard slurped more coffee. "Like that expensive suit you have on under that fancy coat." He eyed Steven's pin-striped suit peeking out from under his unbuttoned coat. "Or those expensive alligator shoes you have on. I'm sure they cost a fortune."

"Look Rich, I'm not a penny-pincher or a coupon cutting kind of guy." His jaw clinched. "Do you realize how hard it was for me to get rid of those condos? They meant a lot to me. Besides," he shrugged, "I've been cutting back in other ways. I even parked my own car at the hospital, instead of using the valet."

"That's not going to cut it." Richard's eyes narrowed. "Let's get serious here. You need to cut out big things, like you did with the condos in Florida. You need to get rid of one of those expensive cars, or that fancy country club membership."

"Oh, no." Steven sat straight up. "Emily used to love going to the country club when we first married. I'm hoping she'll love it again. I can't give that up. And for your information, I did sell one of the cars."

"Which one?" Richard pushed his glasses up his nose.

"The Audi S7." Steven scowled like a child.

"Why didn't you tell me that?"

"I sent you an e-mail." Steven frowned. "I was too upset to talk about it."

The keys on Richard's computer clicked as he typed. "Why you did, didn't you."

"You got a good price for it, too. But that's still not going to be enough." Richard shook his head. "If you won't get rid of the club membership, then maybe you'll consider selling the convertible Jaguar." He pushed his glasses up again.

"I can't do that." Steven shook his head. "Richard, this is getting ridiculous." He stood. "I'm not that bad off. Even if I were, this case I'm working on is big. If I win, I may make partner and get a bonus."

"If you win." Richard looked up at him. "There's no guarantee that you're going to win."

"I realize that." Steven paced the tiny office, back and forth.

"So yes, it's good that you sold the condos and the one car. Now, you have to stop doing things to counteract all the good you're doing."

"What does that mean?" Steven stopped pacing and stood rooted in one spot.

Richard swirled the squeaking computer around so Steven could see. "Your bank records show you withdrew fifty thousand dollars. You're in no position to drop fifty thousand here or forty thousand there, like you used to. I know fifty thousand doesn't seem like much to you; but, that was in the old days. You can't do things like that anymore." His high-pitched voice turned soft. "At least, not right now. Like you said, maybe you will make partner and it will turn things around. But until then, you have to watch every penny."

"I understand what you're saying." Steven shook his head. "But you're acting like I'm broke. I'm not. I'm having a little financial setback, that's all."

"Yes, but that little financial setback will turn in to a giant setback if you don't control your spending now."

"Are we done here?" Steven was annoyed. He felt like a man on death row with no way out.

"Yes, for now." Richard stood. "By the way, I didn't get to mention it earlier. I'm glad your wife is home now, even if she can't remember everything."

"Thanks. Me, too." Having Emily in his life was the only thing that kept him smiling these days.

"Are you going to discuss this with her?" Richard asked.

"Of course not." Steven's eyes widened. "As far as she's concerned, it's life as usual. She can have anything her heart desires. Just like when we first married." He shook Richard's hand and then turned to leave the room.

"One more thing, Steven," Richard called out.

"What now?" Steven mumbled, turning back toward him. He couldn't handle any more bad news.

"You never told me what the fifty thousand was for." His glasses slid down again. "Is there something I should know?"

"No." He couldn't tell Richard what the money was used for. Richard would say he was being frivolous. And he knew in his heart, Richard would be right.

He grunted at Cynthia—the blonde haired, blue eyed secretary—as he stormed past her. Back in the day, he would have tried to be coy with her. Those days were over. These days, he was trying to keep his head above water and to keep his marriage on track.

Steven understood everything Richard had said. But he couldn't get rid of the other cars, the club or even the expensive clothes. He couldn't get rid of the things he had worked so hard for. Steven had strived to have the things his father couldn't. He had strived to have money and to be a well-respected man in the community. He had strived to have a woman in his life that meant something to him, a woman who would always be in his corner. Steven had been able to attain all these things and he had been happy, for a while. He'd been content, until he blew it with Emily, the first time.

Now, he had Emily in his corner again; and, he had to find a way to keep her there. Steven couldn't have her back and then lose his wealth. He needed to have everything, all at once.

Why on earth hadn't he followed his financial advisor's suggestions? Instead, he thought he'd known it all, and of course he hadn't. He made a few bad investments, unbeknownst to Richard. Now, because of those bad decisions, he could lose everything he'd worked so hard for. His arrogance could now cost him everything. Steven's hand shook as he took the car key from his pants pocket. Fumbling, he tried to hit the alarm button on his remote.

He needed to keep his money problems a secret. He couldn't do anything out of the norm. The routine had to be as similar as possible to the first year he and Emily were married. Any deviation from that pattern could cause her memory to resurface, and he couldn't have that. Maybe it was stupid, but then again, maybe it wasn't. If Emily knew his funds weren't up to par at the moment, it might cause a shift between them. That shift could cause her memory to return. That shift could cause him to lose her forever. Just thinking about it made a cold rush of air chill his bones.

Steven's phone buzzed in his pocket. It was Jerome.

CHAPTER FOURTEEN

"Where are you headed?" Robert's co-worker, Paul, stood next to him at the mirror.

"What makes you think I'm headed somewhere?" Robert quickly washed his hands, trying to avoid any further conversation.

"You're moving like you have fire under your feet," Paul said. "And, you had on a black suit before and now you're wearing black jeans."

"I didn't realize you paid attention to my wardrobe. Don't you have a wife at home?" He chuckled. "Should I tell her that you're into me?"

He whipped out a small brush from his briefcase. The brush swooshed as it went through his short hair.

"And, you're in a good mood." Paul's brown eyes looked darker in the bathroom light. He used his hand to brush back his low cut hair. "What brought all this on?"

"If you must know, I'm meeting Emmie."

"I'm happy for you, man." Paul patted him on his back. "I know how hard you've been working to get her back into your life. It's just…" He paused.

"Just what?" Robert's eyebrows slanted together.

"I know she's with her husband. What if she never remembers you? I mean, you can't meet, in secret, forever."

"Maybe we won't have to." He put the brush in his briefcase and slammed it closed. "She fell in love with me once before. Who says it can't happen again?"

"I hope it all works out for you."

"Thanks, man. I appreciate it." He grabbed the briefcase and headed for the door.

"How's the driving going?"

"Better," Robert said, softly. "Thanks for asking."

His steps were quick and his stomach was in knots. The sun was setting and the cold wind ripped right through his bones. His old car had been totaled in the accident. He thought buying a truck this time would help him feel more secure. So he bought a silver Chevy Tahoe. It didn't always work. Sometimes, he felt paralyzed, or frozen, and his breathing became heavy. When Robert turned the key in the ignition, all he saw was Emily searching for the ring, and her head hitting the dashboard.

"Thanks for meeting me." Robert smiled and sat down next to Emily on the sofa in her apartment.

"You don't have to say thank you. I wanted to come."

Two weeks ago, they'd had their first meeting at her apartment. The encounter went well. They talked, ate Chinese food and watched a movie on demand. She hated to lie, but she'd told Steven she was spending the day with Monica. She'd told him the same exact lie today.

"Do you have on a vanilla fragrance?"

"No." Emily shook her head. "That's the wall plug in. The apple and cinnamon one you put in wore off."

"Well, it's nice." Robert's gaze was strong.

"Yes, it is." Emily stood. "Are you hot?" she asked, walking past him.

She took off her cardigan sweater and a T-shirt showed underneath.

"No, I'm fine. Is something wrong? You seem fidgety."

Robert was right, her stomach was filled with butterflies.

"Here, sit back down." He reached for her hand.

Emily let him lead her back to the sofa. His palm was warm and strong. She enjoyed his touch.

"I thought we could do something different this time. I don't want you to feel like every time we're together you have to talk about yourself. Or, I have to tell you stories of what we did together. So I brought something with me." He grabbed his briefcase from the table.

The latches popped open and he took out a board game.

"What is that?"

"Something that I hope will help you relax."

"It looks like Scrabble." She scooted back on the sofa. "You realize that I used to be a teacher." She grinned.

"Is that supposed to intimidate me?" His eyebrow rose. "Because I thought you couldn't remember."

"I can't." She tilted her head to the side. "But I'm sure all my knowledge is still in my head." She touched her fingertip to the side of her head. "And, I'm sure I know lots of extraordinary words."

"Extraordinary. Wow, you're starting with the big words already. We haven't even started playing yet." He slid down onto the carpet and spread the game pieces out on the table. "By the way, you are still a teacher. Don't forget that, okay."

"I won't." She slid down onto the carpet beside him.

They played for what seemed like hours. Emily relaxed and had fun.

"What kind of word is *Scyphozoa*?" Robert's jaw dropped. "That's not a real word."

"Yes, it is. It's sometimes used to refer to the true jellyfish."

"I don't believe you." He playfully tapped her knee.

"Let's check the dictionary then." She stood. "I'm sure I must have one around here somewhere."

"I have one right here." He grabbed her hand and pulled her back down. "On my cell phone."

There was a clicking sound as he hit the letters on his dictionary app.

"Did you find it yet?"

"I'm looking. Stop rushing me." He smiled. "So, it is a word."

"See, I told you." She leaned in and tapped his nose.

His eyes broadened.

"Did I do something wrong?"

"You used to always tap my nose like that."

"I don't remember that, but it felt natural, so I did it."

"Maybe that's a sign that your memory will return soon," he said, with a smile.

Robert brushed a strand of hair behind her ear. Their eyes met and Emily watched as he moved closer to her. He leaned in and cupped her face. She felt the warmness of his hand, and relaxed into him. Robert pulled her even closer, and Emily allowed him to kiss her on the mouth. She kissed him back, as a tingle moved up her spine. She closed her eyes and felt the heat of his breath kissing her neck. She moaned. Emily felt the ripples in his muscular chest rubbing up against hers. This was the closest they had ever been recently, and even though she enjoyed it, Emily knew it was wrong.

"We shouldn't be doing this," she said, pulling away from him.

"How can you say that? We're engaged." Robert's breaths were jagged and he kissed her cheek. "We mean something to each other."

"But I—"

"It doesn't matter if you can't remember. I can feel you shivering when I touch you. I can see the brightness in your eyes when we're together. I know you feel something for me. Even if you never remember, it doesn't mean we can't start over."

"Maybe we should go." Emily pulled away from Robert and stood.

"If that's what you want."

"Yes, I think it's for the best."

She watched him leave and she locked up and left as well. Their time together was supposed to help her remember. But Robert wanted to start over with her, and that was something Emily was unsure of.

✦

"I went to the printer and had the flyers made up." Emily placed the boxes down on the table.

"Thanks for picking them up," Samantha Martin said.

"I wish I could do more." Emily sat down across from her. "It's nice feeling useful again, even if it is running errands."

"It's so nice having you back," Whitney Collins added. She sat at the table as well.

"Thank you," Emily replied.

The women were gathered in one of the conference rooms at the country club, women Emily was—or used to be— friends with. Whitney looked exactly the same. Her dark eyes glistened and her hair was still brunette, but Samantha was a different story. Samantha's blue eyes looked bolder than Emily remembered, and her long hair was bleached a lighter shade of blonde now.

They weren't her close friends, but they did work a lot of fundraisers together. Emily wore a dark knit dress with high heels and a jacket. She noticed Whitney had a flowered dress on that gathered at the waist, and Samantha had on a blue dress that ruffled at the bottom. Now that April had arrived, coats were discarded.

The country club walls were a vibrant yellow and filled with paintings of mountains and sunsets. The ceilings were high, and the scent of lilac was in the air. The tennis courts and golf course were out back. There was also a swimming pool, a sauna and a spa. There were several clothing stores and places to eat. There was a workout room as well as yoga classes.

Now that Emily could drive again, she wanted to fill her days with something meaningful. She was on a leave of absence from her teaching job until her memory returned. The country club was filled with a lot of rich women who liked to gossip; but, it wasn't only that, they also did good work. They helped people and sponsored charities. Emily wanted to get back to that again. When she mentioned going to the club to Steven, he was all for it.

"Yes, we missed you so much," Samantha said. "It's a shame that horrific car accident is what brought you back to us."

"Yes, I missed you, too." Emily smiled. "Even though, I still can't remember ever being gone. I'm missing a lot of years."

"That must be maddening, not being able to remember parts of your life," Whitney said.

"Yes, it is." Emily nodded.

"You know, when you and Steven separated and you stopped coming here, it hurt us. Even though you two weren't together, you could have still visited," Samantha said.

"I don't remember that. I'm sorry if I cut you out of my life like that." She swallowed hard. The conversation made her stomach uneasy. "How do you like the flyers? I think the colors came out nicely." She opened the box and took one out.

They were having a golf tournament to raise money for repairs to Rolland Public Elementary School. It was damaged by a fire, part of the building was destroyed, and the students were relocated to other schools. They wanted to reopen the building as soon as possible, so any money raised would be of help. The elementary school wasn't far from the high school where Emily used to teach.

The members of the club will donate money to the cause and they can also play in the tournament. They will charge ten dollars per member and fifteen dollars per nonmember. There will be snacks and beverages sold along the course to raise money as well. Afterward, there will be a banquet and those who want to attend will be charged a reasonable rate with the money also going to help rebuild the school.

"The colors are wonderful," Samantha said. "You were always good at picking out colors. I like the blue, it reminds me of the morning sky."

"Please help us by helping our school and our children. I like the way it reads as well," Whitney said. "The red lettering is bold. It really stands out."

"Thank you," Emily said. She was happy the ladies were pleased.

"You know, the entire time you and Steven were separated, all he did was talk about you," Samantha said, then sipped some of her tea. "He kept telling my husband that he was intent on winning you back because he missed you so much." The tea cup clanked as it hit the saucer on the table.

"Do you two know why we were getting divorced?" Emily asked. Her voice was shaky. She reached for her cup of tea, hoping the cinnamon apple aroma would calm her. The steam was hot to her lips.

"We heard rumors," Whitney said.

"What were the rumors?" Her legs shook under the white table-cloth. Maybe she shouldn't have asked.

"Steven cheated on you," Whitney said, then cleared her throat. "I mean we don't know who the women were—"

"Hopefully, with no members here," Samantha chimed in.

"That's all you know?" Emily asked.

"Yes." Samantha nodded. "Why, what else would there be?"

"Oh, nothing." Emily shrugged.

Apparently, they didn't know about the abuse. Anita hadn't mentioned it in their conversation either. Monica did say she hid the bruises well. It shouldn't even matter since Emily was putting that part of her life behind her. But she was curious as to what people who'd spent time around them knew about their relationship.

"There was a new member who joined right after you separated," Whitney said, with narrowed eyes. "Her name was Amanda. She had heard Steven was going through a divorce and she started making conversation with him. But Steven wouldn't pay her any mind. He kept saying he only had eyes for his wife." She shifted in her chair. "And that he knew you two would get back together."

Emily remained quiet and took it all in.

"Steven's such a good-looking man," Samantha said, then drank more tea. "As well as generous. It's a wonder he didn't have more women falling all over him. I'm sure you don't know this. Right after you two separated, he anonymously donated twenty-five thousand dollars to cancer research at the hospital. The reason I know is because he joked around with my husband, Tim, one day about it. They were debating who would get the bigger tax write-off and Steven said he would because of his donation."

The conversation went from making Emily queasy to pulling at her heart strings. Her eyes watered; she knew the real reason for his donation. Steven's mother had died from breast cancer and a cure was something near and dear to his heart. Maybe she would stop by Macy's later, buy Steven's favorite Armani cologne, and then surprise him with it.

"Are you alright, Emily?" Samantha asked, placing her hand over Emily's on the table.

"Yes, I'm fine. It's—"

"Well, hello ladies," Steven said, walking up. "Am I interrupting something?"

"What are you doing here?" Emily's eyes widened. Steven looked nice in his black silk suit.

"I thought I'd surprise you." He leaned down and kissed her forehead. "Is it alright if I steal my wife for the rest of the afternoon?"

"Certainly," Samantha said. "We can finish up here."

"Are you sure?" Emily asked. "We still have to get the flyers distributed."

"I'm sure we can handle that. Go with your husband." Whitney waved her hand. "We insist."

"See honey, they insist." He clutched her hand, and helped her up from the table. "We'll take my car and pick yours up later."

She didn't know what to make of his mysterious behavior, but Emily was glad she was there at the club instead of off with Robert. Robert had called her after she'd left the printers and asked if they could meet after he got off work. Emily said no because she needed to meet the ladies at the country club. After the closeness they'd shared the last time, she was a little afraid to be alone with him.

⚬

Steven wasn't a stupid man. He knew something was off between him and Emily. Ever since she had gone to her apartment, things had changed. Even if he hadn't paid Jerome to follow her, Steven would have known something was off because Emily was more distant and jittery.

Jerome had told him the day he had followed Emily and Monica to her old apartment, Robert showed up. Since then, he'd had Jerome follow her a few more times. But she ended up at stores. Steven was overjoyed when Emily told him she wanted to go back to the country club and help fundraise. Her wanting to regain parts of the life they'd shared together showed promise for what their future may bring.

Steven had almost told Jerome to stop following her, but was glad he hadn't. Jerome had caught Emily at her old apartment with Robert when she claimed to be visiting her sister. So when Emily told him she was going to the country club today, Steven didn't believe her. Not caring if his hands were kept clean, he cut out middleman Mitch, and again called Jerome directly. Jerome was slow in reporting back. His jealousy got the better of him, so Steven decided to check and see if Emily was at the country club himself. He knew he shouldn't have, but he let Leonard handle the brunt of the workload while he left work early.

Steven should have been furious. He was being lied to and possibly cheated on. His pride overtook his anger. He knew he could win her heart, if he could keep her away from Robert. He wasn't even sure what she was doing when she met with Robert; maybe they just talked. He had no idea and he didn't care. So today was a new day and he was going to have a new plan of attack. He would work his magic on his wife. He would play with her insecurities;

maybe that would do the trick. Steven did love Emily; so what if he had to use underhanded methods to keep her.

⁓

"Are you alright? You're acting a little strange." Emily put her seat belt on. She sat in the passenger seat of Steven's Cadillac.

"Why would you think that?" He put his seat belt on and pulled out of the parking lot.

"I don't know." She shrugged. "You're really quiet."

"Everything's fine." Steven gripped the wheel.

They drove for a few minutes in silence. She placed her hand on top of her knee to try and stop it from bouncing up and down; but, it wasn't working. She wondered where they were going. It was five p.m., and Steven acted mysteriously eerie.

They pulled across the street from a large brick building. At first, she couldn't make out what it was. Blinking a couple of times, it looked like a school to her. In fact, it looked like a school she had passed many times before during the years she could remember—Hill High School. She could see a banner outside of the school with the school's mascot on it. She blinked, trying to make it out; it looked like some kind of bird with multicolored feathers.

"This is the school where I worked," she said, turning to look at Steven. "Isn't it?"

"Yes, it is." He smiled, brushing a strand of hair behind her ear. "You told me Monica said I deliberately kept you from things that might help you remember. I need you to know that I'm not trying to do that."

"You don't have to prove anything to me."

"I feel I do." His voice softened. "Tonight will be an evening filled with me taking you to places to help you remember. If that's alright with you?"

"It's fine with me." Even though her stomach did flip-flops, she nodded in agreement.

"So, do you remember working here?" He turned his attention out of her window.

"No, sadly I don't."

"This might help." He took something from his pocket.

"Your cell phone?" Her voice was high-pitched.

"No, silly. I have a video for you to look at. It's on the cell phone."

"Oh." She smiled.

He leaned toward her so she could see the tiny screen and hit play. She saw teenagers, about twenty of them, sitting in a classroom. She saw a male teacher sitting at the head of the class.

"I see my student Maggie in the front row. That must be my class. H-How did you manage to do this? I mean, get them on video."

"I called up to the school last week and asked Christina if it would be possible for me to come and record your old class. I hoped if they sent you a message it would jog your memory."

"I can't believe you did this." She blinked. "That's so sweet." Her eyes watered.

"If your eyes are watery, you won't be able to see the message." He leaned over and wiped her cheek.

The video was about five minutes long, long enough for her students to say how much they missed her, and how they couldn't wait for her to come back and teach again. They told her how much they had learned from her. Hearing their kind words made her heart drop to her knees. It was hard to believe she was loved so much by a group of people she couldn't remember. She was still dabbing away tears when Steven told her it was time to move on to the next location.

About forty-five minutes later, they ended up in the parking lot of a tall white building. It had a revolving door out front, and people were coming and going.

"I'm not sure what this building is." She shook her head.

"Well," he frowned. "It's the building where your divorce lawyer's office is."

"M-my divorce lawyer." She bit down on her lip. "How do you know that?"

"When you served me with the divorce papers, her name and address were on the envelope." He shifted under his seat belt. "Her name is Cora Watson. Does that mean anything to you?"

"No. I can't say that it does." She shook her head. "I'm sorry."

"Why are you sorry?"

"I'm sure coming here can't be good for you. This is where I spent time talking to someone about divorcing you."

"It's fine. This is about helping you remember."

After the first two stops, they decided to go to the little Italian restaurant they had always frequented for dinner.

"There's one more place we need to go." Steven reached over and grasped her hand. They had finished eating and they were seated back in the car.

"Steven, we don't have to do this anymore." Her heart pounded. "Can we go home?" She didn't know what this last place would be, but she didn't feel good about it.

"This will be the last place and then we'll go home." He gripped the steering wheel to pull out of the parking space.

The car hummed as he turned onto the street. It was after seven p.m. and it was still light out. It seemed to Emily like they'd been driving for hours when they pulled into a cemetery.

"W-why are we here?" She began to panic.

"This is where our daughter is buried." His seat belt clicked as he unlatched it. "I know you don't remember." He leaned over and took her hand. "But I would like you to see where she's buried."

"I-I don't want to do this." She shook her head. "I don't need to see where she's buried. What would be the point?" Her eyes watered. "Please, Steven, I really don't want to do this."

"I know your sister told you I pushed you, but I didn't. I snatched your arm and when you pulled away, you slipped. I will regret that day for the rest of my life. I should have never been fighting with you at the top of the steps."

"You already told me this when we got home from the hospital a few months ago. You don't have to explain it to me again."

"I want to." Leaning in, he took her chin in his hands, and lightly kissed her lips. Then, he pulled back and wiped a tear from her cheek. "I need us to do this." Her seat belt snapped as he unlatched it for her.

Emily couldn't stop shivering. She watched Steven open his door and proceed to her side of the car. Her shaking continued and her heart pounded into her ears as he reached for her hand. Her knees felt like jelly. As nightfall approached, a cool breeze was in the air.

They walked, hand in hand, over to the cemetery plots. The more they walked, the tighter Steven gripped her hand. It smelled of old wood and moss. The grass didn't look cut in some areas. The wind had blown branches all around. Some headstones looked kept up, while others didn't; some headstones housed an abundance of flowers, while others had dirt lingering on them. Her legs wobbled as they continued their walk. Like a child on a long trip, Emily wanted to ask how much farther but decided to keep quiet.

"Here it is," Steven somberly announced, when they reached a gray headstone way in back.

Emily stood silent while watching Steven's every move. He bent down on his knees and pulled her hand to help her bend down with him. She still trembled. A cold rush twisted over her body. When Steven said he wanted to help her remember, Emily had no idea this was what he had planned for her. Her thoughts could have rattled on for hours just so she wouldn't have to embrace where she was, but Steven put his arm around her shoulder which helped center her back in reality. The warmth of his body helped her stop trembling. She was grateful for his touch. Emily couldn't bring herself to look at the headstone. There was silence as she knew Steven was giving her time to gather herself.

"Lindsey Montgomery." Steven broke the silence. He read the name on the headstone. "That's the name you wanted for her." He lifted her chin so their eyes met.

"Yes, I r-remember saying if I had a little girl that would be the name I would pick for her." She stared at the ground.

"This is your first time here."

"I know." She glanced up. Her knees were hurting so she maneuvered her weight to sit down on the ground.

"No, not since the amnesia." He sat down on the ground with her. "This is the first time you've ever been here. You refused to come. You said you didn't have to come to a grave site to remember our daughter. You also said it was too painful."

"Well, someone's been coming." Emily gestured at the bouquet of multicolored flowers sitting on the headstone.

"They're from me." His voice softened. A tear trickled down his cheek. "I promised I would come here once a month…"

"You've been keeping that promise?"

"Yes, I've been trying my best to."

"That's sweet of you," she said, while wiping away the deluge of tears falling from her eyes. Why couldn't she stop crying?

They sat there, in silence, for what seemed like hours. The sky had grown dark and the air seemed to be thicker. Finally, Emily said she was ready to go and Steven agreed with her. The walk to the car was silent, and so was the drive home.

"Thank you for what you did today." Emily leaned in and kissed his cheek. They had picked up her car from the country club, and were now, thankfully, home in the living room.

"W-where was Lindsey's room?" she asked. There were several bedrooms upstairs and Emily wondered which one would have been for her.

"The room at the end of the hall. It's empty now. I had Anita clean it out after you left me. Now, I keep the door locked. I don't see any reason to go in there; it brings up bad memories. But now, all of that can change since the evening isn't over yet." Steven smiled, pulling his arm through the sleeve of his jacket.

"What else could there be?" Emily asked. She felt the puffiness under her eyes; she was tired and ready for bed.

He walked to the dining room and came back with a tiny box in his hands. It had blue wrapping and a pink silk bow on top. He handed it to her and asked her to open it. Emily had no idea what it could be. Steven plopped down next to her with an odd grin on his face. Trembling hands and all, Emily undid the tiny pink bow. Taking the top of the lid off, she found a pair of white baby booties.

"Were these Lindsey's booties?" Her voice shook as she turned to look at him.

"No, they're for our new baby."

"I'm not pregnant." Her mouth dropped open. "We haven't even been intimate y-ye—"

"I realize we haven't made love since you came home from the hospital." He finished her sentence. "I was hoping that would all change tonight." His voice was low. "I think it's time. Don't you?"

She trembled. His eyes seemed to pierce right through her. He leaned over and nibbled on her ear and she felt her heart flutter.

"Steven, I think it's too soon to talk about having another baby." Her voice quivered as she leaned back from him.

"You're right. I'm sorry." He shook his head. "I'm getting ahead of myself. I'm just so excited about our new life together that I got carried away. We had a good day reminiscing, don't you agree?" He stroked the top of her hand.

"I appreciate everything you did for me today. Going out of your way to help me regain my memory was a nice gesture. I just don't want to ruin it." His fingers felt warm against her skin. His eyes looked sincere.

"I'm not trying to ruin it." His voice softened. "You've been home for months now. You can't tell me you haven't thought about us moving this relationship to the next level."

"Yes, I've thought about it." She felt him gently squeeze her hand.

"Then, what's stopping us?" He released her hand and moved closer to her. "I love you. I want this. And I think, deep down you do, too." Steven gripped Emily's neck and moved her mouth to his.

His kiss felt warm. Her body betrayed her. Feelings awakened in Emily that she hadn't felt since they first married.

"I want our relationship to move forward. Let me take you upstairs," he said, through kisses.

Steven had been nothing but kind and loving all day. In this moment, Emily wanted to feel closer to him. She could tell he really cared for her. She saw nothing but love in his eyes. His kisses made her tingle all over and his touch soothed her. Emily did love Steven, so being with him now felt right. He wanted her to be happy; she wanted the same for him. This is not a mistake, Emily told herself. He took her hand and led her to the bedroom. She shuddered as he removed her dress and laid her down on the bed. He caressed her cheek. Steven's gaze bore into hers. Emily knew, after tonight, everything would change.

CHAPTER FIFTEEN

Emily's hands shook as she drove her BMW down the street, desperately trying to concentrate on the road. Now that she had committed to making things work with Steven, she didn't feel it was right to keep seeing Robert. Yet, here she was driving to meet him. He had called and asked if they could spend some time together, and she couldn't say no, at least not over the phone.

She decided they should meet at the Lincoln Park Zoo in Chicago instead of her apartment. It was twenty minutes north of where she lived. A neutral place might work better for the both of them, or at least for her. Emily's heart fell into her stomach when she pulled up into the zoo's parking lot and saw Robert's Chevrolet truck parked a few spaces down.

She watched him wave and step down out of his truck. He wore black khakis, a cotton T-shirt and a jacket. She paled in comparison with her blue jeans, red blouse and gray hoodie. His smile was infectious; she couldn't help but smile back.

"You look wonderful." He stepped up to her and smiled.

"So do you." She smiled back.

His eyes burned into hers.

"So, what animal would you like to see first?" he asked, breaking the silence.

"Animal?"

"I figured that's why you asked to meet here instead of at your apartment. I thought maybe you wanted to see the animals." Robert had a bleak expression on his face.

Emily could tell what this was. It was his subtle way of looking for answers. He probably wondered why she didn't want to meet at the apartment.

"I don't really want to see the animals." She shook her head. "I mean, I like animals. I haven't been here in a long time." Emily glanced down, then back up at him. "Unless, I came here during the years I can't remember." She smiled. "Did I happen to come here with you?" She playfully tapped his shoulder.

There she went again, touching him, being coy with him. Why did she always, somehow, end up touching him? This was why she didn't want to be alone with him. Sure, it was a playful tap on his shoulder or a gentle touch of his face. She felt so comfortable with him. Being alone with him made her feel things she shouldn't. A neutral place wasn't helping either.

"No." He broke her thoughts. "Out of all the places we went, the zoo wasn't one of them."

"Oh…" Emily threw her purse across her shoulder. Hoping she had avoided his question, she started walking ahead of him. Hearing him clear his throat, she knew she hadn't.

"Emmie, you still haven't told me why you didn't want to meet at your apartment." His voice was soft.

She turned around to face him. Her throat constricted. "To be honest, I feel bad going behind Steven's back. It feels like a date when we're alone. I thought if we came to a neutral place it wouldn't feel like a date. That way I wouldn't feel so guilty." She looked down and back up at him. "When this started, we were only supposed to talk to see if it would spark my memory…"

"And that's all we're doing." He stepped closer to her.

"No," she stepped back. "You know as well as I do, it's more."

"We talk and we eat." His gaze was strong. "If you don't feel comfortable around me, please say so."

"You know that's not it. In fact, I feel too comfortable around you. That's the problem." Tension mounted in her chest.

"Why shouldn't you feel comfortable? We were a couple. We were talking about getting married." He grasped her hand. "There's nothing wrong with feeling comfortable. Comfortable is good."

"No, comfortable is not good." She released her hand from his. "Not when it leads to us kissing like we did last time. And I…"

She knew what she wanted to say but the words wouldn't come out, so instead she said nothing.

He changed the subject, looking bleak.

They somberly walked around the zoo. Emily knew they were both stinging from their earlier conversation. They saw the elephants, which reminded her that the elephant in the room was her unresolved feelings for Robert. The zebras reminded her that life wasn't so black and white. Then, there were the kangaroos that leaped around like her emotions did, from Steven to Robert.

They heard the roars as they walked to the lion house. And they heard the growls as they walked to the bear habitat. As the day continued on, the sun pierced brightly through the clouds and beat down on Emily. They sat down and shared a bag of popcorn, along with hot dogs and bottles of water.

"I've been meaning to ask you," Robert began, turning to her on the bench. "When your sister and I came to visit you awhile back, you were in the greenhouse. I didn't realize you liked to garden."

"That was months ago."

"I know but being out here now, around all the flowers and greenery, made me think of it." He put a handful of popcorn in his mouth and crunched.

"Yes, I like to plant flowers and fresh vegetables."

"I never knew that about you." His eyes were soft. "When I was young, my mom used to have a flower garden. She liked me to help her plant."

"You had a green thumb?"

"Something like that."

"I learn new things about you every time we meet." She gulped down some water. "I thought you knew everything about me." The bottle crinkled in her hands. "It's a nice change of pace that you got to learn something new about me."

"Yes, now that I know that bit of information, if we became a couple again, we could garden together." He smiled.

"Robert," she said, standing. "I don't think we can meet again." She swallowed hard.

"Did I say something wrong?" He frowned.

"The whole point of us meeting was to see if it triggered my memories." She walked over to the garbage can and threw away the water bottle.

There was a commotion over near the popcorn stand. A little redheaded boy cried because his mother wouldn't let him have another bag of popcorn. Eventually, she gave in and handed the man behind the stand two dollars for another bag.

"I asked you a question." Robert walked up beside Emily and put his empty popcorn bag in the garbage.

"I'm sorry, I didn't hear you." She turned to him.

"Are you saying you don't want to meet anymore?"

"I haven't remembered anything. I know you feel that even if I don't, we can start over. I feel like I'm leading you on since I can't do that."

"Why?" He looked hurt. "Why can't you do that?"

"I don't want to hurt you." She shook her head. "I should have told you this when I first got here. I shouldn't have wasted your time, but I thought I would give it one more try and maybe something would resurface. I think it's for the best if we don't see each other anymore. We can remain friends but you should start—"

"Don't do that."

"Do what?"

"Tell me to start over. Or, say I'm a good person and I will find someone new. I found someone and that's you. So I don't need to hear you say it."

She heard the anger in his voice. She knew the anger masked his pain. The sinking feeling in her stomach got worse. Emily didn't want to hurt him, but he was right. Every word he had just said was exactly what she had planned to say to him.

"I'm not going to give up on you," he continued. "Not when I know Steven is all wrong for you."

"I can't keep seeing the both of you; it isn't fair. In the end, someone will be hurt."

"And that someone has to be me?"

"That's not what I'm saying at all."

"Well, that's how I see it."

"Robert, please try and understand. I've decided I need to give my marriage another chance. Steven and I have been intimate."

Those last words she hadn't planned on saying. This was her way of making him understand how serious she was. Emily needed to make it clear to Robert that he needed to move on.

"Did he force himself on you?" His gaze was hard.

"No, it wasn't like that." She turned away from him again.

"So you wanted to be with him? You wanted to sleep with him." His voice softened.

"Yes, I did."

Emily saw the pain in Robert's eyes, but she couldn't lie to him.

"If that's what you want for your life, then you will never hear from me again."

He threw his open water bottle into the garbage. The water splashed up into the air and some water spots landed on her arm. He turned to walk away; she reached for his hand.

"Robert, don't be like that." Her voice was high-pitched. "I still want us to be friends."

"What's the point in remaining friends, if we never see each other or talk to each other? It makes no sense," he said, pulling away from her. "I will stop paying the rent on your apartment. If you want, you can pick up the rest of your things from there. I will give my set of keys to Monica. I have to go. Take care of yourself." His face was red and his eyes were cold. He turned and walked away.

Robert walked fast, like he was on hot coals, and Emily let him leave because she didn't know what else to say. There was nothing else she could say to make the situation better. Her chest burned, like she had swallowed fire; and even though she still couldn't remember him, she felt sad. Somewhere deep down inside Emily knew Robert was once the most important person in her world, and now that world was shattered.

⨍

"You missed your last few appointments," Dr. Robinson said. "I was a little worried. Ever since the social worker stopped visiting you, I depend on these meetings to see how you're doing. Do you need me to send her back out again?"

"No, there's no need for Mrs. Hopkins." Emily shook her head. "I'm driving now and everything's getting back to normal."

"Then, what's the problem?" Dr. Robinson turned on the portable fan on her desk. The air swirled around.

"I feel like coming here is not helping my memory return." Emily bit her lip. "Actually, nothing is."

"I hope you know that's not the only reason you come here, Emily." She clasped her hands on her table. "The ultimate goal is to have your memory return; but even if it doesn't, I'm here to listen and make sure you readjust to your life. Losing parts of your memory is a traumatic event, and it helps to talk to a professional, who won't pass judgment, rather than a loved one sometimes."

"The last time I was here, I told you I was trying to make my marriage work because that's the life I remember."

"You said that wasn't the only reason."

"No, it's also because I still love Steven. He's changed. My family refuses to believe that. But I know how he treats me. And I've heard stories from people who were around him while we were estranged, and they all say that he missed me and he was sorry." Emily twisted her hands.

"Why do you seem upset?"

"I was meeting with Robert to see if my memory would return after talking and spending time with him."

"That wasn't working?"

"No, it wasn't, so I decided to stop meeting with him. I felt he wanted more than I could give and it wasn't fair to him."

"That's an honest and fair reaction."

"I'm glad you think so. My sister, Monica, was furious. She hasn't spoken to me since I told her my decision."

"I'm sure your sister will come around, she's worried about you."

"I hope so. I knew saying goodbye to Robert would be hard. I didn't know it would be this hard. I can't stop thinking about him."

"Emily, I can't tell you what to do in your personal life—that's up to you to decide. My job is to access your brain behavior. I know your memory hasn't returned, but you're making great progress. Although you can't resume your teaching duties, the charity work you're doing is a healthy activity that you can be proud of."

"Thank you."

"You're adjusting nicely to normal life. And as long as you feel you're in a safe environment, and that your mental health is not being compromised, then I'd say you should stop being so hard on yourself."

"I'm in a safe environment. Steven has even been trying to help me remember."

"That's good, as long as things keep progressing this way. But as your therapist, I need to say if you ever feel threatened you must leave."

"I don't think it will ever come to that, but I promise I will."

"If you need anything before our next session, don't hesitate to call."

"I won't," Emily said, standing. Her straw purse dangled from her shoulder.

"One more thing," Dr. Robinson said. "Don't worry so much about Robert. I feel, in time, that situation will work itself out, and you'll be able to move on."

Emily gave a weak smile. "I hope so."

CHAPTER SIXTEEN

"That's fine, sir," Robert said into the phone. "I understand, Mr. Mullins. I realize Chad is more qualified." His tie constricted his neck, so he yanked on it. "Yes, maybe next time," he mumbled. The phone thumped as he slammed it down.

There was steam coming from his ears and, for a moment, he forgot where he was. He stood from his honey colored laminate desk and, with one swift movement, knocked all of the papers off his desk onto the concrete floor. The plastic picture frame of his mother and his golden salesman of the year trophy went with them. It was like a gust of wind blew through his office.

"Robert, are you okay?" The commotion brought Paul into his office.

"No...yes...I don't know." He shook his head as he bent down to pick up the papers from all over.

"Here, let me help." Paul bent down beside him.

"You don't have to do that."

"It's okay, man. If you don't mind me asking, what happened in here?"

"I didn't get the sales manager position." Robert stood. He placed the stack of papers back on his desk. "I guess I let my anger get away from me."

"You've been doing that a lot lately. Ever since—"

"Don't even say it."

"Since you and Emily called it quits."

Robert glared.

"Sorry, I mean she called it quits." Paul patted him on his back. "Things will get better."

"I hate when people say that." He frowned. "But I know you're trying to help."

"Word around the office is there'll be other positions opening up soon. You can apply for one of them." Paul smoothed out the jacket of his gray suit.

"Yeah, I know. I thought this promotion would help me move on and keep my mind off of…" He sat down at his desk. "Anyway," he shook his head. "Not that I'm not happy to see you, but what brings you in here? I hope the whole office didn't hear my tirade."

"No one heard it. I came in to tell you that you have a visitor." His eyes narrowed. "She's in the waiting room."

"Why didn't Margaret call me?"

Margaret was the office receptionist.

"She tried but—"

"I was on the phone."

"I was walking past, so I told Margaret I'd save her a trip back here by telling you myself."

"Do you know who it is?" He hoped it was Emily.

"I think her name is Kelly."

"Kelly?" Robert repeated her name and swallowed hard.

"Is everything okay?"

"Yes." Why was his ex-girlfriend here? "You can send her in."

Paul had to be mistaken. Why would Kelly be in town or at his office? Maybe he was jumping to conclusions. Maybe it was a different Kelly altogether.

He heard the office door open and there stood Kelly, his ex-girlfriend, staring right at him. She was tall and thin and as beautiful as always, dressed immaculately in a short blue dress suit. Her hair was still amber colored, but her brown eyes appeared lighter than he remembered next to the green walls.

"K-Kelly, what are you doing here?" He felt his heartrate climbing. Last he heard, she had moved to Los Angeles. She wanted a fresh start after the loss of her little sister. He had also heard she wanted to start over after they had broken up.

"I moved back here a few months ago. My mom was sick and my dad couldn't take care of her by himself."

"I'm sorry, I didn't know." He brushed his hand through his hair. "Come in and close the door."

"Are you sure?" She stepped closer to him. "I don't want to bother you." She glanced around the office.

"You're not bothering me," Robert said, clearing his throat. "You used to always say that."

"I guess I'm still the same." She smiled.

Their gazes held for a moment.

"Why don't you sit down?" He pointed to the chair across from his desk. "I have a few minutes." He walked over to the window and the blinds clicked as he opened them more to let the sunlight in.

The room was quiet for a moment.

"It's good to see you," he continued. "Please excuse the mess." He straightened some papers around his desk to make it look neater.

"I wasn't so sure you'd feel this way, after the way we left things." She sat across from him. "It's good to hear you say that."

"So, how's your mom now?"

"She's much better." She crossed her legs. "Her lupus is in remission. Pretty soon, she should be able to take care of herself."

"That's good." He smiled. "When will you be going back to Los Angeles?"

"Trying to get rid of me so soon?" she said, her eyebrow rose. "I just got here."

"No, nothing like that." He shifted uncomfortably in his seat. "When you said your mom was getting better, I assumed you'd be leaving soon."

"No, I'm actually going to stay here."

"Permanently?" His eyes widened.

"Yes, permanently. Is that a problem?"

"No." He cleared his throat. "Not for me, it isn't."

"I feel like I need to be close to my family. My parents are older now, and with my mom being sick—you never know how much time you have with the people you love. My life in LA wasn't that great anyway. I didn't care for my job, and I didn't have many friends. I wasn't dating anyone." She uncrossed her legs. "I went there for all the wrong reasons. I was running away from you and I shouldn't have done that."

"Really," Robert said. His fingers trembled as he loosened his tie. His throat felt constricted. "So what brings you to my office?" He didn't mean to be blunt, but if she'd been in town for months, he wondered why she showed up now.

"I heard through the grapevine that you broke up with your girlfriend."

"Technically, she was my fiancée. I guess that doesn't matter now." He mumbled. "What else did you hear?"

"I heard she was in a terrible car accident which, ultimately, led to the break up." She blinked. "Anyway, the reason I'm here is I thought you could use a friend. I went by your condo a few times, but could never catch up with you; so, I thought I'd have better luck at your office. I don't mean to be blunt, but I figured if you're not seeing anyone, and I'm not, what's the harm in going out—as friends, of course," she added.

"I don't know if that's such a good idea." He frowned. "Things didn't end so well with us."

"Because you didn't want to get married." She played with the silver chain around her neck. "But that's water under the bridge now. What's the harm in two old friends having dinner?"

"I guess there's no harm," he said. Something felt off to Robert, but he couldn't put his finger on it.

Maybe this dinner with Kelly would distract Robert from the pain of losing Emily.

❧

Emily made her way down to the lobby of the hospital. The month of May had rolled in with unpredictable weather. Some days it was warm, other days it was a little cooler. She zipped up her jacket because the wind looked like it had picked up since she came inside. She'd stop by the country club on her way home to see if she could help some more with the fundraiser.

"It's a shame the only time I get to see my sister is when she comes to the hospital."

She heard Monica's voice.

"Were you not going to stop by the pharmacy to say hello to me?" Monica questioned. She wore her lab coat and her arms were folded.

The pharmacy had glass windows so Monica must have seen her walking by.

"I didn't think you were speaking to me," Emily said. "And, you know you'd see more of me if you came by the house."

"I'm not coming by as long as you're with Steven."

"Monica, you're being stubborn and childish," Emily said. Like a pot on a stove boiling over, she felt her pressure rising. "Don't you have to get back to work?" She glanced into the pharmacy where a line of customers waited.

"I'm on a break. Veronica can handle things until I return. Walk with me to the cafeteria."

"Sure," Emily said, following behind her.

"I miss you," Emily said, with tears in her eyes. They were in the stairwell on the basement floor. It was dank and musty; she didn't care.

"I miss you too, Emily, but I feel what you're doing to Robert is wrong."

"I never meant for Robert to get hurt, but I realized something.

If I really loved him, then my memory would have returned when I was with him; and, it hasn't."

"That's what you're basing this on? That's nonsense." Monica rolled her eyes. "I don't think that's the real reason."

"It is."

"Who are you trying to convince, me or yourself?"

"What do you mean?"

"I think you're scared because even without your memory, you feel things for Robert. So instead of acting on them, you're staying with Steven since that's what's familiar to you. And since he hasn't abused you in the few months you've been back home with him, you have made up this fantasy in your mind that you two are going to live happily ever after. I think you're afraid of taking a chance with Robert. That's what this is really about."

"You don't know what you're talking about." Emily brushed a strand of hair behind her ear. "Yes, I'm attracted to him. Yes, I feel something when I'm around him. But it's more like lust or mutual attraction. I don't love him."

Emily felt like she was being grilled in front of a courtroom full of people. She paced back and forth in the tiny stairwell.

"Why can't you understand that I all I want is a good marriage that lasts? Like Mom and Dad had." The tears in her eyes threatened to spill over. "And, like you and David. Why can't I have that? Don't I deserve that?"

"Yes, you do." Monica clutched her hand.

"Then I need to fight to make my marriage work. Steven is different now." She squeezed Monica's hand. "Please tell me you understand."

Monica sighed, loudly, and shook her head.

"What's wrong?" Emily asked.

"You said those exact words back when you and Steven were having problems." Monica released her hand. "You always forgave him."

Emily blinked. "I did."

"What is it? Are you remembering something?"

"No." She shook her head. "I don't remember anything."

"Maybe, you saying those words is a small sign that your memory is going to return."

"I doubt that," she said.

"I should get back to the pharmacy."

"You didn't get your break."

"I don't have time now." She hugged Emily. "Are you coming?"

"I'm going to grab a bottle of water from the cafeteria." She waved as Monica walked back up the stairs.

"One more thing, Emily," Monica said, turning around. "I know you don't remember. I always told you that you can fight as hard as you want to save a marriage, but it's not going to work if the marriage is one-sided and you're the only one trying. You both have to fight in order to save it. You finally realized that once you lost the baby. I know you say things are different now. I hope you're right."

Could Monica be right? Did remembering a simple phrase she used to say mean something? Maybe it meant nothing at all. She couldn't get her hopes up. One thing Emily did know was her marriage was no longer one-sided and, hopefully, it would stay that way.

"You're late tonight," Steven said. He unzipped her jacket and helped her take it off. "You normally beat me home. Is everything okay?"

"Yes. The country club took a little longer than I expected."

"Anita went home already. She left dinner in the stove for you. I can warm it up if you like." He brushed a strand of hair out of her eye. He still had on his silk pin-striped suit from work.

"That's alright. I'm not hungry." She plopped down on the living room sofa.

"Do you want to talk about what's bothering you?" He sat next to her.

"Nothing's bothering me."

"Well, if you won't talk about your day." His eyes slanted. "I'll share mine with you. I went to see Cora today. She needs you to come down there sometime next week. You know who I'm talking about right, Cora Watson?"

"Yes, you took me by her office." Her voice was shaky. "Why would you go see my lawyer?"

"Now that we're back together, it's been bothering me that the divorce is still pending."

"I don't understand."

"You remember a few months back when we went to the post office and had your mail forwarded here?"

"Yes, it made sense since I'm living here now."

"The other day, when the mail arrived, I saw a letter from Cora and I opened it."

"Why would you open my personal mail?" Her face felt hot.

"I know it was wrong, but seeing that it was from Cora made me edgy. With the divorce still pending, seeing the letter made my head spin. That was the worst time in my life, and I was anxious about what she had to say."

"Steven, you shouldn't have opened my mail," she admonished. But she was curious. "What did it say?"

"When I went to see her, she said she'd heard about the car accident and had been trying to give you some time. But now that some months had passed, she decided to get in touch with you. Your old cell number was shut off. Since she didn't have your new cell number, she sent you this letter."

"That doesn't answer my question." Emily frowned. "I want to know what the papers were for."

"The divorce is still pending. She wants to know if you still want to go through with it. If you don't, then she wants to discuss a request for dismissal."

"Why wouldn't you tell me about this?"

"I didn't want to bother you with it, sweetheart. Now that we're back together, I know you don't want the divorce anymore. So I figured I'd go down to her office and sign off on the papers."

"Since you went behind my back and handled everything already, why do I even need to go to her office?" Her teeth clenched. How dare he?

"Only the person who filed for the divorce can be the one who signs the request for a dismissal."

"I'm surprised—you being a lawyer and all—that you didn't know that already." She stood. Her face was still hot. She didn't appreciate him going behind her back the way he did.

"I knew that, but I figured we could work around it, somehow." He pulled on her hand. "Please, don't be mad. I'm sorry. I didn't want to drudge up bad memories. Why drag you down there if I could handle everything on my own? Please, tell me you understand."

"I understand you not wanting to bring up bad memories. I don't like you going behind my back. And I don't like you opening my mail."

"I'm sorry." He stood. "I promise, I will never do it again." He gave her a quick kiss.

"Fine," she said, shaking her head. "I'm not hungry. I'm going to take a shower."

She turned to go upstairs. Her throat burned. Why was she so furious? He'd done nothing wrong the last few months. And now, he made one mistake by opening her mail and trying to handle the situation without her. Was it simply a nice gesture like he said? After all she didn't even remember Cora. Her whole body was numb. Emily's head pounded through her ears and she didn't know why.

⁖

"Don't you think you should talk to Emily before cleaning out her place?" Monica placed the dishes from the cabinets in a brown box.

"I'm the one paying the rent. Why do I need to consult with her?" Robert replied, packing the coffeepot. He should have wrapped it in paper but he didn't and it clunked as it landed in the box.

"That's your hurt talking." Monica swiped at the beads of sweat on her forehead. "Not you."

"Maybe it's both." He shrugged. "What does it matter? She doesn't want, or need, this place anymore." He picked up the metal toaster and it clanked, landing next to the coffeepot in the box. "Besides, she does already know. The last time Emmie and I met, I told her I was going to stop paying for the apartment. And when I came here and informed the manager, Mr. Barkley, that I wasn't going to pay for the place anymore, he said that Emily had to give him thirty days' notice and sign a form. So he wanted me to tell her this, but I—"

"You refused." Monica raised an eyebrow.

"No, I told him it was best to contact her directly. He called while I stood in his office. She told him she knew I wasn't paying for the place anymore, and if he e-mailed her the form, she would sign it and e-mail it back." He placed the silverware in a different box. They clashed as he dropped the knives and forks in. The conversation made his ears hot, and he used a little more force than he would have liked to put them in. "I guess she signed her name with an e-signature, using her home computer. She was able to handle the entire transaction from home."

"Did she realize you were standing there?"

"Yes, Mr. Barkley had us on speakerphone." The spoons clinked in the box next.

"I guess my question to you is," she paused to wipe her hands on her pants, "If Emily knows about all of this, then why are we the ones packing instead of her?"

"Mr. Barkley wants the place empty as soon as possible so he can get a new tenant. Emily said she'd have Steven help her, but I told her, while we were on speaker, that I would do it."

Monica grinned.

"Don't look at me like that."

"Your last act of chivalry toward my sister."

"No, that's not what it is." He shifted his weight. "Actually, I don't want Steven here. This was the place where Emmie and I spent so much precious time together." His voice was soft. "I didn't want

Steven invading it and treating it like it was nothing. Not when it meant so much to me and Emmie."

"I understand. I can see Steven coming here and tossing everything. He would have loved every minute of it."

"Anyway, since the movers have all the big stuff already out in the truck, I thought you could go with them to put the things in storage. You can sign it into your name, and when Emily's ready, you can give her the key or she can go with you to get her things from the storage unit. Once we're done with the little stuff, we can put it in storage as well. I will pay the movers. Emily can reimburse you, and you can give the money back to me—or keep the money. I don't really care. I just want to be done with this."

"So that's the main reason I'm here." She folded her arms. "To put my name on Emily's storage unit, so you don't have to."

"Why would I want to?" he said, scratching his neck. The more they talked, the more he felt like he was breaking out in hives. "That would involve me seeing her again. And you know I can't do that—especially not now."

"Why, what's happening now?"

"I started seeing Kelly again." He took in a breath than continued. "At first I didn't want to go out with her. I felt like I was using her to take away the pain of losing Emmie. I told her that; she said she didn't mind being the rebound. I know that sounds crazy." He cleared his throat. "She still has feelings for me, and she believes—in time—my feelings for her will resurface as well."

"Wait a minute." Her eyes were wide. "I need you to start that sentence over. Are we talking about your ex-girlfriend, Kelly? And if we are, when did she come back to town?"

"She has been here for months because her mom was ill. She heard that I broke up with my girlfriend-fiancée. At first, she was scared to see me, but finally she got up the nerve and tracked me down at my office."

"Where did she get all this information from?"

"She said she heard it through the grapevine."

"What does that even mean?" Monica tapped her fingers on the counter.

"She said some friends that we used to go out with told her. I don't really keep up with any of my old friends. I sort of neglected them, once I fell in love with Emmie. It's really not a big deal how she found out. Word got around and she found out."

"Don't you think that sounds a little fishy?" Her eyes narrowed. "She broke up with you because you didn't want to get married, and now—all of a sudden—she's back, happy to be the rebound? That's just weird."

"Monica, you always think everyone's up to something."

"I'm serious, why would she show up now?"

"It's like she said, she heard I was single. And since she knows I wanted to marry Emmie, she probably figures I've grown emotionally. She probably figures—"

"You'll marry her since you're on the rebound." Monica finished his sentence for him.

"I guess, if you want to put it like that. I don't care," he said, reaching for a glass in the cabinet. The sunlight from the window hit the glass, making it glisten. "All I know is her presence in my life is helping me. We even started working out together." He placed the glass in the box. "I'm not saying I'm going to run off and marry her, but right now she's what I need."

"I wish things had worked out with my sister. Whatever you decide, I want you to be happy."

"I know that," he said, smiling. "Thanks." There was a ripping sound as he tore off a piece of tape to seal the box.

"We're about done here." Monica pulled out the vanilla fragrance plug in.

Robert felt a tickle in his throat. His key would go back to the office, and this would be the last time he'd step foot in this place. Everything was gone, but the memories would always and forever be in Robert's heart.

❦

"Did you have any trouble finding the place?" Cora asked. "I realize with your memory being impaired, you may not remember your way around town the way you used to."

"No." Emily shook her head. "I used GPS, along with the directions you gave me; they both helped." She scooted back more in her chair. She had chosen to wear her cotton khakis and her hooded sweater. She wanted to be comfortable yet look professional. "Steven drove me by here recently, so I kind of remembered where it was."

"I'm glad to see you're out of the hospital and doing better. How do you feel?"

"My memory hasn't returned. But I feel much better."

"After an accident like that I would hope every day would be a good day because you're still breathing."

"I agree." Emily smiled.

She didn't mean to but Emily found herself staring at Cora. She was a small framed woman. Her smile was warm and her eyes were kind. She saw why she had picked Cora to be her lawyer. The room was also nice, the walls were a rose color, the air was calm and smelled like cinnamon. It was cheery and nothing like she thought a fancy lawyer's office would be. Steven's office was the complete opposite, dark and overbearing.

"All you have to do is sign right here and then there won't be a divorce." Cora placed the papers in front of Emily and handed her a pen. "I know you can't remember, but if your memory returns and you decide you still want the divorce, you'll have to start the process all over again."

"I understand," Emily said, nodding.

She clutched the pen; her hand shook.

"You seem nervous. You don't have to do this today. We can always reschedule, that's not a problem."

"No, it's fine. I want to get this over with," Emily said, leaning over and signing the papers.

"That's funny. Those are the exact words you said the last time you were here."

"Really." Her eyes shifted up. "That is funny."

Emily left Cora's office with a lump in her throat. In the past week she had repeated two phrases that she had said in her former life. Could that mean something? She felt nauseated. She'd been trying not to focus on Robert, but every day she thought about him and how badly she felt for hurting him. Emily hated to admit it. She missed him and the time they spent together. What could it hurt if she went by to see how he was doing?

Emily rounded the corner so quickly her tires screeched. Robert's condo was in the opposite direction, so she turned the car around. Monica had driven Emily by there several times, hoping it would jog her memory. Hopefully, he'd be home from work by now.

Finally, she turned on to Dover Street. The closer she got, the more her knees turned to jelly. Once she was parked across the street from his condo, her mouth felt dry. She blinked a few times, someone had beaten her there. A small, four door Chrysler sat in his driveway with the motor still running.

Unless her eyes were playing tricks on her, there was a woman in the front seat. She felt a hammering in her chest. Why would a woman be sitting in a car, in his driveway? She took in a deep breath and tried to remain calm. Maybe she was selling something. Or maybe she had the wrong address. Her eyes widened when the woman got out of the car. Who was this woman on his porch? The door opened and Robert stepped outside. He embraced the woman with a tight hug. Why was he hugging her? What did this mean? Her stomach felt hot. Emily still couldn't see the woman's face, only the back of her head.

All of a sudden, the woman raced back to her car to retrieve something. Then, Emily saw her face. It was Kelly, Robert's ex-girlfriend. Her mouth dropped open, watching Kelly walk back up on the porch with something in her hand. They both went inside and Robert closed the door. Why was Kelly there? What was Robert doing with his ex-girlfriend? Her heart pounded through her ears. Wait a minute. Why was she so upset? Why was she jealous? How did she even remember Kelly? No one had mentioned Kelly since before the car accident. Emily remembered Kelly from when she had first started dating Robert. She had found a picture of Kelly in Robert's wallet. When Emily had confronted him about it, he said it was a picture of his ex-girlfriend. He'd said he'd forgotten it was in there. Then, he had crumbled it up and threw it away.

Wait a minute. If Emily remembered Kelly. And she remembered Robert having a picture of her. Did that mean her memory was returning? Dr. Robinson had said any little thing could jog her memory. She had already repeated a few phrases which she took to mean nothing. Was seeing Robert with his ex-girlfriend the trigger she needed? Emily's throat constricted and her hands shook. She couldn't stay there anymore, she needed to go somewhere to think. Her hands still shook as she put the car in gear. The roar of the car seemed louder than usual. She hoped Robert wouldn't look out to see what the commotion was. Her imagination ran wild; the car was probably no louder than normal. And if it wasn't, Robert was probably too consumed with Kelly to even notice.

Emily needed to go where she felt safe. She ended up, across town, at her old apartment. Robert had cleaned the place out for her. She still had a few days left on her thirty days' notice, so what was the harm in going inside? The keys clanked as they dangled together. Her hand shook as she unlocked the door. Her legs felt weak beneath her as she slowly walked up the stairs. Once she reached the top, Emily stood there, searching the living room. She didn't know what she was looking for, but she couldn't get enough air.

The room was cold and empty; she shivered. Walking to the dining room, she stood where the long wooden chest used to be. She leaned against the wall, dwelling on the place all the pictures used to sit on the chest. She closed her eyes, trying to remember each and every photo. Now, they held a special meaning. She had a flash of Monica introducing her to Robert. Her heart raced like she was in an out of control speed boat. Emily had another flash of their first date.

Like a lightbulb turning on and off, there was one flash after another. Emily sank to the floor, her head pounding, her heart racing like mad. There was her engagement ring in the glove compartment. Steven coming to the school, telling her he didn't want the divorce. Robert sharing he was trying to get the sales manager position. There was her English class. Steven shoving her into a wall, later saying how sorry he was. She and Robert eating at their favorite restaurant. Robert kissing her softly on the lips. Robert saying how much he loved her, and her saying the words back to him. Everything came roaring back like a tidal wave. The floodgates opened; her life with Robert and her past with Steven suddenly became real again.

She remembered Robert's condo. It always smelled like lemons because he cleaned his furniture with Lemon Pledge. There was the smell of mint candy. Steven chewed on it to calm his stomach before a big case. The smells were strong, like they were here and now, but she knew they weren't. Then, all of a sudden, the most awful memory of all was right there in her mind's eye—falling down the stairs and losing the baby.

All the good and bad memories were there. They were all in her head. But what was she to do with all of this information? It felt like a noose around her neck and she started gasping for air. Emily had to get ahold of herself. She took in deep breaths to try and calm down. What was wrong with her? She should be overjoyed that her memories were returning. She was, and she wasn't.

Everything was so confusing now. Was she supposed to leave Steven now that she remembered all the horrible things he had done? Was she supposed to run back to Robert now that she remembered all the love she had for him? Robert looked like he had moved on with Kelly. At least that's what it looked like a few hours ago. But how could he have been so angry with her a few weeks ago and now all of a sudden be with Kelly? Had he been in touch with Kelly all along? And then, there was Steven. He had changed. He'd been so good to her, lately.

Emily's head was spinning. Her stomach cringed like she would vomit. Her temples pounded. And she felt dizzy, like she was on a roller coaster. Tears were streaming down her face and getting caught in her throat. The once thin air in the room was thicker, choking her. Emily didn't know what to do; and, she didn't know who to talk to about it.

CHAPTER SEVENTEEN

"Emily...Emily...sweetheart, it's Steven. I know you're in there, open up the door."

Emily raised her head up. She blinked a few times. She was groggy and felt like she'd been hit by a bus. She held her head in her hands, trying to figure out where she was. Light seeped through the blinds. Her watch read nine a.m. She must have fallen asleep on the floor.

"Emily!" Steven shouted again. "Please open the door."

She stood and tried to get her bearings. She wiped her hand through her hair and licked her lips. Was last night a dream? No. Emily remembered everything. Her entire life with Steven. And with Robert.

"If you don't open the door, I'm going to call the manager. If he doesn't come, then I'll call the police." He banged again. "I don't know if something has happened to you, if you're hurt. I should break the door down."

"Steven, stop yelling." She flung the door open. He stood there in dress pants and a button-down shirt. "You're going to wake the neighbors."

"I don't care about the neighbors." He pushed the door open and brushed past her. "I'm worried about my wife." The door made a thump as he slammed it behind him.

Emily didn't know what to say, so she leaned against the wall and stared at him. A flash came to her of Steven yelling at her that he was her husband and she would do what he said.

"What's wrong with you?" He touched a hand to her cheek.

She flinched, but her feet remained frozen.

"Why are you trembling? What happened?"

Emily felt his arm wrap around her waist, and her breath hitched. She broke away from him, and ran up the stairs into the living room. Steven grabbed her elbow, but she moved so fast his fingers slipped and let go. Emily didn't know what to do or where to go. Tears flowed down her face like a faucet. Another flash came of Steven shoving her into the wall of their bedroom.

"Emily, what's going on? Please talk to me."

Steven grabbed her hand, but she pulled away. Another flash came. Steven had just lost a case and when he came home, he had needed comfort from his wife; Emily had been working late at the job he felt wasn't necessary.

Emily couldn't stop shaking. The blinds crunched as she backed up against the window. She felt like a rat caught in a trap. Emily bit her lip so hard she swore she tasted blood.

"Why are you looking at me with fear in your eyes?" Steven touched her waist. "Did something happen last night? Has someone hurt you?"

"Y-yes, someone hurt me." Emily's voice quivered.

"Who?" Steven's hand moved to her cheek. He wiped a tear away.

"Y-you did." Emily moved her face so his hand would fall away. "You hurt me."

"I don't even know what that means."

"I remember." Emily took in a breath and looked Steven squarely in the eye. "I remember everything. Every awful thing you've ever done to me." Her voice got louder. "It's all in here." She pointed at her head. "Everything's clear now."

"No, it's not clear. If it was, you'd also remember that I was honest with you about everything I've done. And that I've apologized, over and over again, for it. And you forgave me. You said if your memory came back you would still give me a chance because we were starting over."

Her head pounded, and his words were a blur.

"I want you to leave." She walked to the other side of the room. "I need time alone." She swiped at the tears stinging her eyes.

"Emily, please. I know this is a lot to process. Please, let me be here for you. Let me help you. I'm not going to let you push me away. I love you."

"How did you even know I was here?" Her voice was still shaky. How had he found her? Did he have her followed?

"You've been gone all night, so I was worried." He rubbed the back of his neck. "I've been calling your cell phone and not getting any answer, so I called the last place you were." He put his hands in his pockets and took them back out. "I spoke to Cora and she said you were fine, you signed the papers and left. I called your sister, but didn't get an answer. So I decided to drive around to any place I thought you might have gone. I even went over to Robert's condo to see if your car was in his driveway. I don't know why," he said, shrugging. "I mean, I know you can't, or didn't, remember him; but, I had a bad feeling that you might be there. There was a brown car in the driveway that wasn't yours."

"You know where Robert lives?" She had moved far away from him and had leaned on the wall in the dining room.

"Yes, back when I was a lesser man, I had you followed. I found out where he lives."

"Now that you've explained yourself, you can go."

"Please, don't look at me that way. You can't be afraid of me. Can you honestly say in the last few months I've given you any reason for alarm? Given you any reason to be frightened of me? Please, come home with me."

"I want you to leave, so I can be alone."

"Fine." He shook his head. "I'll leave the apartment, but I'm not leaving you here alone. It's Sunday, and I have nowhere else to be. I'll sit out in the car until you come to your senses and realize that I would never harm you. "

"Steven, you don't have to do that."

"But I do." He turned toward the steps. "I can't drive home and leave you in this condition. You're shaking and trembling and your eyes are all red. I'm not going to leave you this way." He walked down the steps and the door slammed behind him.

Emily slid down on the carpet and laid her head against the wall. Like a river, her tears flowed nonstop.

⋙

"How is she?" Mitch asked.

"Not good. Her memory is back."

"Is that a bad thing?" Mitch asked.

"I don't know yet." Steven sat in his car, staring up at her window. "She's all rattled and she looked at me with fear in her eyes, like I'm some kind of monster." The window rustled as it rolled down so he could get some air. "I need to get her to go home with me."

"If the apartment is still in her name, she can still stay there."

"I realize that, but the apartment is all cleaned out, and she told me everything was going to be put in storage. She has about three days left, and then it won't be her apartment anymore. Unless, she signs a new lease." He tapped his fingers on the leather steering wheel. "That can't happen."

"What do you want to do?"

"I need a favor. Does your cousin Sheila still need an apartment?"

"I think she does, but that's not the area she's looking in."

"I know it's across town, but it's a nice place that I'm sure she can afford. I'll put down the deposit and pay the first and last month's rent."

"Can you afford to do that with your financial situation?"

"Don't you worry about that. I'll have to make do."

He knew he couldn't afford it, but he couldn't afford to let his marriage go to ruins either. Not after he worked so hard getting Emily back.

"Even if my cousin agrees to this, you know it's going to take time for her to be approved. They have to do credit reports and background checks. Emily could get the apartment back before then."

"Emily's not going to get it back." His tone was loud. "She has no money and no job, at the moment."

"What about the money in your bank account?"

"After she left me, I was livid and I didn't handle it well. I transferred all the money in our bank accounts to an account with only my name on it, before she could take any money out. Of course, she would have gained it back during the divorce proceedings; but, as you know, the divorce never happened. Once she came home from the hospital with me, I transferred some of the money back into our joint account so she could feel we were one unit again. But I'm not stupid. I didn't transfer it all, just in case something like this happened. If I feel she's leaning in the direction of taking money out, I will get to it before she can. Don't worry. I'm on top of it."

He hung up the call with Mitch and headed for the manager's office. He had to move quickly, just in case Emily decided to emerge from the apartment.

A short stocky bald man with dark eyes, wearing a loud yellow shirt, sat at a desk. He was on the phone, so Steven waited for him to finish. He noticed the plaque on the desk had his name followed by the words 'apartment manager'.

"May I help you?" he asked, hanging up the call.

"Hello. Mr. Barkley, is it?"

"Yes, that's correct."

"I'm Steven Montgomery. My wife, Emily, rents an apartment here."

"Yes, her papers are on my desk. I'm trying to rent out her place."

"No takers yet?"

"No." Mr. Barkley shook his head. "A few people have inquired, but no one has signed a lease yet. Why do you ask?"

"I have someone in mind. Her name is Sheila Emery, and I need you to hold the place for her."

"We're not in the habit of holding apartments for people. If someone else wants it, and their money—and credit—is good, we're obligated to lease it to them."

"I realize that." Steven's tone was rough. His fist clinched. "I don't care if you rent the place out to Sheila or whoever else wants it. I don't want you renting it to my wife again."

"I cannot discriminate against your wife because you ask me to. She was a wonderful tenant. She never gave us any trouble. She's welcome to rent the apartment again, if she would like. "

Steven felt like fire came from his ears. His first impression of this guy as a wimp, apparently, was wrong. He didn't like to be wrong. And he didn't like this opposition. He would have to move on to other methods.

"I know you're only doing your job. And you're doing it well." Steven's jaw tightened. "But you will have a tenant in that apartment soon, so you won't be missing out on any money." He slid a roll of five, one hundred dollar bills across the table. "I'm going to ask you again, nicely. If she wants to sign another lease for that apartment, or any other apartment in this facility, I need you to tell her no. Here's another three hundred for your troubles." The money screeched across the table. "That's eight hundred dollars in total. You can count it if you don't believe me."

"No, I believe you."

"This will be our little secret. Do you understand?" Steven's eyes narrowed.

"Yes, I understand," Mr. Barkley said. He took the money and it made a crinkling sound in his hands.

"Glad to hear it." Steven nodded, turned, and walked away.

Emily opened the blinds and peered out. She couldn't believe Steven still sat in his car. She thought he would've gotten annoyed by now and left. She had tried calling Monica, but she didn't pick up. David hadn't either, and Dr. Robinson was out of her office. Emily knew she had to go down and confront Steven. Sure, he was quiet now; but, what if he made a commotion?

She grabbed her purse and threw it over her shoulder. Emily wanted her cell phone nearby in case she had to make a call. Her heels clicked along the pavement as she headed straight for Steven's Bentley.

"Have you come to your senses? Are you coming home with me?" Steven slammed the car door.

"What are you still doing here? Why can't you leave me alone?"

"Because no matter what you think about me right now, you're my wife and I'm worried about you. Do you know how much it hurts me to see that look of fear in your eyes?"

Not knowing how to respond, she folded her arms and remained silent.

"Yes, okay, you may remember what I've done in the past; but what about lately? I'm the same man you've lived with for the last few months. I'm the same man whose been sleeping by your side. And I'm the same man you've been making love to. Can you honestly say during that time I have harmed you."

"No." Her voice shook.

"Then how can you think I would harm you now?" Steven reached for her hand. "Please, Emily, come home with me. I love you."

"Don't touch me," she said, and pulled away.

"Fine. If you don't want me to touch you, I won't. But this is ridiculous." He rubbed his forehead. "You're my wife. I can't just leave you here. You have no clothes here. There's no furniture, no bed for you to sleep on. At least come home, shower and change into fresh clothes. If you're so frightened of me, Anita will be there, so you won't be alone with me. Please." His soft tone matched his eyes. "You can drive your car and I can follow you in mine. I'm begging you."

Steven hadn't hurt Emily in the months after her car accident.

He had been nothing but gentle and kind. Yes, there had been some overprotectiveness. But besides opening her mail and going to her lawyer's office, he had done nothing else wrong. Emily had slept on the cold, hard floor all night; she was tired and would like a change of clothes. This was no longer her apartment; well, in three days it wouldn't be. Monica wasn't picking up; neither was David. Even if they did, there was no room for her at David's parents. She needed to be strong. What was the harm in going home with him?

"Fine, then," she said. Her eyes were misty as she took her keys out and walked to her car.

She saw the pleased look on Steven's face, like he'd just won a million dollar prize. Just because she was going home with him now didn't mean she had to stay forever. Emily had a lot of things to think through and she needed sleep in order to do that. If she felt unsafe, at any time, Anita will be there. That thought made Emily feel better.

❧

"Where am I?" Emily asked. She was groggy and wiped the sleep from her eyes.

"You're at home, sweetheart." Steven sat on the end of the bed. "You refused to sleep in our bedroom, so you stayed in the guest room."

Emily looked around and saw the plastered green walls and the flowered bedspread. The room smelled like lilac. The blinds were closed, yet she could tell it was daytime because light peered through them.

"What time is it?" she asked.

"It's almost four p.m. You've been asleep for almost twenty hours. You were exhausted when I brought you home yesterday. So after I left for work this morning, I had Anita checking on you. And I called every hour to get updates on how you were."

"S-so you've been to work and back." Emily glanced around the room again. "And I've been asleep all this time?"

"I'm worried about you." Steven moved closer.

"I'm f-fine." Her voice trembled and so did her body.

"After everything that happened, I think you need to make sure everything's okay. I made an appointment with Dr. Robinson. I told her it was an emergency—a happy emergency—because your memory has returned." He smiled. "I thought we'd go see her together, unless you'd rather Anita take you. I don't think you should drive alone."

"A-are you honestly happy about my memory returning?"

"I'm not happy that you're frightened of me." His face dropped. "And, I'm not happy that you're looking at me like I'm a monster. But I'm happy that your memory has returned because that means you feel whole again. I know that's what you wanted."

"Just because I came home with you doesn't mean everything's okay between us." She scooted back on the bed and pulled the covers up to her chin.

"I realize that. You still need to get checked out. No matter what, I love you." His eyes watered. "We had good times. You can't deny that. I'm praying the good outweighs the bad because the bad was years ago. I'll say it until I can't say it anymore, I've changed."

His eyes were sincere. Emily had a flash of them holding hands and laughing in the car. Another flash of them making love. Steven's touch was gentle and soothing. Another one came of them in their favorite restaurant, talking about how much they missed their parents.

"Please, let me take you to see Dr. Robinson." His voice was soft.

"Fine," she said. "You can take me." Emily gripped her trembling hands together under the covers.

On her way in, Emily stopped at the pharmacy to tell Monica the good news; but, she wasn't at work. Veronica told her, Monica had taken a few days off. Emily then had David paged, but was informed he was off duty as well. Anxiety swelled in her chest.

Now, she walked back down to the hospital lobby, feeling light as a feather. The earlier tightness she felt, going into Dr. Robinson's office, was now gone. Her CT scan and MRI brain scan came back normal; she couldn't ask for any better news than that. The lobby lights were bright. Emily saw Steven, waiting for her. As soon as he saw her, he stood and smiled.

Dr. Robinson's words replayed in her head.

"Now that you remember everything, are you afraid to be around him? And now that you remember everything, do you still want a life with him? Do you feel he has truly changed? Would you like to try again with Robert? You do what's best for you and don't let anyone sway you."

She couldn't give Dr. Robinson any solid answers then, and looking at Steven standing in front of her now, the answers still weren't clear.

"Did everything go alright?" He had such love in his eyes.

"Yes, it did." She cleared her throat. "Dr. Robinson said I don't have to see her for regular visits anymore. But if I need anything, I can always make an appointment."

"That's good to hear. You ready to go home now?"

"Steven—"

"I know." He held up his hands. "You're not sure if our home is your home anymore. I get it."

She stopped paying attention to what Steven said because, just then, the revolving lobby door whizzed, and Robert and Kelly walked in. They were hand in hand. Emily felt a gnawing in the pit of her stomach. Robert looked handsome in blue jeans and a gray shirt. Kelly looked beautiful in a white flowered knee length dress.

"Are you ready to go?"

She felt Steven's hot breath in her ear. She wasn't sure if he'd noticed them, too; but, he was just as eager to leave as she was.

"Yes," Emily nodded, "I am."

❧

"Thanks for coming with me to see my mom," Kelly said. "I was so scared when she spiked a fever."

"It's fine. I'm always here for support." Robert's smiled faded.

"What's wrong?" Kelly asked.

"Emily's over there with Steven."

"I hope she's alright."

"I'm sure she's fine." He cleared his throat. "Steven's with her." He couldn't stop glaring at them. He noticed Emily had on a pink dress that ruffled at the bottom. She always did look good in pink.

"Do you want to go check on her? If she's at the hospital, maybe she's not feeling well." She rubbed his shoulder. "I can head over to the gift shop and you can meet me there."

"No, she doesn't need me anymore. Besides, we're here to get flowers for your mother and that's what we're going to do." Robert reached for Kelly's hand.

CHAPTER EIGHTEEN

"I don't understand," Emily said. "I was just there a few hours ago. I even used my key to get in. How could you rent my apartment out that fast?" Her voice was high-pitched.

Her mouth went dry because she realized she'd been asleep for over a day. What seemed like a few hours to her was actually a lot more.

"Do you have anything else available? No…well, I appreciate you checking. Thank you. I'll return the key first chance I get," she said, hanging up the call.

The door whirled open and Steven walked in.

"I'm sorry to barge in. I knocked and you didn't say anything."

"I didn't hear you. I was on the phone." She stood. Her hands were sweaty. She wiped them on her dress.

"Anita has dinner ready." He stepped closer. "Is everything alright?"

"I need you to sit down." She pointed at the plush chair across from her bed.

She sat down on the bed and wrung her hands. She was nauseous, like she had gone for a swim right after eating.

"You don't have to say anything. I know this is the part where you tell me you're leaving me and going back to Robert." He shook his head. "The new man I've become means nothing to you."

She saw the love in his eyes, changing to hurt, then sadness. His glare went right through her, like she was a wolf in sheep's clothing.

"I'm sure you have your bags packed." His voice was full of pain. "That's why you ran straight upstairs when we got home. You were packing, weren't you?"

"No, I'm not packed. And I'm not running back to Robert. But I do feel like I need to be on my own. So I called the manager of my apartment building; but, he said my apartment had already been leased."

Emily knew she couldn't go to Robert—that was made clear by seeing him locked hand in hand with Kelly earlier.

"Then why can't you stay here? At least for a little while, until you find a new place. It's going to take time to look for a new apartment. Stay here while you search. I'm not going to hurt you, Emily. Please, tell me you believe me." His voice shook.

"I've seen the changes in you. I've seen your vulnerable side, and the side of you that isn't always out for money. I've seen the side that's sweet and kind, and doesn't have to be in control of every situation. But then there's the other side of you that scares me. I do still love you, but that doesn't mean we should be together."

"Where will you go?" He frowned. "Please, don't say a hotel."

"What's wrong with a hotel?"

"Why would you choose to stay in unfamiliar surroundings when you can just stay here—in a place that you're used to? All your things are here. Why would you drag your belongings to a hotel when it's not necessary? I don't know how many times I can reiterate that I won't harm you. You can take our bed and I can sleep in here. If that doesn't make you feel comfortable, then I will take our bed and you can continue to stay in here, like you did last night."

Emily paused for a moment because she didn't know what to do. Monica was still living at her in-laws. There was her friend, Christina, who she now remembered. But Emily didn't want to intrude on Christina and her husband, either. She didn't feel close enough to her country club friends to stay with them. She didn't want her problems to turn into her friends problems. She needed to handle this on her own.

"I'll stay here while I look for another apartment, but if I feel unsafe in any way, I'm leaving. I can easily get money from the bank, or use my credit card and stay in a hotel." Was she making a mistake? Only time would tell.

❧

"I thought we could talk before I left for work." Steven walked into the kitchen. "You were honest with me yesterday about wanting to move out," he said, sitting down across from Emily. "I wanted to be honest with you about some things."

The smell of bacon wafted in the air. Emily noticed Anita walk out when Steven sat down to talk to her. His face was serious and his tone was somber, so she stopped eating her eggs and put her fork down.

"I know we're not technically together," he said, motioning his fingers to use air quotes. "You consider us roommates, so this isn't your problem. But we are still legally married, so I thought it was time you knew." He cleared his throat. "I've been lying to you for months. I should've told you this before, but I was too embarrassed, too proud."

She saw the anguish in his face. His eyes were soft and his voice was weak.

"Just tell me what it is."

"I thought money could bring happiness." He stood. "You know, when I was a child, I didn't have much. I promised myself, when I grew up, I would make something of myself. I'd buy whatever I wanted. I'd give my family a good life."

"I know all of this, Steven. What's wrong?"

"I know you don't care about having money the way I do, but it means everything to me. I don't want to have nothing, like my father. But I couldn't be happy with the success I made of myself. I tried to invest, so I could have more." He lowered his head. He walked back to the chair across from her and sat down. "I made a few bad investments, and I lost a lot of money. That's why the Audi has been missing for months—"

"It's not in the shop?"

"No." He shook his head. "That was a lie. I had to sell it. Richard, my accountant, wanted me to sell a few more cars but I refused—"

"What else did your accountant say?"

"He said I should sell the house and downsize, and let Anita go. But I refused to do that. I figured if I won a few more cases, I'd make partner and get that bonus. I was counting on it. So far that hasn't happened." He stood again and walked toward the kitchen window. "I don't know what's happening to me. When I was younger, I won every case I tried, but now..." His words drifted off.

Emily sat there, not knowing what to say, or how to feel. The air was getting thick in the room. She knew he was suffering and she didn't know how to take his pain away, or why she even wanted to. She felt horrible, but evil thoughts crept in. Was he making up this story so she wouldn't look for an apartment and leave? Did he think she would stay if she felt sorry for him and what he was going through? Emily needed to know if his story was true.

"Steven, it's okay." She stood and walked to him. "I'm sure it's not as bad as you're saying. Why don't we go to see Richard together? Then, I can see the damage for myself."

"You would do that for me?" Steven turned from the window to look at Emily.

"Yes, I would do that for us." She gave a half smile. "You shouldn't have to go through this alone. We're still legally married, so the trouble with our finances affects both of us." The money was acquired during their marriage and Emily needed to know what was happening to it.

Before she knew what was happening, Steven wrapped his arms around her and squeezed. Like a needle popping a balloon, she could feel all of the air being sucked right out of her. Emily should have pulled away; instead, she embraced him. Steven was like a man who had lost his best friend and had nothing else left.

∽

Emily glanced around the dark room. The walls were dark and smelled of musk. She had only been to Richard's office once, when she and Steven first married; but the air was just as thick now as it had been back then.

Steven had on cotton khakis and a cotton, button-down, woven shirt. He looked different without one of his expensive suits on; he looked vulnerable. Steven kept a tight hold on Emily's hand. His palm was sweaty and shaky, yet she decided not to pull away. The situation wasn't as dire as he made it out to be, at least not to her. Maybe that was because money didn't mean as much to her as it did to him.

"We want to keep the house…" Steven's voice drifted off.

"And our maid, Anita, of course." Emily cut in. "She's been with us for years. She's family."

Emily noticed Steven cringe when she agreed with Richard that two more cars needed to go.

"I think the convertible Jaguar and my BMW can go. We'll get something cheaper."

"No," Steven said, placing his hand on her knee. "I insist we keep the BMW. That's your car. I bought it for you when we first married and even if we're not together anymore, I want you to keep it."

His grip tightened on her knee and even though she had on blue jeans she could feel the hotness of his hand. This was a big change for him. When they first separated, he took her car away and threatened if they divorced it would no longer be hers. But now, he knew that she still planned on leaving him, and he wanted her to keep the vehicle.

"I think we should sell the Cadillac XTS," she said.

"That's good," Richard said. The keys clacked as he typed

something into his computer. "Steven can keep his Bentley Continental GTC, and Emily will keep her car. That way each of you will have one car."

"And that's all we need," Emily said.

Once all of that had been decided, Steven quickly stood. Emily knew he was ready to go. She squeezed his hand, yanking him back down to his chair; they still had more work to do.

They decided not to renew their membership at the country club. Emily would miss helping out with the fundraisers; but, she wouldn't have time for it anyway. Emily planned on going back to work.

Steven would have to cut back on his need to splurge on high-priced suits.

She saw the sadness in his eyes as they drove home.

"Are you alright? I know that was tough for you."

"It was made better, knowing you were by my side and supporting me. I'll be fine as long as you're with me." He reached for her hand.

"Steven…" She pulled her hand away.

"I noticed you kept saying 'we'. 'We' could keep this and 'we' could sell that." His hand gripped the steering wheel; he turned into the driveway. "I have to say, it felt good hearing you say that. It was like we were one again. I hope it stays that way." His somber face turned up into a smile.

That was the first smile she had seen on his face all morning. It was nice to see his vulnerable side show through. Steven didn't show it much; but when he did, it reminded Emily that he could be human.

৯৯

Emily stood in the hospital gift shop, her stomach in tight knots because she still hadn't been able to reach Monica. David had finally answered his phone and he said Monica was fine, just really busy.

He was abrupt and vague. Emily got the feeling something else was going on. She needed to find out what was happening with her sister.

Veronica said Monica was on a break and had walked over to the gift shop to get a candy bar. Emily thought that was strange since Monica didn't like chocolate. When they were kids and their mother would give them treats for being good, Monica never wanted anything chocolate.

"Hi, stranger," Emily said. She finally spotted Monica, in her lab coat, standing in line paying for a chocolate bar.

"Hello," Monica replied. Her face dropped as if she was surprised to see her.

She waited for Monica to pay before she spoke again.

"I've been trying to get ahold of you," Emily said, as they walked out of the store. "I called and called and got no answer."

"David said he spoke to you and told you I was okay."

"He did, but he kind of rushed me off the phone, and I didn't feel good about the conversation."

"There's no need for you to worry. My phone broke and I haven't been feeling that well lately, so I haven't had a chance to get a new one. It's not a big deal."

"It's a big deal to me." Emily's eyes softened. "You took care of me after my car accident, so maybe it's time I took care of you. What's wrong?"

"My stomach's been a little queasy and—"

"Are you pregnant?" Emily's smile spread from ear to ear.

"Why would you jump to that conclusion?"

"You're eating chocolate. You hate chocolate. So you must be having a craving."

"Just like when we were little," Monica said, shaking her head. "You always had to figure everything out."

"That must mean I'm right."

"Yes, you're right." The paper rattled as Monica ripped open the candy bar and took a bite.

"Why didn't you tell me?"

"You have a lot going on right now, dealing with your memory loss," she said. "And, living with Steven." She rolled her eyes. "Besides, I only found out a few days ago."

"You still should have told me. How far along are you?"

"About five weeks." Monica patted her stomach.

"This is so exciting. I'm going to be an aunt. I'm so happy for you." Emily's eyes watered. "If my baby had survived, your little one would have a cousin to play with. Lindsey was so tiny. I remember you didn't want me to look at her, but I had to." A tear graced her cheek. "She was so small and pale—"

"How do you know that?" Monica had a shocked expression on her face. "Did you get your memory back?"

"Yes, I did." Emily's throat was dry.

"When did this happen?"

"About a week ago." She wiped her face. "Probably around the same time you found out you were pregnant."

Monica moved closer and grabbed Emily's hand.

They ended up walking to the corridor behind the gift shop. There was less foot traffic, more privacy.

"That's why I've been trying to reach you, to tell you the good news."

Some small children ran down the hallway, distracting their conversation.

"I'm sure Robert is elated about this." Monica turned her attention back to Emily.

"Robert doesn't know."

"I don't understand." Monica tapped her heel on the concrete floor.

The stern look on Monica's face reminded Emily of her childhood, when her mother scolded her for doing something wrong. Only now the roles were reversed; Monica did the scolding.

"He's back with Kelly and I wasn't sure if I should come in between that. I've hurt him so much already. If he's happy, do I have a right to ruin what he has with her?"

"I don't think you should worry about what he has with Kelly. As far as I know, I don't think it's serious. He's seeing her to get over you."

"You knew about Kelly?"

"Yes, I found out recently. You shouldn't let that stop you. I believe what he had with you is so much stronger than anything he could have with her."

"That's what I hoped, too—"

"So, why haven't you gone to him?"

"It's only been a few days. I'm still trying to figure everything out. And Steven has been so kind to me. How could I up and leave someone who's been there for me and taken care of me for the last few months?"

"Weren't you scared once you remembered everything?"

"Yes, I was afraid—very afraid, at first, and angry. I thought about all the things he put me through in the past..." Her fingers clinched. "But that was a long time ago. And the more I thought about the last few months, the less afraid, less angry I became." She bit her lip. "Yes, at times I still feel a little scared—not because of the way he is now, but because of the memories I have. I know you probably think I'm crazy, but I believe he's changed or, at least, he's trying to. On top of everything else, Steven informed me that he, or we, are having some money problems. He's been down about it."

"There could be one crisis after another with him; so if that's the reason you're staying, you'll never leave him."

"It's not the only reason. Everything's confusing right now. I do plan on looking for an apartment and getting my job back."

"I'm glad your memory is back." Monica reached for her hand and squeezed. "I'm glad that you want to stand on your own two feet again. And I know that you say Steven has been good to you lately; but, I have to say, I believe you belong with Robert. Kelly or no Kelly, I think you need to talk to him and see where you stand."

"Monica—"

"No, you have your perfect chance to see him while Steven's not hovering around. Robert's here, in the hospital. He's been in the ER since this morning. I saw him earlier on my lunch hour."

"I don't understand." Emily's voice quivered. "I saw him here a few days ago with Kelly and he looked fine."

"Don't get upset. It's nothing serious or I would've told you as soon as we started to talk."

"What happened?"

"Robert can tell you." Monica glanced down at her wristwatch. "I have to go. I'm sure Veronica is wondering what's taking me so long."

Emily's knees felt weak. What if Robert didn't want to see her? What if Kelly was there? What if Monica was wrong and Robert and Kelly's relationship had progressed into so much more? Like a drum, her heart beat loud and fast. Was Monica right? Was this her chance to tell Robert her memory had returned? Was this her chance to tell him she still loved him? Was this her chance to win him back?

Emily stopped at the front desk and asked a short brunette haired nurse what room Robert Johnson was in. The nurse asked who she was to him, and she blurted out fiancée. Where those words came from, she didn't know. They were no longer engaged; they were barely even friends anymore. The nurse smiled and pointed her in the right direction.

Feeling like a tightrope walker on a thin wire, she walked to his room. Knowing she might fall at any moment made her stomach churn. Emily wiped the tiny beads of sweat from her forehead and took in a deep breath. She saw through the glass window that he was alone. Kelly was nowhere around. Hopefully, she'd have time to talk to him before Kelly arrived.

Standing outside his room, she heard the beeping of the machines next to him. It reminded Emily of her days in the hospital, and it made her want to cringe. Taking in another deep breath, she slowly walked in. Robert was so still, it looked like he could be gone from this world; but, the heart monitor hooked up to him showed otherwise, and so did his chest rising up and down. Deciding not to wake him, Emily sat in the chair beside Robert's bed to watch him sleep.

"Emmie, what are you doing here?"

His voice was groggy but soft. Hopefully, she hadn't awakened him. He had a little stubble on his cheeks, and on his chin. She was too far away from him the other day to notice it. But now, staring at him, the hairs made him look sexier than usual, and she felt a small tingle go up her spine. Emily's gaze lifted to Robert's, his pale green eyes were just as beautiful as always. It seemed liked decades ago since she had seen them.

"Monica told me you were in the ER." She stood and walked closer to him. "I hope you don't mind that I came."

He remained silent, so she continued. "How are you feeling? What happened?"

Her body went numb because his green eyes seemed to pierce right through her. Was he mad that she was there? Maybe he wanted Kelly by his side instead of her. His expression was neutral. She couldn't tell what he thought.

"I was stupidly playing basketball with some guys at work while on lunch." He finally said, breaking the tension. "I think I aggravated my rib injury." He frowned and let out a groan while rubbing his side. "I'm sure it's fine—it only hurts a little."

"I'm sorry that you're hurting." She wanted to reach out and hold him. She wanted to touch his face, but she knew she couldn't. "I wish there was something I could do to help, to make you feel better."

He opened his mouth like he was getting ready to say something, but then he quickly closed it.

"Why were you playing basketball anyway? Basketball was never your game. You always preferred football."

"It was stupid. The guys dared me that I couldn't win, and like a child, I had to show them I could. I figured I'd be okay." He shrugged. "Basketball is easier on the bones than football. I guess I was kidding myself." He rubbed his side.

"I guess you're right." Being so close to him made her stomach bounce around. She wanted to tap his nose the way she used to; but she couldn't, so she kept rambling. "How have you been? I haven't seen you in a while…"

"Emmie, why are you here?" His tone changed.

"I was worried, and I wanted to see how you were."

"You shouldn't have come."

"I don't understand." Her voice cracked.

"I haven't spoken to you in months. So I don't know why you're here now." His face turned red.

"I thought we were still friends."

"Well, we're not."

All the love Emily used to see in Robert's eyes had turned to hate. Maybe she was being overdramatic, but that's what it looked like to her. If it wasn't hate it was dislike. No matter what he felt now, maybe that would change when she told him about her memory.

"Robert, please don't be this way. I wanted to tell you—"

"I think you should go." He cut her off.

"If you just let me finish," she paused, biting her lip. "I wanted to say—" A ringing sound cut off her thoughts.

She glanced down at the table next to his bed where his phone was. Noticing Kelly's name appear made her throat burn. Her eyes saddened as she glanced back at Robert. He groaned, leaning over to grab the phone from the table. A frown appeared on his face as he laid his head back on his pillow.

"I have to take this," he said, sighing and looking away.

She knew their conversation was over when he turned away from her. Kelly's phone call was more important to him than what she had to say. She felt tears forming. Emily turned to leave before Robert could see the wetness hitting her cheeks.

CHAPTER NINETEEN

"I've been in contact with the school board and the superintendent of Hill High about getting my job back," Emily said, sitting across from Steven at the dining room table.

"What did they say?" Steven's fork clanked as he laid it on his plate.

"They'd like to have me back. Since school will be out in about a month, they feel it best if Mr. Nathan finishes out the school year. The students are used to him now, and it would be silly for me to come back for only a month."

"That's only fair." He cleared his throat. "Going back now would be disruptive to the class."

"They did say I could come back in September. I need to speak with them again, but they said there might even be something for me this summer. They already had another teacher lined up, but she may not be able to do it. Then, I could teach summer school."

"That's wonderful news." Steven smiled. "I'm happy for you."

"Are you really happy for me, or are you just saying that?" He had been so wonderful lately, yet it was hard to know if he was sincere or if it was just an act.

"To show you how serious I am, why don't we throw a party, to celebrate?"

She was taken aback by his enthusiasm. It was a pleasant

change—a big change, as well. Sometimes, it was hard to believe this was the same man.

"We can't afford a big party right now. Not with our finances." She stood and cleared the table.

"I'm surprised—and glad—to hear you say 'we'. It *almost* makes me feel like we're a real couple again." He followed behind her.

"I sometimes feel that way, too." She couldn't believe she had said those words out loud.

She hated to admit it, but she did feel closer to him. Even though they were still sleeping in separate rooms, he was tender and caring. They were still husband and wife, on paper; but, oddly enough, it seemed like it mentally and physically as well.

"I hoped you would feel that way." He smiled. "I know you want to move out, but I hope that changes, too."

"I can't give you any answers on that right now." She placed the dishes in the sink. "I need for us to take it slow, like we've been doing." She rinsed the plates off. The water was cool on her hands.

"I'll go as slow as you need." He kissed the top of her forehead. "I'm grateful that you're even considering it. As far as the party goes, why don't we hold off until after you start back teaching, and then, we can have a small dinner with your sister and David?"

"That's fine." She pursed her lips together.

"Did you call Dr. Robinson about the other thing we talked about?"

"Yes," she said, drying her hands on a towel. "I explained to her that I still had trouble going into Lindsey's room and going to the cemetery. I told her every time I try, my chest tightens, like I'm having a panic attack."

"What did she say?"

"Just because my memory came back doesn't mean I'm going to automatically be able to do those things. I couldn't do them before the memory loss; and now that the pain is fresher, it's understandable that I still don't want to. She recommended a therapist, off-site, who specializes in situations like mine."

"Can you make the appointment for two? I'd like to come and work on my issues as well."

She felt her face stiffen. Did he honestly want to work on his issues?

"Lindsey was my daughter, too." His face was sullen. "You don't have to answer now, but please, think about it."

Even though things were different between them now—better—she wasn't sure if she wanted them sharing their feelings together with a therapist. That was something she wanted to do alone. Maybe she was scared if they went together it would bring them even closer. She wasn't sure if she wanted that because she still hadn't forgotten about Robert. He was never far from her thoughts. She constantly wondered where he was and what he was doing. But Robert was with Kelly now, and Emily had to move on as well.

❧

"Are you sure you want to do this, man?" Paul asked, walking into Robert's office.

"Yes, I'm sure." Robert plopped down at his desk. "What's the big deal? It's only six p.m.; I work late all the time."

"That's not what I'm talking about." The door clunked as he slammed it behind him.

Robert raised an eyebrow. He remained silent, waiting to hear what Paul had to say. Ever since Robert had gone to the emergency room, Paul had been on him that he worked too much and needed to take some time off. But he disagreed. The doctor said he had reinjured his bruised rib bones. Robert had been given pain medicine, and he'd been using an ice pack at home. He wouldn't be playing basketball anytime soon, that's for sure.

"I heard you accepted that job offer." Paul sat down in the chair across from Robert's desk. "Are you sure you really want to relocate to New York?"

"Why wouldn't I be?" He shifted in his chair. "I lost out on that sales manager position that I wanted." He placed his one foot over his knee. "And, you're the one who told me I should go for this one when it posted."

"I know I did; but at the time, I didn't realize this position was in New York."

"I think it's a good thing. It's more money, and my parents live there. It'll be nice to catch up with them. Besides, there's nothing left for me here…" His voice drifted off.

"You talking about Emily?"

"Yes, among other things."

"What things?"

"I don't know, man," Robert said. "I lost Emmie. I got back with Kelly for the wrong reasons. It's just that…" He shook his head. "Kelly could never replace Emily. And it was unfair for her to be in a one-sided relationship."

"You told me she didn't care if she was the rebound. You said she wanted to be with you."

"I know, and that was alright for a while; but, I knew eventually Kelly would want more than I could give, and I couldn't live that way. I'm glad we were able to remain friends, but I know now that it's time for me to move on. I need to start over, and this is my opportunity to do so."

"I'll miss you, buddy." Paul stood and extended his hand.

"Yes, and I'll miss beating you at basketball." Robert smiled, shaking his hand back.

"Now I know your dreaming because I believe I beat you."

"You remember it your way, and I'll remember it my way." Robert stood. He smoothed out his suit coat. "Besides, I'm not leaving for a few more weeks. I have a lot of packing to do."

"If you need any help, I'm here." Paul turned toward the door.

"Thanks, man. I appreciate it." Robert waved and sat back down at his desk.

He couldn't believe he was leaving Precone. He was leaving his friends, his home. And most of all, he couldn't believe he was leaving Emily. But it was for the best. It was time he started over. A new atmosphere would do him a world of good. She had moved on and it was time for him to do the same. Maybe a change of scenery would help Robert get over Emily.

CHAPTER TWENTY

E mily stood in front of Steven's office building, watching land-scapers work their magic on the grass. She loved the smell of fresh-cut grass. The bright sun blazed down, making her skin hot. Things had been so good with them lately she decided to surprise Steven with lunch.

When she reached his office, his secretary—Rachel—said Steven was in a meeting; but, she could buzz him, so he'd know Emily was there. She didn't want any special treatment, and she didn't mind waiting for him to finish. The office had been updated since they were married. The warm camel colors soothed her, and so did the soft gray carpet. There was a flat-screen television on the wall, showing a news program. She wished the colors in Steven's office matched the reception area, but he chose to keep his office on the dark, drab side.

The swooshing of the glass office door opening caught her attention. A tall, heavyset man with dark hair—and darker eyes—came in. Emily didn't like the way he looked. The man made the little hairs on the back of her neck stand up. He had on a black T-shirt, black denim pants and a black leather jacket. This was strange since summer was nearing, and the weather was almost eighty degrees outside. Emily tried glancing back at the television, but the man talked so loud it was a distraction. It was like listening to classical music while the person next to you was listening to hip-hop. The man seemed cagey, and Emily couldn't keep her eyes off him.

She wasn't trying to be nosy, but she heard the entire conversation. The man said he needed to see Steven right away. It was important. Apparently, Rachel knew the man; she called him Jerome. This Jerome must have been on a first name basis with Steven; he kept using it. Emily listened as Rachel told Jerome that Steven was in an important meeting and couldn't be disturbed. Jerome went on to say that Steven told him he would be in a meeting with his real estate agent at noon, but he should be done by now.

Emily's chest pounded, like a bomb ready to explode. She no longer cared about the bizarre man standing there. She wanted to know why a real estate agent was in Steven's office. They had decided not to sell the house since their finances would be in order without doing that. Steven told Emily that he'd be working on his important case all day. This wasn't an important case. What was going on?

Her heart continued to pound in her ears as she watched Jerome check his watch like he had somewhere to be. She only saw the side of his face, but he seemed annoyed. Jerome leaned on Rachel's desk and tapped his fingers.

Steven's office door rustled open and Emily's eyes widened. A short, thin woman with sandy hair walked out of his office. The woman's steps quickened as she walked past Jerome, and swung open the outer glass door to the hallway. Emily continued watching as Rachel stood and walked toward Steven's office door. Before Rachel could reach the door, Jerome flew past her, almost knocking her over. The door banged as he slammed it behind him. Rachel then turned toward Emily and mouthed she was sorry. Emily mouthed back that it was fine. What just happened?

Maybe she should leave and go home? Obviously, Steven was too busy having secret meetings to go to lunch. But Rachel had already seen Emily and would surely tell Steven she had been there. Leaving was out of the question. Her head was spinning, so she tried watching television again. The news talked about the latest scandal of the day. Finally, she heard the swish of Steven's door and saw Jerome walk out. Rachel gave her a look, and she stood, knowing it was her turn to enter his office. Emily's fist clinched as she walked in.

"I didn't know you were here." Steven's eyes widened. "Did you just get here?"

"No, I've been here for a while." She sat down in the cushioned chair across from his desk. "You were pretty busy, so I told Rachel not to disturb you."

"I wish she would have told me anyway. My wife should always come first."

"It's fine. I didn't mind waiting."

"What brings you here?" He loosened his striped tie.

"I wanted to surprise you and take you to lunch. The school board called me this morning and said the summer school position is all mine. I thought we could celebrate."

"That was fast," he mumbled under his breath. "I thought it would take them more time to come to a decision."

Emily was surprised at his abrupt tone and eye rolling, but she continued, "I guess today wasn't such a good day since you're so busy."

"No, we can still go." He glanced down at his watch. "It's only two. I could eat."

"I'm not hungry anymore." She wrung her hands. "I need to ask you a question."

"You can ask me anything. What is it?"

"Who was that woman I saw leaving your office a little while ago?"

"What woman?" His brows drew together.

"She was short with sandy hair. She walked out about forty-five minutes ago."

"Oh, her." He looked uncomfortable. "Her name is Candace Hatton."

"Who is she?" She noticed beads of sweat forming on Steven's forehead.

"She's an old real estate friend of mine." He stood.

"Why would you need a real estate agent?" Her foot shook already knowing his answer.

"I was going to surprise you with this, later." He put his hands in the pockets of his pants suit and took them back out. "I got a job offer from a law firm in Atlanta. I have a friend who works there. He said I could make partner in only a few years. So I was thinking of selling the house. We could move there and start over."

"When were you planning on telling me this? Once the moving vans were in front of the house?" She stood.

"Emily, it's not what you think." Steven shook his head. "It was just an idea. I planned on discussing everything with you first."

"I don't believe this. We're slowly finding our way back together. Now you want us to move."

"I thought a move might help us."

"But my family's here and my job's here." She brushed her hand through her hair. "I can't believe you would even consider this."

"You left out Robert." His face hardened.

"What?"

"You heard me." His eyes narrowed. "You don't want to leave because your precious Robert is here."

"That's not it at all. I'm going back to work. My doctors are here and my sister's here. I told you she is pregnant. Monica needs me."

"Your sister has a husband to take care of her. And as for your job, you haven't worked in almost a year. You can get another teaching job in Atlanta."

"This is my home."

"Sweetheart, our home is wherever we are." Steven walked to her. "Your actions, recently, have proven to me that we're starting over. I think a move will do wonders for our relationship. A new atmosphere could change everything." He grabbed onto Emily's hand and squeezed. "You can always come and visit your sister. Why can't you see that?"

"But what about—"

"Lindsey's grave." He squeezed her hand tighter. "I already

thought about that. We can have it moved to a nice site in Atlanta. That way, we can visit her whenever we want. See? I already thought of everything."

"I don't know if that's such a good idea." Emily pulled her hand away. "This is all a little too much for me." She wiped her eyes. "I came here to take you to lunch, and now I find out you want to move to another state."

Feeling like she'd been hit by a train, the urge to leave his office was great. She needed to clear her head. The thought of moving her daughter's grave made her skin crawl. How could Steven even think of doing such a thing? And moving so far away from Robert? Sure they weren't together, but at least Emily knew Robert was close by.

"Why are you getting so upset? I thought this was a good thing." Steven tried to grab Emily around her waist, but she pulled away.

"I need some time to think about this." She stepped back.

"Even though we haven't been intimate since your memory returned, I'm still your husband. And if I'm not mistaken, when I told you I loved you the other night you said you still loved me, too."

"I said I still had strong feelings for you."

"It's the same thing." His face turned red. "I don't see what there is to think about."

Feeling a buzzing coming from her purse made her ignore what he said. Instead, she reached down and retrieved her phone.

"Don't answer that. We need to finish discussing this."

"It's David. This could be important." She turned away from him. "It will only take a minute," she mumbled.

She turned back to Steven. "I have to go."

"What's wrong?"

"I-I don't r-really know. David said Monica was admitted into the hospital. " Her hands shook trying to put her phone back in her purse. "Something may be wrong with the baby." She headed for the door. "He wasn't sure."

"Wait a minute." Steven grasped onto the strap of Emily's purse to pull her back. "Are you sure you're okay driving? I can take you in my car."

"I'll be fine." She ripped her purse from his grasp.

"I still want to go with you."

"Why? You don't get along with my sister. You've never cared for her."

"That was in the past. I care for you. I don't want you to be alone." His tone was sincere. "I'll meet you there."

"That's fine." She turned and headed for the door. There was no time to argue with him. She needed to get to the hospital and find out what had happened to Monica and the baby.

The women's center was right around the corner from the nursery. Going up to that floor made her stomach churn. It brought back memories of her horrible time there, when she lost her little girl. She tried to shake off those feelings as she stepped off the elevator since this time was about Monica, not her.

Emily's heart nearly stopped as she turned the corner and saw Robert standing in front of Monica's room. He looked immaculate in a gray suit and tie. He had probably come straight from work.

"Is Monica alright?"

"I don't really know." He shrugged. "David called me, and I raced over here. But when I got here, he was already in the room with her. A nurse said I had to wait for David to come out. I'm sure she'll be fine." His eyes were soft.

"You can't know that for sure."

"Try not to worry." Robert wiped a tear from under Emily's eye.

His touch was familiar, and his gaze overpowered her. For a moment, it seemed like old times—times when he would take her in his arms and tell her everything would be alright. But Robert's soft gaze turned hard when they both heard a familiar voice behind them.

"How's your sister doing?" Steven walked up behind Emily and touched the small of her back.

"I don't know anything yet." Emily's eyes continued to water as she turned toward him. "David's in with her now."

"Maybe we should go sit in the waiting room." Steven pressed harder on her back.

Emily noticed the two men didn't acknowledge each other.

"There's no sense in standing in front of her room. I'm sure David can find us in the waiting room," Steven continued.

Emily stood frozen, not knowing what to do. She wanted to see Monica. She wanted to stay with Robert. But she felt a warm hand grab hers. Steven tightened his grip, and she felt him jerk her toward the waiting room. Feeling like a prisoner in shackles, she followed him. Why did she have to follow him? Why was she letting him tell her what to do? She wanted to stay with Robert and wait for David to come out. Emily didn't want to make a scene, but she was angry with herself for going with Steven.

The waiting room was crowded. It was filled with the chatter of people talking, and the screech of children crying. The smell of coffee and donuts wafted in the air. Steven led her to two seats across from the flat-screen television. Feeling like all of the energy had left her body, Emily plopped down, trying to drown out the noise. She stared up at the television. She was desperate for more information on her sister's condition.

Emily needed to feel like she was doing something, so she decided to call Anita and tell her what had happened to Monica. Anita always liked Monica and would appreciate the call. Emily finished her conversation and hung up when she saw Robert entering the waiting room. He took the last seat that just so happened to be right across from her and Steven. She didn't know if that was a good thing or not.

Her stomach had butterflies. Emily felt Robert's gaze on her, and she couldn't stop looking at him, either. There was still an enormous pull between them; there was no denying it. Steven sat right next to Emily, reading a magazine; but, she couldn't stop staring at Robert. She knew now what she'd known all along. Robert was the man Emily wanted to be with.

CHAPTER TWENTY-ONE

The doctor finally came out and gave them good news. Monica and the baby were doing fine. Monica's stomach pain was a bad reaction to something she had eaten. Steven was on his cell phone, so Emily slid past him to visit Monica. After her visit with Monica was over, she walked back out to the waiting room to tell Robert he could go next. She never got to speak to him. Steven stood, obstructing her view.

"Now that we know your sister's alright, I have somewhere I need to be. I would never leave you here with him…" He glared over at Robert, who walked out of the waiting room. "If it wasn't an emergency," he said, mumbling. He leaned over and kissed her cheek. "Please, give your sister my love."

Emily watched Steven leave the waiting area and then headed back to Monica's room. The door whizzed open, and Robert walked out.

"I'm glad she's alright," he said, brushing past her.

"I am, too." Emily had to get Robert's attention before he got away. "Your visit was quick."

"I have to be somewhere."

"It seems like everybody does," she mumbled. "It's such good news that the baby is okay." Being so close to him sent goose bumps up her arm.

"Yes, it is." He smiled. "I'm happy for both of them. They'll make wonderful parents."

"I think so, too." She glanced down at her shoes and then back up at him. There was so much more Emily wanted to say to Robert, but it was hard getting the words out.

"I should be going. It's getting late."

"Robert, can you wait a minute? I want to talk to you."

"I guess." He shrugged.

"Now that Monica's going to be alright, and we're alone, I …" Her voice trembled. "I wanted to say…" Emily tried to continue, but she noticed Robert checking his watch. "Am I keeping you from something?"

"Yes. I need to get home and finish packing."

"Are you going somewhere?" Her tone was high-pitched.

"Yes, I am." Robert looked back at his watch.

"Are you going on vacation?"

"If you must know, I accepted a job offer in New York. I'm out of here in a few days."

"You were going to leave town without telling me?" Emily's face dropped. "If Monica wasn't in the hospital, I wouldn't have seen you." Her body felt numb. "H-how could you do that?"

"How can you have your memory back and not tell me?" Robert snapped back at her. His eyes hardened.

"How did you know?"

"I'd have to be an idiot not to know. When you came to visit me in the hospital, you said football was my game, not basketball. I never told you that during our recent time together. So the only way you would know was if your memory was back." He roughly brushed his hand over his forehead.

"Robert, please let me explain." She moved toward him; he stepped back. "I wanted to tell you that day in your hospital room, but you were with Kelly and—"

"Just because I was dating Kelly is no excuse. You should have still told me. Do you know how hurt I was?"

"But Robert—"

"No, let me finish." He shook his head. "I always thought if your memory ever returned, you would come running to me, you'd be so happy to share the good news with me. I thought you'd come back to me, if you remembered all the love we shared. Boy," He threw his hands in the air. "Was I an idiot! You remembered and chose to stay with Steven."

"If you would just let me explain…" She heard the pain in his voice, and the hurt in his eyes was unbearable.

"There's nothing to explain. You made your choice. And now, I've made mine. I'm leaving town, and there's nothing else to say." Robert walked away.

"I didn't choose to stay with Steven. I stayed there, temporarily, and then it turned into something longer," she rambled. "My love for you never faded. It's just, you had moved on and…" Her voice drifted off. She didn't have the right words to explain.

"I guess you should know…" Robert turned to her again. "I'm no longer with Kelly. I broke things off with her because I was still in love with you. You would have known that if you'd have come to me, but you didn't. I know you said you tried telling me at the hospital; but, somewhere deep down inside, I believe if you really wanted a life with me, I would have been the first person you called once you remembered."

Emily felt numb, so she stood there.

"Your silence tells me everything," he continued. "Take care of yourself. I have to go." Robert turned and walked away. This time he didn't turn back. He kept walking until he reached the elevator.

Tears streamed down Emily's face. Should she try and stop him? He was so angry with her. What else could she have said to make him stay? Everything he'd said was true. Even if Robert was with Kelly, Emily should have immediately gone to him and told him the truth. Robert had every right to leave town and start a new life.

Emily's knees wobbled as she stepped inside the elevator. Now that she had seen for herself that her sister was alright, she would leave and give Monica and David some alone time. Emily also wanted some time for herself, so she could gather her thoughts. As the elevator dropped, her heart went with it. Emily knew nothing would ever be the same again. Her life with Robert was truly over.

Her car was hot, and the apple and cinnamon air freshener made it smell like an apple pie was baking in the backseat.

Emily put her hands on the steering wheel and rested her forehead against the leather. What a fool she'd been. A rapping sound suddenly came from her window. Shocked, she found Kelly standing there. Emily rolled down her window and stared at Robert's ex-girlfriend.

"I know you don't know me," Kelly said. "I'm a friend of Robert's. Could we talk for a moment?"

A cold rush went down Emily's spine. She couldn't imagine what Kelly would need to talk to her about. Her hands shivered as she opened the car door and stepped out.

"I know who you are. So if this is about him, you don't have to worry—" Emily's voice cracked.

"No, this doesn't have anything to do with Robert." Kelly cut her off. She spoke, quickly. "I went to your house and your maid, Anita, told me you were here. I've been hoping to catch you."

"Well, you caught me. So what is this about?" Emily closed the car door and turned back to face Kelly.

"It's about your husband, Steven."

"What about him?" Emily's stomach churned. What could she possibly know about Steven?

"A few months ago, I quit my job to come back here and take care of my sick mom. Anyway, a man approached me here one day and said he had a unique opportunity for me." She was talking fast, so she took in a breath. "He said he knew things about me. He knew I had once dated a guy named Robert. He offered me thirty thousand dollars to get back with Robert. I knew Robert was dating you. We kept in touch, for a little while, after I had moved. Robert told me all about you, and your soon-to-be ex-husband, Steven.

After Robert met you, his calls and texts stopped. I never heard from him again."

"What does this have to do with Steven?" Emily was getting impatient. She started to sweat. "Was he the man who approached you?"

"No." Kelly shook her head. "Anyway, this man told me that you and Robert had broken up. And like I said, he offered me thirty thousand dollars to keep Robert distracted, so he wouldn't think about you—or try to get back with you, I guess." She took in another breath. "I feel terrible because I told him I'd do it. I needed the money. I wasn't working, and my mom was sick. And I missed Robert, so I wanted to be around him. It wasn't hard for me to fall for him again." She shakily brushed her hand through her hair. "As time went on, I started to feel guilty about what I'd done. I was planning to tell Robert about everything—the money, and the man's offer. But—"

"But what?" Emily's eyes narrowed.

"Before I could, he dumped me. He said he didn't want to hurt me, a second time. He wasn't over you. He said he tried, and tried, not to think about you. He tried telling himself what was the harm in having fun with me. But in the end, he said it was wrong. He was still in love with you. And even though you two would probably never get back together, it was wrong to lead me on. I should have seen it coming." She shook her head. "The entire time we were together, all he did was talk about you."

Emily was happy to hear that, but she had no idea what any of this had to do with Steven.

"Where does Steven fit into all of this?"

"I'm sorry. The guy who gave me the money, his name was Jerome. After Robert broke it off with me, I met with Jerome. I didn't know if he would want the money back, since things didn't work out between me and Robert. I also kept wondering why he cared so much about you and your relationship with Robert. So after we spoke, I followed Jerome. He went straight to some office building—it was a law firm. I followed him upstairs. He went straight to an office with a plaque on the door that read, Steven Montgomery." She let out a breath. "I'm sorry. I think Jerome is working for Steven."

Emily couldn't believe what she heard. Was Steven up to his old tricks again? "So if all this is true, then Steven paid you to keep Robert away from me."

"Yes, that's what I believe. I searched for your address, on the internet, to find you because I thought you should know."

"Thank you." Emily blinked. "For tracking me down and for telling me this." She extended her hand to Kelly. "I appreciate it."

"You're welcome." Kelly embraced the handshake. "I guess I should be going now." She let go of Emily's hand and turned to walk away.

Emily leaned on her car, for a moment, trying to gather her bearings. Jerome was the strange man, dressed in all black that day at Steven's office. The man who made a scene at the front desk. Jerome worked for Steven. Everything Kelly said had to be true. This was exactly the kind of thing Steven would do.

Once she was home and parked in the garage, Emily's leg wouldn't stop shaking. She wasn't sure what to do with the information Kelly had just laid in her lap. She had to make a phone call to confirm something. The call was brief; then, she made another call to Anita.

The plan was to wait for Anita to arrive before Emily confronted Steven. She didn't know how his interaction would go, and she may need backup. It was after midnight, so the house was dark. The only light she saw was the thin line of light seeping under the bedroom door. Emily walked into the room to find Steven sitting on the bed. He was still dressed, in his suit, looking over some papers.

"I didn't think you would ever make it home." He looked over at her.

"Sorry I'm so late," was all she could think to say. Emily was still trying to process everything Kelly had told her earlier.

"Since your sister's alright, and we're both still up, maybe we could talk about the move." Steven shifted on the bed. "I was writing down everything that will have to go with us. A lot of things we can just leave here until we're settled in Atlanta."

"What are you talking about?"

"Us moving to Atlanta. We discussed this earlier." He stood.

"We discussed it, but nothing was finalized."

"Well I finalized it once I left the hospital. That was part of the emergency I needed to take care of. I figured your sister and David are starting a new life, and it's time we did as well. So when I got home, I e-mailed the firm in Atlanta and told them I would take the job." Steven walked toward Emily. "I'll have Anita start packing up some stuff in the morning. I'll turn in my resignation letter. I'm only handling one case right now, and I can let Leonard take it over. After that, we can be out of here."

"This is insane." Emily stepped back from Steven. Robert was moving; now, Steven wanted to move. All this talk of moving made her head spin. Maybe she was going crazy.

"What's wrong?" Steven reached out to grab her hand.

"Everything." She pulled away from him. "Who's Jerome?" Emily blurted out.

"What?" Steven's eyes widened.

"You heard what I said. Who's Jerome?"

"I don't know who you're talking about."

"So now, you're going to lie to my face." Her skin was hot.

"Sweetheart, what's wrong with you?" He tried to look innocent.

"You're what's wrong with me." Anger took over. "Since you're not man enough to say it, I will. Jerome is the man you hired to keep tabs on Robert. Jerome is also the man you gave fifty thousand dollars. He gave thirty thousand of it to Kelly, so she would distract Robert. And I take it the other forty percent was his cut for finding her." Steven opened his mouth, but Emily kept talking. "Don't even try to deny it. On the way home, I spoke to Richard. Yes, it was late; but, he was still up. And he said he remembers you taking out fifty thousand a few months back, and you never told him what it was for. But he remembers telling you that you didn't have money to spend frivolously anymore, not the way you used to."

"Where did you get all this information?"

"It doesn't matter. What matters is you're not denying it. And instead of being sorry, you want to know where I got my information."

"Would it matter if I was sorry?"

"Honestly, it wouldn't. First off, I wouldn't believe you. And secondly, I don't care anymore. I realize this isn't where I belong."

"I take it you belong with Robert."

"That's no concern of yours."

"This is what you've wanted all along." He shook his head. "You've wanted a way to get out of this marriage, so you could run back to Robert. Now, you've finally found it, your way out." His eyes saddened. He walked to the bed and plopped down, all the while looking defeated.

"You're wrong, Steven. I did want this marriage to work. For such a long time, all I prayed for was that our marriage would work. But now, I know it's too late. My heart is with someone else. It has been since my memory returned." Emily headed for the door, but there was one more thing that needed to be said. "Steven, I'm going to file for divorce, again." She turned back to face him. "And no matter what you may think, I do want you to be happy. You should take that job in Atlanta. It can be a new start for you. Maybe you'll find happiness there."

"And that's it?" He stood. "You think you can up and leave me." Steven's steps were quick as he walked toward Emily. The sad look in his eyes turned to anger.

Something bad was coming. Emily turned to run toward the door. Steven grabbed the strap of her purse and yanked her toward him. Ripping the purse from her hands, Steven threw it on the floor, and grabbed Emily around her elbow.

"After everything we've been through," he continued his rant, "after everything I sacrificed for you." His grip moved from her elbow to her upper arm, and he turned her toward him. "I stayed by your side when you were in the hospital, and I prayed that you would get well. All I did was worry about you which, by the way, didn't help my already failing reputation at the law firm. And on top of all of that, I brought you home—to our home—and remained patient while you slept in a separate room."

"Steven, please, you're hurting me." His grip was tight around her arm, and Emily could feel Steven's nails, digging into her skin. She squirmed, but he didn't let go.

"I would have done anything to make you happy." He ignored her cries to let go. "I tried to make things work, even though I knew you were still pining away for your stupid Robert. I would have done anything to save our marriage." His face was red. He screamed at the top of his lungs. "And this is how you repay me? This is how you treat me? This is the thanks I get?" Steven started to twist Emily's arm.

Like she was stuck in a cage and couldn't get out, Emily couldn't seem to break the strong hold Steven had on her arm. Her eyes welled with tears. His grip got tighter, and his voice got louder.

"You're hurting me!" Her arm felt like it was being sliced in half with a knife.

"Let her go." Anita walked in.

Emily was grateful to hear Anita's voice, but Steven's grip was still tight, and she felt the hotness from his breath on her face.

"Steven, you don't want to do this," Anita continued. "Let her go, now, before I call the police." Her tone was serious.

Emily felt his grip loosen. Eventually, he released her arm.

"Just go, then," he shouted. "Both of you, get out of here." He angrily waved his hand. "If you expect a peaceful divorce, don't hold your breath. I can tie up this divorce for years." His nostrils flared. "By the time I'm done with you, your precious Robert may not even want you anymore. And if you think you're getting any money from me, you can forget that, too. I'm done being Mr. Nice Guy."

For a minute, Emily stood there shaking, not knowing how to respond. She felt Anita's warm hand behind her back.

"It's alright, Ms. Emily." Anita's voice was soft. "Here's your purse. Let's just go."

Her insides quivered, like she was falling with a parachute; but, somehow, she managed to take the purse from Anita and turn to walk away. The bedroom door shook as Emily slammed it behind her.

Once she was outside, Emily thanked Anita and hugged her goodbye. She got in her car, realizing that Steven would probably try and take it back; but, it was hers, for now, and she wasn't going to worry about that. But what she did need to worry about was the fact that she had nowhere to go. Monica was in the hospital, and she didn't want to bother her. And once again, she couldn't intrude on Christina and her husband, either. Anita had a small apartment that she shared with her elderly sister, so that wasn't an option. Her savings account only had about fifty dollars in it. Emily always meant to save better, but other expenses always came up. Her joint account with Steven was not an option, she was sure he had either transferred the funds or placed a hold on the account so she couldn't get to it. Emily did have one credit card with a small limit. She could use that to stay in a hotel for a few days. She groaned. Her thoughts were scrambled as she rode around.

After driving for what seemed like hours, Emily somehow ended up in front of her old apartment building. She was able to park right in front of her old door. The place was no longer hers, it belonged to someone else now. Maybe it was stupid for her to come, but she was drawn there. Emily needed to see the place she had always felt safe in, the place where she found her independence. And it was the place where she spent so many precious moments with Robert.

Turning off the roaring motor and taking off her seat belt, Emily leaned forward to get a better look. A light was on in the kitchen window. It made her wonder who lived there, now. Was it a single woman in her first apartment? Maybe a couple who had just married? Could it be a family? Yes, it was small; but, a family could live there; they could make it cozy, make it their own.

Emily felt herself nodding off, so she rolled down the window— a crack—to get some air. It was almost two in the morning, and she needed to shut her eyes, for a moment. Laying her head back onto the headrest, she let out a soft groan. The last thing Emily remembered was a full moon, off in the distance of the black sky, as her eyelids got heavier and heavier.

✍

Emily was half asleep when she heard a familiar voice call her name. A dream, no doubt. The voice sounded just like Robert's. The familiar voice said her name, again, followed by a tapping sound. Fluttering her eyes open, Emily realized it wasn't a dream. Robert rapped on the outside of her car window. Groggily, she tried sitting up. She heard him call out her name, again.

"Emmie, are you alright?"

Slowly, everything started coming back to her—her argument with Steven; her leaving him, for good; her driving around, for hours, and ending up at her old apartment; her wanting to close her eyes, for a few minutes, and falling asleep. But why was Robert here? And why did he have a worried look on his face?

"Why are you sleeping in your car at this time of the afternoon?" he asked, through the crack in the window.

"Afternoon?" She woozily mumbled.

"Yes, afternoon," he said. "Unlock the door."

"Sure." She blinked a few times. "What are you doing here?" she asked, reaching for the door handle and unsteadily stepping out of the car. "And, what time is it?"

"The better question should be, what are you doing *here*?" He reached for her hand to help her stand. "I'm surprised the neighbors didn't call the police when they saw a woman sleeping in her car at one in the afternoon."

"I'm surprised, too." She gave a half smile. Emily wondered how she must look to him. She brushed her hands through her mangled hair. "What are you doing here?" she asked, again. Her voice was shaky.

"Anita called and told me what happened between you and Steven last night. She was worried. She didn't know where you'd gone. She felt horrible for not asking you to come home with her, but when she tried to call you, there was no answer."

"My ringer was down low. I never heard it. But I had no idea she had your number."

"Apparently, she was able to track down Monica and David at the hospital, and they gave it to her."

"Oh. I wish she hadn't bothered them, or you for that matter. I'm fine. And I'm surprised you would drive all the way here looking for me. Why did you think I'd be here?"

"To be perfectly honest, I didn't know you'd be here." He cleared his throat. "I was already on my way here when she called me to see if I'd seen you."

"W-why would you be on your way here?"

"Do you remember me telling you that I come by, once a week, to check on the place?"

"Yes, but I figured—"

"You figured I stopped doing that. Well, it may sound stupid." Robert shrugged. "But I still come here quite often, just to look at the place. We spent so much time here together. It's where I felt my happiest. I believe I was here more than I was at my own place."

"I believe so, too." Emily let out a small chuckle.

"Anyway, it may sound ridiculous, but I wanted to look at the place where I had my happiest moments, one last time."

"It doesn't sound ridiculous." She shook her head. "Funny, I guess that's the reason I came, too. And I had nowhere else to go." She mumbled that part, so he wouldn't hear her.

"Robert, I'm so sorry," Emily blurted out.

"No, I'm the one who's sorry." He gripped her hand. "I've been so harsh toward you, lately. I should have let you explain at the hospital, yesterday." He stroked her hand. "I was so hurt when you said we couldn't meet anymore. And once you came to visit me, and I could tell your memory had returned. I was devastated that you didn't care to share that good news with me, devastated that you chose to stay with Steven."

"I know and I'm sorry, but if you let me explain why—"

"There's no need to. I think I finally understand. After Anita told me what happened, I replayed our last few conversations, in my head. And I realize now that you were trying to tell me when you came to visit me in the ER, but I was so angry, I wouldn't let you speak. I kept interrupting you, and then, when Kelly called me—"

"I thought you were happy with her." She cut him off because she had to get her point across. "I'd made your life miserable, and if she brought you some happiness, what right did I have to come between you two."

"You should've known Kelly could never fill the void you left in my heart."

"But how was I to know that? You were so mad at me."

"I know. I realize that, now. Just like I realized, yesterday, I shouldn't have said the things I did at the hospital. You're right. You didn't know what my relationship was with Kelly, just like I didn't know how you felt once your memory returned. I'm sure you were conflicted, confused, and even scared. I know Steven was putting on his best act to be there for you, to play the dutiful husband. And if you thought I was happy with Kelly, why wouldn't you try to make things work with your husband. I wish I had realized all of this sooner." Robert glanced down at Emily's arm. "Before he had a chance to hurt you." He rubbed her arm. "Does it hurt?"

"No, it's fine. It's just a little red where he twisted it. It looks worse than it really is."

"Are you sure? I can take you to the hospital."

"No, Robert," she said. "There's no need for that."

"Well, you should get your bruises documented and file charges against Steven with the police."

"I will."

It felt good being close to Robert, again. But there was an uneasy feeling in Emily's stomach because she knew the real question she wanted to ask. But she wasn't sure if she should. Before Emily could open her mouth, Robert started speaking.

"What are your plans, now? You can't stay in your car."

"No, I can't," she said, smiling. He still rubbed her arm, and it felt nice. "I'll start working at the high school when summer classes begin. I was able to get my job back. Then, I can start looking for my own apartment. Too bad my old place is taken." She glanced back over at her old building. "I loved it here."

"Where will you go, in the meantime?"

"I don't really know." She shrugged, pulling her arm away. "Everything happened so fast that I haven't had time to think straight. I have enough to stay in a hotel, for a few days, until I can figure everything else out."

"What about your sister?"

"I don't want to intrude on her and David. They're busy now that Monica's pregnant. Besides, they're still living with David's parents while their new house is being built."

"I know there's not much room at his parent's house, but I feel your sister will need you now that she's pregnant. What could it hurt to stay there? Even if you had to sleep on the sofa, it's only for a little while. It's not forever."

"That's true. I'll be making money soon; so, it will only be for a few weeks, until I can save for my own place. I feel like I'm truly starting over." She blinked. Thinking about everything made her eyes misty.

"There's nothing wrong with starting over. Starting over is moving forward, and it's good to move forward."

"Yes, it's good to move forward."

"There's no reason to go back since that brings back bad memories that need to be forgotten, bad memories that we need to move on from."

"Yes, bad memories that we need to move on from." Emily kept repeating every word Robert said, like she suddenly forgot how to think for herself.

The only sound that could be heard was the whirring of the strong wind, howling against the trees. They both fell silent. Emily glanced up in the sky.

"I wonder if it's going to rain." Those were not the words she wanted to say, but those were the words that came out.

"So, we're really going to stand here, now, and talk about the weather?"

"I don't know what you want me to say, Robert. You're going on and on about forgetting bad memories, and I'm sure I'm the bad memory you're talking about."

"If you heard me right, I said I understand everything now. And I also said, I wish I had realized it sooner." His eyes softened. "Because I already gave up my condo, and the buyers are excited to move in. And I've already committed to relocating to the office in New York for at least six months and—"

"You don't have to say any more." She shook her head, cutting him off. "I know you have to go. I don't expect you to renege on your new promotion." She glanced down. "You're not that kind of man. That's one of the reasons why I love you."

"And, if you would let me finish." He lifted her chin. His gaze bore into hers. "No matter what has happened, I still love you, too. And it's good to move forward—you're the only person I want to move forward with. It's not going to be easy. At first, it'll have to be long distance. I can come here to visit you, on weekends, and you can come to visit me. And, after six months, maybe I'll relocate back here. Who knows," he said, shrugging. "Maybe you'll want to relocate to where I am. What I'm trying to say is, I never loved anyone the way I love you, and I want to try and make this work. I want to be here, to help you through this ugly divorce with Steven and for anything else you might need. That is, if you'll have me."

"Of course I will, as long as you'll still have me," she said, leaning into him and kissing him, softly, on his lips.

"That being said," he mumbled, releasing the kiss. He leaned away, and lifted her chin so their eyes could meet. "If we're both committed to making things work between us, I would like to properly ask for your hand in marriage, since I wasn't able to do it, before. Now, I don't have a ring but—"

"You don't have to do this now," she said, cutting him off, and shaking her head.

"No, let me finish." He took her hand. "Will you Emily take me Robert as your fiancé?" Robert continued to ramble. "Like I said earlier, it will have to be long distance, for a while; and, of course, we'll have to wait until you're divorced, but will you marry me?"

"Yes, yes." Her eyes widened. "I will marry you."

Robert squeezed Emily's hand, harder; and, Emily leaned into Robert and kissed him again. Her heart melted like butter. He kissed her back, even harder. It felt like ages since they had touched, and she savored every minute of it. This was everything she could have hoped for, and more. They were going to have a fresh start; and even though things would be difficult, at first, she knew they'd make it work, this time. They would be honest with each other, and they would make sure there were no misunderstandings between them. Their path was clear. They would be married, one day. Emily and Robert loved each other, and love was all they needed.

Dear Reader,

Thank you so much for purchasing and reading my novel. I hope you enjoyed reading it as much as I enjoyed writing it. I would be grateful if you left an honest review. Let me know if you loved it or hated it. I love to receive feedback.

If you have any questions for me please contact me through my website www.ljeppsauthor.com. I would love to hear from you.

ACKNOWLEDGMENTS

I have to thank my sister and brother-in-law for believing I could write a novel.

Thanks also for the kind words and encouragement from my friend, L.W.

Thank you to all my hard working beta readers who believed my manuscript was good enough to be published and to Helen, my copy editor, proofreader, and beta reader. Her help encouraged me to do better, and made me believe I could self-publish this novel.